Penny Freedman studied Classics at Oxford before teaching English and Drama in schools and universities. She has a PhD in Shakespeare Studies and lives with her husband in Stratford-upon-Avon, where she lectures on Shakespeare and indulges her passion for the theatre. She has two grown-up daughters.

THIS IS A
DREADFUL SENTENCE

PENNY FREEDMAN

Matador
5 Weir Road
Kibworth Beauchamp
Leicester LE8 0LQ, UK
Tel: (+44) 116 279 2299
Fax: (+44) 116 279 2277
Email: books@troubador.co.uk
Web: www.troubador.co.uk/matador

ISBN 978 1848764 200

British Library Cataloguing in Publication Data.
A catalogue record for this book is available from the British Library.

Typeset in 11pt Book Antiqua by Troubador Publishing Ltd, Leicester, UK

Printed in Great Britain by the MPG Books Group, Bodmin and King's Lynn

Matador is an imprint of Troubador Publishing Ltd

This book is dedicated to all my former students, who taught me as much as I taught them.

Foreword

I lived very happily for thirty years in the city which was the inspiration for Marlbury and I have many good friends there. I would not want anyone to think that Gina's jaundiced view of the city is mine. The characters who appear in these pages bear no relation to any of that city's inhabitants, and the places of learning have only the most superficial resemblance to prototypes there.

This is a dreadful sentence.
All's Well That Ends Well, Act 3 scene 2

1

WEDNESDAY: *Conditional Clauses*

'If I had known England was so cold, I would not have come'
'Excellent!'

If I had known England was so cold, I would not have come.

My pen squeaks on the whiteboard as I write; it's running out of juice.
'Farid?'
'If you had a better coat, you would not be cold'
Laughter.
'Very good'

If you had a better coat, you would not be cold.

'Valery?'
'If I had not got drunk last night, I would work better now'
More laughter.

If I had not got drunk last night, I would work better now.

'Spoken from the heart, Valery?'
A silence. Valery shrugs. Now I look at him, he does look a touch grey, his hair unkempt, his clothes if not slept in, certainly

not fresh off a hanger. Not your business, Gina. You've done your mothering, remember?

Four thirty in the afternoon and we're doing conditionals – the perennial *if*. Their English is pretty good but conditionals still catch them out, as they do foreigners in general. Listen to *The Today Programme* or *The World at One* any time and you'll hear foreign diplomats and politicians speaking quite beautiful English, until they launch into hypotheticals and then everything goes pear-shaped. What they need to bear in mind is that tenses in English are not so much about time as about probability and uncertainty, actuality and unreality. I don't tell my students this: this linguistic philosophising would freak them out – as it may you, I realise. Do stay with me, though. You will need to follow some of this if you're going to keep up with my story, and the story is a good one: it has international criminals and fiendish plots as well as love, lust, revenge – and English grammar. What more can you ask for?

In place of linguistic analysis on this Wednesday afternoon in Seminar Room 5, I am simply drilling my students in the conditional forms, like Skinner's rats. I move on round the table. My class has segregated itself along gender lines, as do most classes of students, eastern or western, Islamic or not. And after the first week they sit in the same places every time. It's a comfort thing. There are thirteen students in the class and I usually make a fourteenth round the long table that has been created by pushing small tables together. Today there are only thirteen of us, though - Ceren, the Turkish girl, is off sick. I'm not sitting down. I'm on my feet at the whiteboard writing up their sentences with a black board-writer which is rapidly running out of ink. I think it's best that I don't sit down. There is a surprising fear of the number thirteen in some cultures – triskaidekaphobia, as we linguists like to call it – and not just the *ooh it's Friday the thirteenth* frisson. In Japan, hotels have no room thirteen and no thirteenth floor in high-rise blocks. So I'm staying on my feet, though it won't actually do any good:

today will prove to be unlucky for at least one of us, anyway – as unlucky as it's possible to be.

Later on in this story, I shall be asked by the police to draw a sketch of our positions round this table in this seminar room, so I see no reason why you shouldn't see it now. I've indicated where Turkish Ceren usually sits, but her chair is empty today.

Denis   Laurent

                    Valery
Desirée
                    Atash
Christiane
                    Farid
(Ceren)
                    Ahmet
Yukiko
                    Asil
Irina
                    Ekrem
          Gina Gray

So, as I move on round the table, it's Ahmet's turn. He is ready with his example, smiling cheerfully.

'If my father was a rich man, I wouldn't need to work.'

'*If my father was* - or what would be more correct, Ahmet?' Denis, the Frenchman, offers a clue.

'*If I were a reech man da da da da da dum….*'

'Thank you, Denis, for that musical contribution. Yes. *If I were*. OK, Ahmet? The last remnant of the English subjunctive. You will hear people say *If I was*, but in this class, we aim for - what?

'Perfection,' they carol dutifully.

'Exactly.'

If my father were a rich man, I wouldn't need to work.

3

'Asil?'

'If I drove more slowly, I didn't crash the car.'

Patience, Gina.

Asil gazes at me. He is forty or so, a college teacher. He has done a stint of teaching in one of Turkey's remoter mountain regions and now he is being rewarded with a government-sponsored couple of years in the UK, doing an M.Phil at the University College of Marlbury. My job is to get his English good enough for him to write a dissertation on Turkey's claim to membership of the E.U. Affable and willing, he has, as we say in the trade, plateaued as far as English Language is concerned. He is one of half a dozen, all sent to us by the Turkish government, three of whom are in this class. Ahmet, his friend, is rather brighter than Asil, but then there is Ekrem. Ekrem was a mystery to us all initially - surly, idle, stupid - until we realised that he is the spy in the group – there to keep an eye on the others. And he is not enjoying it. He is bored by the work, and being known to be a spy must hamper his social life somewhat, I imagine.

We unpick Asil's sentence, discourse on the difference between *If I drove* and *If I had driven* and reach an acceptable version.

If I had driven more carefully, I would not have crashed the car.

Asil beams uncomprehending approval and I turn to Ekrem for his sentence. He is a bit younger than the other Turks – middle thirties, I suppose – but he is already running to seed. His belly bulges over the belt of his trousers and his heavy face is jowly and dark with stubble. He speaks without expression:

'If I want, I can have.'

Something in the air, the merest stillness of breath. More than irritation, I think; we are used to this kind of thing from Ekrem, after all. What then? Plough on.

4

'That's not an unreal condition, is it, Ekrem? I asked for examples of unreal conditions. Yours is an open condition. If you say *If I want,* you might want something or you might not. We don't know.'

He ignores me, gazes at the ceiling, drums his fingers on the table. Part of the problem, I know, is that he needs a cigarette. He suffers after an hour without a nicotine fix. We all sit and consider his horrid little sentence. I look round the table to where the women sit. Irina, to my left, is looking across at Ekrem with an inscrutable expression. I grasp the nettle.

'Irina, can you turn Ekrem's sentence into an unreal condition?'

Irina qualified as a doctor in Russia but is here, I learnt recently, at her parents' expense, to escape the attentions of an ex-husband turned stalker. I can't help admiring her. She's got nothing going for her in the looks department, but it doesn't seem to bother her. She's got the build of a shot-putter, nondescript features and the kind of dead white skin that seems never to have seen the light of day, but I applaud her decision to dye her flimsy hair an improbable shade of red and to team it today with red lipstick, a pink polo-neck and a purple padded gilet which threatens to turn her into the Michelin man. She has impact; she refuses to be defeated by the genetic chance that made her to be ignored. She's built up that physique, working out on the rowing machine at the gym; she's turned her flat, mousey hair into an orange halo; she has no truck with the mantra that dark colours make you look slimmer, but selects from a rainbow palette. She will be noticed. And she seems to be perfectly comfortable with herself, at ease in her skin. She also has a great voice: if you couldn't see her, you would say it was sexy. We all laughed incredulously when we first heard that her ex-husband was obsessed with her, but I think she may be great in bed. She shifts now and puts up a protesting hand. Her voice is richly guttural, emphatic on the breathy aspirates of *he*, as she says,

'He makes no sense anyway. He must say what he wants.'

'Yes, Ekrem. *Want* can't stand alone, can it? It needs an object.'

He lowers his gaze from the ceiling, glances at me, then at Irina, then along the row of women who face him, a basilisk stare. Then he raises his arms in an expansive gesture of dismissal which encompasses conditional sentences, the English Language, this room and all its occupants. I call up reinforcements.

'Any suggestions about what Ekrem might want?'

The women remain frozen under his gaze but the men oblige.

'Money'

'Success'

'Fame'

'Love'

'Sex'

Laughter from the Y-chromosome team. Among the X-team, I see Christiane Becker regarding them with the strangest of looks. Mingled astonishment and contempt, I would say, with a touch of – something else. I hastily go for the money option and get Laurent, the silent Swiss, to produce a sentence before moving on.

If I wanted money, I could have it.

'Good, Laurent. And Denis? What have you got for us?'

'If I had a gun, I would kill you'

'OK. Nothing personal, I assume?'

Denis smirks. He is tall for a Frenchman and broad-shouldered in his perfectly cut English tweed jacket. He has what I think of as continental hair: it is thick and wavy and will turn a distinguished grey. It doesn't trickle apologetically from his scalp in the way of so many Englishmen's hair, announcing that it's only there temporarily and baldness will

6

not be far behind. His beauty is marred only by a smugness in the set of his mouth – a hovering half-smile that is beginning to irritate me after six months of it.

If I had a gun, I would kill you.

'Desirée?'

Desirée and Denis form the bridge between the male and female halves of the class. They are in fact an item, though I'm not sure that they'll last. Denis de Longueville is seriously aristocratic (I learnt this from Desirée) while she, I guess, is not his class. She is immaculate, though: chicly suited, hair and maquillage just so at all times, a shaming contrast to my vaguely ethnic scruffiness. The dress code in this room is unusually flexible, actually: the Turks wear grey suits – government issue possibly; the two Iranians (Electronics students – studying how to blow us all up, we teachers joke nervously) are stylish in dark shirts and leather jackets; Laurent the Swiss and Valery the Russian wear standard student jeans and sweatshirts; Denis wears English tweeds. On the distaff side, German Christiane is in jeans and a Fair Isle jumper; Yukiko wears black trousers and a cashmere sweater in pale pink; Irina wears the pink polo-neck and padded gilet. If Ceren were here she would, no doubt, be wearing her usual East-West fusion outfit of jeans and sweater with a patterned cotton scarf round her shoulders. To complete the picture for you, I am in a long skirt, suede boots, a black sweater and a turquoise blue Indian scarf.

'Desirée?'

'If I were a man, I would be happier'

'Ah! Wouldn't we all!'

If I were a man, I would be happier.

'Christiane?'

Christiane looks at me with her clear blue eyes behind

7

studious little spectacles. Her normally calm face is more animated than usual.

'There is a line in Shakespeare – *Much Ado About Nothing*. I think Beatrice says, "*If I would be a man, I would eat his heart in the market-place*".'

I am shamed as ever by how much Germans know about Shakespeare. When did I last bandy Schiller quotes with anyone? Fortunately, I know this quote.

'Actually, it's an old construction she uses, Christiane. She says, *O that I were a man* – in other words, *if only I were a man*.'

'OK. If only I were a man, I would eat his heart in the market-place.'

If only I were a man, I would eat his heart in the market-place.

'Very good. And Yukiko?'

'If I were in Japan, I would soon be enjoying the cherry blossom.'

'Oh, Yukiko. That's why you're wearing the pink sweater.'

If I were in Japan, I would soon be enjoying the cherry blossom.

I stand back from the board and we gaze solemnly at the sentences. So sad, unreal conditions, life's *if onlys*.

If I had known England was so cold, I would not have come.
If you had a better coat, you would not be cold.
If I had not got drunk last night, I would work better now.
If my father were a rich man, I wouldn't need to work.
If I had driven more carefully, I would not have crashed the car.
If I wanted money, I could have it.
If I had a gun, I would kill you.
If I were a man, I would be happier.
If only I were a man, I would eat his heart in the market-place.
If I were in Japan, I would soon be enjoying the cherry blossom.

'Look,' I say, 'how sad we are. Atash didn't know how cold England was, and he didn't buy a good coat, and now he's here, freezing. Valery got drunk and now he's regretting it. Ahmet's not a millionaire's son, so he has to keep working. Asil drove too fast and crashed his car. Ekrem hasn't got lots of money. Nobody, I hope, will give Denis a gun. Desirée and Christiane aren't going to turn into men, and poor Yukiko won't see the cherry blossom this year. It's a good thing it's the end of the lesson or we'd all have to kill ourselves. Home time. Have a good evening. I'll see you all tomorrow as usual.'

But one of them at least was going to have a very bad evening and I wouldn't see them all tomorrow. And nothing would ever be quite usual again.

2

THURSDAY: Investigation Day One

The call came just after nine a.m. The desk sergeant who took it could hear the sounds of someone throwing up in the background. The voice on the recording was shaky, breathy when Detective Chief Inspector David Scott listened to it. He could smell the man's sweat.

'An accident ... or something. We haven't ... we can't – open up far. It's a mess. It's a bloody mess ... and I don't think I can ...'

'Where are you speaking from, sir?'

'The library ... the college ... Marlbury College, the library – Social Science library. They called me in, see...'

'And you are?'

'In the library. They rang. They rang through. I'd only just come on duty.'

'Your name, sir. Can you give me your name?'

'White. Tom White. Thomas.'

'Right, Mr White. Now just keep as calm as you can and tell us what's happened.'

'Between the bookshelves. Stacks they call them. You can move them ... move them together with a handle affair. Saves space, you see – you can get more books in. Blood. They saw blood, coming from underneath. I moved them apart – just a bit – and it fell out. I haven't looked close like, but he must be dead. Poor devil must be dead.'

By ten thirty a.m., uniformed police were stationed at the doors of the Social Science library and Scott was watching while the police pathologist made an initial assessment of the body. The smell, he thought. You never quite got used to the smell of violent death. Not just blood, but urine, shit and usually someone else's vomit. That was here now: someone had thrown up in a waste paper bin and the high, sour smell was everywhere.

Scott went into the library office. A young woman and a middle-aged man were sitting there, both clutching mugs of tea, both visibly shocked. He sat down beside the woman.

'Miss Kitchin?'

'Yes. Carol Kitchin.'

She was paper-white and making a visible effort to keep her voice steady.

'I'll try to keep my questions to a minimum for now, Miss Kitchin. I know you've had a nasty shock.'

She bowed her head in acknowledgement of the shock and the sympathy.

'You're the assistant Social Science librarian?'

'Yes.'

'And you opened up the library this morning?'

'Yes. Either the Social Science librarian does it or I do.'

'Can you tell me exactly what happened this morning? Take your time.'

'I came in through the staff door as usual, took off my coat, switched on the computer, then went down to the main door to open it.'

'And what time was that?'

'Just before nine. I like to be prompt. I could hear there was a group of students outside waiting to get in. There always is.'

'But you didn't open the door this morning?'

'No. As I was walking down I saw the blood.' Her voice wavered and she took a gulp of tea.

'And the blood was around the base of the first set of stacks?'

11

'Yes. I knew right away that there must be something dreadful there, but I never thought ... I vaguely thought it was some horrible practical joke – a dead cat or something.'

'Could you see anything there? Did you investigate?'

'No. I didn't want to go near it. I got straight on to Security. And Tom came.' She turned and smiled wanly at the middle-aged man beside her.

'What did you do while you were waiting for him?'

'I didn't have to wait long. He came right away. I think I just went into the office and sat down.'

'So, Mr White, what did you find when you got here?'

Tom White's face was blotchy red in contrast to Carol Kitchin's pallor, and he was breathing noisily.

'Do you mind if we go outside for this?' he asked. 'I could do with a smoke.'

'Would you mind coming outside, Miss Kitchin?'

She stood up.

'I'd like to. I'm afraid I was sick in the waste paper bin when the – when the body fell out. I feel I ought to clear it up, but we were asked not to touch anything.'

'Don't worry about that. My officers have dealt with worse.'

They went out through the staff door into the foyer of the Social Science block, of which the library was a part. Scott waited until Tom White had taken a few shaky drags on his cigarette before he asked,

'What did Miss Kitchin say to you when she phoned, Mr White?'

'I'm not sure. Just could I come and look at something in the library. There was blood and she didn't want to look at it herself.'

'And you went right away?'

'Yes.' He turned to Carol Kitchin. 'You sounded pretty upset.'

'And what did you find?'

White took a deep pull on his cigarette.

'There was blood, like she said. I didn't know what it was but the only thing to do was to open up the stack.'

'So that's what you did?'

'Yep. I took it slow and it was hard to move at first, but then there was a sound and it just fell out onto the floor.'

'The body?'

'Yes.'

He turned away for a moment, concentrating on his cigarette. Carol Kitchin had her eyes closed and was taking deep, controlled breaths. Scott waited until White turned back towards him.

'Did you touch the body at all?'

'No. It was a mess – the head and that – a bloody mess. I knew he had to be dead. Poor devil had to be dead.'

Back in the library Lynne McAndrew, the pathologist, had just finished her initial examination of the body. She stood up from her cramped position between the stacks, grimacing and flexing her knees.

'Well?' Scott asked.

'Well, he's been dead for about twelve hours, I would say. He's at maximum rigor mortis. He was crushed. And he was alive and standing up when he was crushed. See the way his arms are raised? He was trying to push the stack back as it came towards him. I'll know more about what actually killed him when we do the autopsy. It could have been asphyxiation, but there's a lot of blood. I'd say it was probably ribs piercing the lungs There are some head injuries which happened after death. Whoever turned that wheel went on turning it after he was dead. And we know who our body is. His wallet was in his pocket.'

Scott flicked it open and looked at the student ID card. Name: Ekrem Yilmaz. Date of birth: 24.11.70. Nationality: Turkish. He took a plastic evidence bag from his pocket and sealed the wallet into it.

'Any chance it was an accident?'

'Someone moved the stack without realising he was there, you mean? I don't see how it could have been. He'd have shouted, wouldn't he? And even supposing the person turning the wheel was deaf – which I guess is possible – they'd be bound to feel the resistance.'

'Have you seen anything like this before?'

'Well I've seen people crushed, of course, but it's mainly from above. Even if the force comes at them laterally, like a runaway truck, it'll knock them over first and then crush them. I did once see a child crushed against a wall by a car that went out of control and mounted the pavement.'

'So what's your feeling about this? Are we looking at what the press will want to call *a frenzied attack*?'

'I suppose. I just wonder how frenzied you can be with that thing. How fast can you actually turn it?'

'There's another set of them further down there.'

He turned to look at a younger man just entering by the main library doors.

'I'll get young Tyler to try his strength on them.'

Detective Sergeant Mark Tyler raised a questioning eyebrow and said, 'The SOCOs are here, sir.'

'Good. If you're finished, Lynne, we'll get him photographed and taken away and then the SOCOS can get to work. Meanwhile, Sergeant Tyler and I will take a look round here.'

The room was L-shaped: bookshelves, including the movable stacks, stood in ranks all along the longer dimension, and at the end was a glazed door controlled by a swipe-card security panel. Beyond that was a lobby with coat-hooks and toilets and double doors to the outside world; at the other end was the librarian's desk and behind it a door into the library office. From the office, another door led into a short corridor with a staff toilet opening off it and a door at the end leading to the foyer of the Social Science block. The shorter dimension of the L led along from the main doors and contained more bookshelves and reader's bays with connections for laptops. At the far end there was an emergency exit. Now he was no longer focussing on the bloodied corpse, Scott started to take in the quality of the place. University libraries had certainly changed since his student days: beautiful wood had gone into all these bookshelves and tables and the walls were no plain magnolia. *Lilac Mist*, the colour chart would have called it. It was echoed in the heathery upholstery of the chairs. He commented on this to Tyler, who looked unimpressed.

'Our friend there has messed it up a bit, though, hasn't he, sir? I don't reckon anyone's going to want to work in here for a while.'

'I don't reckon anyone's going to be able to. But there'll always be the ghouls who'd like to. I haven't talked to the College Principal yet but he needs to understand that this stays closed for as long as it takes.'

'Any chance we'll need to clear the whole campus, sir?'

'I don't think so. This is the crime scene and it's easy to isolate. So many people mill around outside, there's no chance of picking up forensic even if we had the place to ourselves.'

The body had been between stacks near the main doors. It had now been bagged and was being taken out and the SOCOs had gathered to move in. Scott had a few words with them and returned to Tyler, who was tentatively testing the wheel controlling the stacks at the other end of the room.

'Go on then, Mark. See how fast it'll move'

Tyler was a big man, broad-shouldered and fit. With his ruddy complexion he looked, Scott thought, as though he had grown up on a farm, though he was actually a taxi driver's son from Milton Keynes. He spun the wheel with as much force as he could muster and the stacks moved smoothly together. Smoothly but not fast.

'It's quite hard work, sir. '

'Yes, I don't think we're looking for a female killer.'

'Not the style for a woman anyway, sir. Can't imagine a

female doing something like this even if they did have the strength.'

'Well what a sweet old-fashioned lad you are, Detective Sergeant. Not true, I'm afraid. Some women are capable of anything. Look at Lady Macbeth.'

'Sorry, sir, I thought we were talking real life here, not Shakespeare.'

'Shakespeare knew a thing or two. But you're right. I can't see a woman doing this.'

'I'll tell you what strikes me - why didn't he get out? I really put my back into turning that wheel but there'd still have been time for someone to get out, even if they'd been down the far end of the shelves.'

'Dr McAndrew says he was alive when he was crushed, and standing up but I suppose he could have been drunk or drugged – slow off the mark. We'll have to wait for the autopsy results.'

'And what was he doing in there or how did someone get him there? I take it it happened after the library closed last night. No-one could have done it with other people around, could they? Students don't study that hard so as not to notice someone being bumped off.'

'The library closes at ten – it says so on the door – and Dr McAndrew puts time of death around ten. Maybe he and the murderer somehow stayed around after it closed. A prearranged meeting, possibly, though why here? We need to know about access: what was locked, who had keys, which librarians were on duty, what they saw. Get going on that, will you, Mark?'

Scott took a look round the library office, noting the duty rota on the wall. He left the office, looked into a staff cloakroom on his right and went out through the door to the central foyer of the Social Sciences block, guarded at the moment by a uniformed constable. The place had the air of an atrium: glass roof, vigorous plants standing in terra cotta pots. Against the back wall was a glassed-in booth where a uniformed porter sat. Mark Tyler was finishing a conversation with him and came over to report.

'Well that's quite clear. It's not a librarian on duty in the evenings, it's one of the students – postgrads, he says, often foreign students – non-EU – who aren't allowed to do other jobs. If they have any problems, they call the porter on duty for help. At nine fifty-five they ring a bell and get everyone out, then they lock the main doors, maybe tidy up a bit, turn out the lights and go out through the office and into this foyer, the way you've just come. They lock the door out to the foyer here, then they hand the two keys – the main door key and the key to the office entrance - in to the porter. He signs for them and the student signs too, with the time. She handed the keys in at 10.10. This guy wasn't on duty last night but I've got the name of the guy who was – Clive Davies – and the student's signature looks like Yukiko Iwaki. Not a signature really – more sort of printed.'

'So could be faked, you mean?'

'Possibly. Do you want to take a look?'

Scott felt a surge of impatience, a need to be doing. He knew there were those in the force who thought he had been promoted too young to DCI; this case, his first solo murder case, he needed to do well. He didn't want to get snarled up in trivia. He turned and called over his shoulder,

'No, I want to talk to Yukiko Iwaki, and to Clive Davies, and to anyone else who was around. I'm going to look around outside. You keep an eye on the SOCOs and let me know if they come up with anything. There'll be people to interview as soon as we can round them up.'

Going out of the building, he lit a cigarette and walked along the side of the library to the main doors at the front. He remembered when the college was a college of education, training teachers, and only half the size it was now. He had come with his primary school class to see *Peter and the Wolf* here and they had been allowed to run around and let off steam afterwards. It was much less open and green now, with new buildings squeezed in between the older ones. He stood and chatted to the constable stationed outside as he smoked and looked across to a group of students standing in front of a garishly-painted building opposite, some also smoking, others just gawping at the police activity. They were wrapped in coats and scarves against the unfriendly wind that channelled between the buildings. He wished he'd put his own coat on and couldn't recall for the moment where he had left it. Grinding his cigarette under his heel, he strode across to the gaggle opposite. They started to scatter awkwardly but he caught up with one of them.

'What is this building here?'

'Student Union.' The reply was surly with a defensive upward inflection.

'Do you know if anything was going on at the Union last night?'

The boy called across to one of the others.

'Know if there was anything at the SU last night?'

'Women's night, wasn't it?'

'Oh, yeah.' He turned to Scott. 'Once a month there's a girls only night.' He smirked. 'I guess they dance round their handbags, don't they? And sing *I will survive*.'

'And is there a no smoking rule in the Union building?'

'Oh yeah. The nanny state's alive and well.'

Scott didn't bother to thank him. He eyed the distance back to the library doors. He bet there were always some smokers outside the Union when there was a gig on, and they'd have seen anyone going in or out of the library after hours. The place would be well lit at night, he could see. It was a matter of appealing for information and jogging memories. Tedious work – a job for the team.

He went back into the library and then out of the emergency exit to check the view from there. The door was securely closed, so no-one had gone out of it last night. Nor in, presumably, since you can't get in through an emergency door unless someone opens it for you from the inside. He made a note to check with the security staff that no-one had found the door open the previous night. There was a three-storey building opposite and he could see seminar rooms on the ground floor. This was obviously mid-morning smoke time: a woman stood opposite without a coat on, puffing hard on her cigarette, huddled against the cold. Turning to go inside, he looked back at her again. He had the most uncomfortable feeling that he knew her from somewhere – and that he wished he didn't.

He noticed that a board behind her declared the building to be the English Language Department. Since his murder victim was a foreign student, he guessed this department might be the place to start looking for information about him. As the woman opposite gave him a vague wave and started off towards the front of the library, Scott crossed the grass, entered the building and found the department office. There a nervous woman fluttered round him, producing a thick file on Ekrem Yilmaz. Although a couple of computers were humming away, this was not the paperless office. He spent fifteen minutes or so looking through the file and then was told that for more information he would need to speak to the Director of Studies *upstairs on the left*.

The nameplate on the door read:

Mrs G. Gray

Director of English Language Studies

He knocked and went in, and there she was again, the woman he'd seen smoking earlier, the woman with a disturbing familiarity. While doing the standard business with the warrant card, he surveyed her: plumpish, large bust, slightly rumpled clothes, big glasses, wry smile, unruly blond hair growing dusty with grey now. He knew who she was.

Shit.

This was all he needed. His first solo murder case and the chance to prove that his early promotion hadn't been a mistake, a time when he needed authority and *gravitas* for Christ's sake, and here he was face to face with his old English teacher and feeling seventeen again. She hadn't recognised him, though. He was just a policeman as far as she was concerned. But she would. Oh yes, she would. At some point in this case, just when he didn't need it, in front of a load of other people, she'd say *I've just realised where I know you from. You were at the William Roper School, weren't you? You haven't changed a bit!* Better to come clean, then. As teachers went, she'd not been bad. Young then, of course, with a decent sense of humour. They'd made jokes about her tits but they quite fancied her really. Get it over with, brush it aside in an *all over a long time ago and I'm a busy man* kind of way, establish his authority and move on. He took a breath.

'You don't remember me, do you?' he said, and only just avoided adding '*Miss*'.

3

THURSDAY: *Unreal Conditions*

It's official. Policemen are not just getting younger, they are actually children. So this is how it goes. It's Thursday morning and I have a clear three hours for getting some admin done. I don't mind admin - I think I'm quite a good director of studies - but given the choice I'll always opt for something teaching-related instead. This morning, though, there are exam entries which must be done, and staffing for next term, and I must make use of the extra hour I've got. Normally, I teach a class at ten, but this morning my colleague, Jenny, has taken them to the Language Lab for an IELTS Listening test and I don't have to teach till twelve. So the plan is to get my head down and work through my in-tray.

I like my office. It doesn't have a view - nowhere has a view on this campus any more - but it has windows down one side and the walls are covered with theatre posters. I don't have photos of children or grandchildren anywhere: I hate that in other people's offices. It seems to shout, LOOK, I'M A PERSON! I HAVE A LIFE! It's no-one else's business if I have life or not, and anyway work is the place where you go to forget about your life sometimes.

The morning goes swimmingly until about eleven, when I don't waste time going over to the Common Room for coffee but make one in my office. I need a cigarette, so I slip out of the building for a puff. I don't take my coat, as a sign of a serious intention to be back in a couple of minutes, so I stand outside shivering (there's a hell of a wind channelling past our building) and surveying what was once the green and pleasant campus of Marlbury College. Back when it was Marlbury Teachers' Training College it consisted of a few human-sized buildings dotted around a tastefully landscaped campus but since it became a university college it has sprouted in all directions. *MARLBURY UNIVERSITY COLLEGE – MOVING FORWARD* read hoardings all over the town as office blocks are bought up, waste ground built on and historic buildings transformed to accommodate the educational phenomenon that is today's Marlbury University College. On the campus itself every inch has been colonised. From where I stand, buildings loom in every direction, shoulder to shoulder like so many colossi jostling for space on a giant dance floor, each bestriding his narrow world.

> . . . . . *and we petty men*
> *Walk under his huge legs and peep about*
> *To find ourselves dishonourable graves.*

I see a man come out of the library's emergency door opposite. He stands looking around for a minute or two, then looks at me with a very odd expression on his face. Perhaps he's wondering why I'm standing here without a coat on in the freezing cold, so I wave my cigarette at him in an explanatory sort of way and take a stroll past him and round the front of the library, just to stop him from staring at me. And as I round the corner, suddenly I'm on the set of CSI.

Actually, stupidly, I do wonder first of all whether I've wandered into something the film department is doing, but nobody's faffing about. This isn't a performance. There are a couple of uniformed police and people in those white all-in-one suits and the front of the building has been wrapped up in white tape. I know I've got my mouth open as I stand there and I'm furious with myself when one of the policemen tells me this is a crime scene and asks me not to get in the way, because I hate people who stand and gawp at accidents. I toss up as to whether to go into the common room, where someone will know what's going on, or to go back to my office and log onto the college intranet. I head back to the intranet. And there I find a message from the Principal:

I am sorry to inform you all that one of our students, Ekrem Yilmaz, was found dead in the Social Science library this morning. The circumstances of his death are not yet known and, as in the case of any unexplained death, the police are investigating. I would ask you all to co-operate fully with the police and to do nothing to hamper their investigation. I am anxious that teaching and the life of the College in general should go on as usual, in so far as this is possible. Mr Yilmaz's family have been informed of his death and we send our condolences to them, as we do to his friends in the College.
Norman Street, Principal

I sit and gaze at the screen. Ekrem is dead, in circumstances suspicious enough to bring out a good chunk of the Marlbury constabulary. My shock and awe are tempered by the consciousness that there is no student I could have spared more easily. *If another student had died, I would feel sad.*

Without quite knowing why, I head downstairs to Seminar Room 5, where I'm due to be teaching Ekrem's class in twenty minutes time. When I was a schoolteacher, a boy in my 'A' level set died. He lost control of his motorbike when on his way to a band practice, crashed into a lamp post and died instantly. For a week his empty desk sat and reproached us until I did the only thing possible and rearranged all the furniture in the room. I think I have some thought of this kind as I go into the room – to remove Ekrem's chair at least – but then I am arrested by what I see on the whiteboard. It reads:

If   *I would kill him*
        I would be happier

It's my writing, of course. As I often do, I forgot to clean the board after the class yesterday. Someone has cleaned everything else off, substituted *him* for *you*, and left this little gem behind. One of the cleaners? Unlikely. Most of them don't know enough English to manage even this incorrect construction. One of the students, then, and with that thought I feel a bit sick.

I trail back upstairs and I'm standing in my office, trying to think linearly because I've got to teach the class in ten minutes, but I have Ekrem's death (murder?) going round in my head, and the weird message on the board, and the feeling that I should have rubbed it off before the students come in, and the worry about how I'm going to deal with the class when one of their number has just met a violent death, when there is a knock at my door. I don't think I say *Come in* but he comes in anyway: tall, expensive suit, funny look on his face, and I recognise him as the smoker who was giving me a funny look half an hour ago.

'Mrs Gray?' he says.

I admit, grudgingly, that I am.

'DCI David Scott.'

He flicks his warrant card at me like they do on the telly.

'I'm in charge of the investigation into the death of one of your students, Ekrem Yilmaz. I take it you have heard about his death?'

I tell him I have, and invite him to sit down. He sits, looks at me with that odd expression once more, rumples his nicely-cut hair, and says,

'You don't remember me, do you?'

I am flummoxed. I scroll back. What did he say his name was? I peer at him.

'David Scott! You were in my first 'A' level class! 1985?'

'Right on the button. *Macbeth, The Knight's Tale, The Mayor of Casterbridge* and a book of poems I'd rather not remember.' He grins and he's all of seventeen. And *he's* going to find out how Ekrem died?

'I'm hoping you'll be able to tell me something about Ekrem Yilmaz,' he says.

I look at my watch.

'I'll be delighted to help but I'm teaching in ten minutes and our instructions from on high are that teaching goes on as normal. I'll be free at one. There is just one thing, though. Can I show you something?'

I head off down the stairs to Seminar Room 5 with him behind me and I show him the message on the board. It takes a while to explain about the other sentences and these being just the relics but he's quite bright and he gets the point and makes a note, though possibly just to humour me, and I just have time to clean the board when the students start arriving.

I need not have worried about Ekrem's empty chair casting a pall: someone has already removed it. Curiouser and creepier. Everyone else is there, including Ceren, who was off sick yesterday. She's not looking well, though: very pale, with the kind of dark circles round her eyes that English people don't get. And she's been crying. Surely she wasn't fond of Ekrem? He was almost old enough to be her father, and nasty with it. She sits between Christiane and Yukiko, who watch her anxiously from time to time. I haven't planned what to say as an opening gambit so I find myself asking, 'How are you all doing?'

They all nod and smile and say OK quite cheerfully. Farid says that Ekrem's death is a very terrible thing, I agree that it is very terrible, and then no-one is inclined to say any more. The waves, it seems, have closed over Ekrem's head.

As we pack up at the end of the class – a gentle trot through a reading comprehension passage on alternative energy sources – I see David Scott through the glass panel of the door, hovering outside, eyebrows raised questioningly. I signal to him to come in and it's clear that he has been busy. He has obtained a list of the students in the class from the office and has scheduled interviews with them through the afternoon. When Christiane asks where they should go, he turns to me and does the boyish charm bit.

'I noticed,' he says, 'that Mrs Gray has a spare office. I was hoping she'd be kind enough to lend it to me.'

It is true, I do have a second office with a communicating door, and either he noticed it when he was in there with me, or he's been back snooping around. I keep all my books in there, and I use it for one-to-one tutorials. I like to think of it as my teaching office as opposed to my admin office. I have no excuse for refusing.

'Of course,' I say brightly and turn to the students. 'You know the office, we mean? Where we have tutorials. Use the door from the corridor, then you won't have to come through the outer office, but if he makes any of you cry, you can come and see me for sympathy afterwards.'

I turn back to Scott.

'I'll let you have the key to the outer door,' I say.

I suggest that we go down to the Senior Common Room for a sandwich and coffee lunch and I freely admit that I enjoy walking in with a good-looking younger man in tow. I find us chairs at a low table in a quiet corner and he pays for my cheese and coleslaw sandwich. As soon as we're settled, he gets down to business – no niceties, no school reminiscences.

'So tell me about the dead guy. What was he like?'

I explain that we believe that he was a government spy, sent to report on the other Turks. On the *nil nisi bonum* principle, I don't add that he was stupid, idle and offensive. DCI Scott will find this out from others of less delicate sensibility, I imagine. I know he wants more but I'm not giving something for nothing.

'My turn now. Tell me what happened to him. We've only had bland words from the Principal. Was it accident, suicide or murder?'

He's eying me, wondering if I can be trusted, wondering what he'll get back in return.

'We can rule out suicide: he was crushed between two of the rolling stacks.'

My jaw actually drops. I thought that was just a cliché, a figure of speech, but I feel it clunk open.

'How? When?'

'We won't know until the autopsy is complete, but we're assuming after the library closed.'

I have a host of questions to pour out but he waves a hand at me in frantic refusal.

'I really need you to keep this quiet. The investigation's –'

'*At a very early stage.* I know. It's all right, I know how to play dumb.'

As a *quid pro quo* I follow up with a few titbits of information about the other students: Laurent, we know has a drug problem (I have spoken to his mother and gathered that he has been sent to England in the vague hope that his problem won't be noticed here); Valery's father was shot by someone in the Russian Mafia shortly before he arrived and he is in no hurry to return home; Irina is here to escape a violent ex-husband; Desirée is here to be with her boyfriend. Sadly, I have to tell him, not all overseas students come here simply for the excellence of our universities and our high educational standards. On the other hand, they work hard; they have very good motivation since failure means being sent home to an uncertain future. He is clearly wondering whether to believe a word I'm saying. I let him wonder. If he's any good, he will soon find out whether he can trust me or not.

He has one last question and I know what it's going to be.

'Do you know of anyone who might have wanted to kill Ekrem?

'Well I don't suppose the other Turks were over the moon about being spied on,' I say, 'but they've never appeared to be particularly homicidal. I, on the other hand, could cheerfully have murdered him on several occasions.'

Not helpful, I know, but I'm really affronted by the obviousness of the question. He'll have to do better than that. As we part, I am not sure whether he thinks the £3.50 he paid for my sandwich and coffee was money well spent.

4

FRIDAY: Investigation Day Two

Scott drove into the station early, fuelled only by double strength black instant coffee and a dubious end-of-loaf slice of toast. Fridays were always like this: the weekend's shopping never lasted through and the milk went off. He would shop properly tomorrow, he promised himself, and eat some decent meals, and do some washing up, and clean the house, and get to grips with the laundry basket. He could even get the car washed. In theory.

As he drove, he gathered his thoughts for the morning briefing. It hadn't been a brilliant idea to use Mrs G's office for interviews. All that Eng. Lit. for a start, lowering at him from her shelves. And he couldn't help wondering if she was listening at the connecting door. Her manner with him was annoying too - that teasing tone. He had a sense of humour, of course he had, but this was a murder enquiry for God's sake.

The team gathered early in the incident room, plastic cups of coffee in hand. He looked around for his core people: Mark Tyler; nerdy Steve Boxer, the computer whizz, looking, as usual, as though he'd got dressed in the dark; ambitious Simon Kerr with his watchful eyes and confident swagger; little Paula Powell, spiky-haired and ferocious. His core team. There were plenty more here, twenty or so, some of them drafted in from around the county, but these were the people he would rely on. A good team, he thought with satisfaction. Tyler had put blown-up copies of the students' passport photos on the board; Scott summarised the findings so far at the crime scene and the results of his interviews with students the previous afternoon.

'Ekrem Yilmaz, age 37. Turkish. Student at Marlbury College. In the UK since last September, registered for a 2-year master's course but apparently really here as an informer for the Turkish government. It was his job to report back on the other Turkish students and their families – political activity, links with Armenian or Kurdish groups, un-Islamic behaviour etc. He was found yesterday morning at nine a.m. by the assistant Social Science librarian at the college when she came in to work. Now this is what the library looks like – just a rough sketch.' He pointed to Tyler's sketch on the whiteboard behind him.

'Some time after ten pm, when the library closed, he was crushed between two sets of bookshelves - rolling stacks, as they're known - here.' He pointed to the x on the diagram marking the position of the body. 'If you haven't come across these, I'll explain. They're a space-saving device for libraries because they mean you don't have to have space between each set of shelves for readers to get in. They can be rolled together or apart as readers want to get into a particular section. This is done by turning a wheel at the end of a set of shelves, here.' Again he pointed. 'There is no question of this being an accident: the wheel must have been turned with considerable force and no attention paid to the victim's protests. We can be pretty sure that the killer was male – Sergeant Tyler here demonstrated for me just how much muscle power was needed to roll the stacks at speed.'

'So it's the mystery of the body in the library. We should send for Poirot.' An aside from Paula Powell, loud enough for all to hear. Cheeky cow.

Above the laughter, he said, 'Thank you, DS Powell. But I don't intend to be the village plod who gets it all wrong, even if you do.'

He turned to indicate the thirteen photos on the board: Ekrem's in the centre, the others clustered round.

'The murdered man and the students in his class. They're not the only suspects, of course, but we're holding on to their passports for the moment. We need to start with people who knew him and knew the way the library worked, so students and staff are in the frame. He'll have known other Turks in the college – the people he was informing on. It's a reasonable working assumption that it was one of these who decided to shut him up, but we have another line opening up as well, which is why we have these people up here. Now, they're all in the same English Language class. They're taking special programmes designed for overseas students. They take masters' degrees which usually take one year, but they take two years over them, improving their English as they go.'

He took up a pointer and circled the twelve faces.

'First thing is, none of them liked him. None of them are sorry he's dead, except possibly this girl – Ceren Vural – another Turkish student, 21, the youngest in the group, doing an M.Sc in Microbiology. She seemed upset, looked as though she'd been crying, but claimed she hardly knew Yilmaz.'

He paused. He could relax a bit now. Even make a joke, maybe, if he could think of one.

'I saw them in alphabetical order, so that's how I'll report on them. Mark will write up the salient facts as we go along. Laurent Amiel.' His pointer found a hairy, scowling youth. 'Swiss. 24. Rich. Studying Law. I'm told he has a drug habit – my informant wasn't specific. He denies it. Refused to show me his arms for needle marks. Said I'd have to arrest him, which I may very well do. Alibi for Wednesday night: he was at a French film at the Film Club. He's given me the names of some people who saw him there.'

'Christiane Becker.' He found her serious, spectacled face. 'German, aged 23, taking a postgraduate degree in Women's Studies. She was at the Students' Union. It was a women only

31

night and all five of the women in the class were there. Irina Boklova,' - Irina's picture showed her mousey-haired and bespectacled - 'now a red-head, by the way. 27. Taking an M.Sc in Biochemistry. Irina is Russian, makes no bones about the fact that she is here in part to get away from her ex-husband, who has turned into a serious stalker. Is there something you want to say, Mark?'

Mark Tyler had stopped writing on the board and was holding up a passport taken from the pile lying on a nearby table.

'Yes, sir. When I was doing the pictures from their passports, I noticed hers. You said Irina Boklova, but on her passport she's down as Irina Yilmaz.'

There was flurry of activity. Heads turned, someone's coffee went over, a murmur of conversation started to rise. It was running away from him. Damn Tyler and his bombshell. He couldn't have told him this before he got started? He'd rip his head off later.

Questions were being thrown at him.

'Could Yilmaz have been the stalker husband then?'

'What nationality is the passport?'

'Are we running checks on these people?'

He held up a hand, thinking furiously.

'All right, let's think about that. It's interesting, but maybe not that significant. In answer to your question, Paula, the passport's Russian – show them, Mark – and she's definitely Russian. I've met her and she's either Russian or a very good actress. The most likely assumption is that she hasn't changed her passport since her divorce and Yilmaz was her married name. Which tells us that the ex-husband was a Turk and she chose not to tell us that. The names are an odd coincidence, but there's no way Ekrem Yilmaz can have been the ex-husband. Think about it. If she came all this way to escape from him she was hardly going to sit in class with him and say nothing. It's possible Yilmaz is a name like Smith or Jones in

Turkey.' He turned to Boxer. 'Steve, check out the ex-husband and see if there's any connection.'

As the muttering subsided, he moved on rapidly.

'Now, the glamour of the outfit.' He selected Desirée's carefully posed photo. 'Desirée Bonfort, French, aged 23. Taking a two-year MA in Comparative Literary Studies. Here with boyfriend, Denis de Longueville - over here.' Again he pointed. 'He's 24, studying European Law, and he's the only one without an alibi for Wednesday night. Says his girlfriend was at the Students' Union so he stayed in his room all evening – they live on campus – watching television. No law against that of course, but he's hazy about what he watched. I asked him why he didn't go to the French film and he said he came to England to improve his English so what was the point of watching French films. He was nervous, though, definitely, the most nervous of all of them. I'm not saying he's our man but he's hiding something. We need to dig for connections between him and Yilmaz.'

He stopped and surveyed the board.

'Then there's this young woman, Yukiko Iwaki. 23. Doing Women's Studies. She's key. Yukiko was on duty in the library on Wednesday evening – they pay students to staff the place in the evenings. She says she saw Yilmaz in the library earlier in the evening but he wasn't there at closing time. She cleared the library at nine-fifty and closed the main doors at ten o'clock.' He turned back to the diagram of the library, using his pointer. 'Then she went out herself through the staff office, here, locked this door behind her, handed the key to the porter in the foyer of the Social Science block – he confirms that - and went over to the SU to join the other girls.'

He broke off as DS Paula Powell raised a hand.

'Yes, all right, DS Powell, I know - the other *women*. If you saw Yukiko Iwaki, even you might call her a girl. She's tiny - weighs about six stone I should think. She certainly didn't kill Yilmaz. And that more or less leaves us the Turks and the

Iranians. These two here, Farid Hosseini and Atash Shirazi, are Iranians, late twenties, studying Electronics. They were both pretty uncommunicative, said they spent the evening at an Iranian Society meeting. All their friends will vouch for them. That'll be a difficult alibi to break. The interesting thing, though, is that Hosseini came back at the end of the afternoon. The Director of English Language at the college could be quite useful to us, I think. Hosseini went to see her and she persuaded him to come back and talk to me. He told me that Yilmaz was not only an informer but a drug dealer. He got coy when I asked who he sold to, but when I suggested continuing the conversation at the station, he mumbled that I should *talk to the French boys*. I assume he means Amiel and de Longueville. The Turks were not helpful, absolutely denied that Yilmaz had been spying on them and claimed to have been at home with their families. They're both early forties and have wives and children with them. Again, difficult alibis to break.'

He scanned the board for the remaining face.

'And finally, Valery Tarasov. Russian, aged 22, studying International Relations. I have information that his father was killed by the Mafia in Russia shortly before he arrived here, and he's desperate not to be sent back. He himself wasn't prepared to confirm this to me, though he did admit that his father died last year. If our dead man was dealing, it's possible there could be a connection with Tarasov. We'll need to pursue that. Any questions or suggestions?'

'Any ideas about what Yilmaz was doing in the library after hours, sir?' Simon Kerr asked.

'Not at the moment. If he was in the library earlier in the evening, it's possible he secreted himself between the stacks there so he could stay after closing time, but we don't know what for.'

'Could it have been some sort of terrorist thing, sir, that went wrong?'

'A bit of arson you mean? A plan to burn the place down because it contained un-Islamic books?'

'Maybe someone found him there. Have you thought about the library staff, sir. Librarians are funny about their books.'

'Oddly enough, Simon, I have thought of that. All the library staff are female – not unusual, I gather. We'll talk to them, of course, but it would be a pretty weird way to deal with an intruder, even if he was brandishing a can of petrol. When we get the SOCOs' report we'll know more about what Yilmaz had with him and that may help. Anything else? No? Then Steve, you start running these characters through the computer. Keep their passports till we know what we're dealing with. Simon and Paula, we've put out an appeal for information from students who were in the library that evening, or outside the Student Union, where they'd have a clear view of comings and goings at the library. They may make contact here at the station, but I've said they can talk to us at the college. I want a team there to take statements. Anything unusual – anything at all - I want to know right away. There's an office in the English department they can use. I'll talk to Irina Boklova-Yilmaz, and to the French boys. Mark, you get a team to check alibis and go through their mobile phone records. And I'd like a word, please, in my office.'

5

FRIDAY: *Relative Clauses*

My legs are unwilling as I pedal the last uphill stretch of my ride home. *Friday night,* I tell them encouragingly, *Annie's bound to go out. I'm going to watch some rubbish on the telly with a glass of wine, have a bath, and go to bed with a Trollope* (Joanna in this case). I enter the house cheerfully, expecting to have time for a cup of tea and a chat with the cat before Annie gets home, bringing her aura of swirling agitation with her. I smell her presence before I hear it. Cigarette smoke. In the sitting room I find her lying on the sofa, eyes half closed, trainer-clad feet on the arm, a litter of dirty mugs and plates on the floor beside her, a children's television programme blaring in the corner. I deal with it well, as usual.

'Get your shoes off the sofa,' I scream. 'How many times have I told you? And you've been smoking. And what's all this mess? And why haven't you been at school?'

She opens her eyes wide and stares at me, contempt oozing from every pore. My sixteen-year-old daughter, Marianne, known to me as Annie and to her friends as Man. She has two modes: one is frenetic, the other passive-aggressive. The latter is in operation today.

'The sofa's shit anyway. You smoke. The mess is my lunch. I couldn't do games 'cos I've broken my ankle.'

'What do you mean, broken your ankle? Let me look at it. Which one?'

She waves a foot, grimacing. I grab it, she protests loudly, I remove the designer trainer and reveal a perfectly normal-looking ankle.

'THERE'S NOTHING THE MATTER WITH IT,' I yell.

'It's REALLY painful.' Her voice rises in injured righteousness. 'They wanted to ring you but I said you didn't like to be disturbed at work.'

Oh fine. So now they have me down as an uncaring mother.

'How did you hurt it?'

'Jumping off a table in Drama.'

'Well you shouldn't be made to jump off tables.'

'God, Ma. I wasn't made to – I just did, right?'

'Well if you had a free afternoon, why didn't you get on with some of your coursework?'

'I was in shock.'

She mumbles this into the sofa back, so I have to ask her to repeat it.

'I WAS IN SHOCK.'

And then I start laughing, and I can't stop. I am hooting with laughter and wiping away tears. I would like to roll on the floor. For a moment I think she might be going to laugh too; there is just a flicker, a twitch of the lips, but she suppresses it and gazes at me with weary pity. I gather up the dirty crockery and retreat to the kitchen.

Peace breaks out over spaghetti Bolognese and when she tells me it is *delish* I am really pleased, until I reflect that she probably wants to cadge money for her evening out. We are just considering ice cream for pudding when I hear a familiar sound – the throaty rattle of a small and ancient car that is being driven into the ground. Annie hears it too.

'Oh sorry,' she says. 'El wants you to baby-sit.'

So let me introduce you to Ellie, my elder daughter, who should be in her second year of reading Drama at Manchester but produced a baby last summer and is intermitting while she decides how to juggle motherhood and a student life. The baby's father is an absence; I've not even been given a name. Ellie is sharing a house with friends from school – the jetsam remaining when the smarter crafts sailed off to university and new horizons. They get by with temporary jobs in pubs and restaurants; they've always got grand schemes for making money without actually having to do a job.

Their house is horrible – a grubby muddle. I feel guilty, of course, that she and my granddaughter are living there rather than under my welcoming roof. There is plenty of room in my house and perhaps I am a wicked woman not to suggest it. Mind you, Ellie has never asked. I can terrify myself in the dark watches of the night by picturing eight-month-old Freda crawling round the house picking up E pills and popping them in her rosy mouth, but I have to hold the line. If they lived here, I'd feel responsible: I'd be up in the night to her, I'd be worrying about her nappy rash, I'd be pureeing carrots in the Moulinex because living on tinned food can't be good for her, and before I knew it I'd be in sole charge while Ellie clattered off back to Manchester. I never really felt I chose motherhood the first time round; I'm damned if I'm going to do it again.

My former husband, Andrew, thinks I should take on Freda and allow Ellie to get on with university. He says I am being *unbelievably selfish*, but I'm not inclined to engage with his moral universe. I heard a short story by Anne Enright being read on the radio the other day, in which she referred to someone's *occasional brother*. It struck me because that is exactly what Andrew was, even when I was married to him – an *occasional husband*.

He is a human rights lawyer (the kind who don't make any money). Throughout our married life he was away, always abroad somewhere on a fact-finding mission or with a commission or just defending some poor bastard against the power of a corrupt state. Many people think he's wonderful, and I'm sure he is if he's the only thing standing between you and cruel and unusual punishment. Our problem, as his wife and daughters, was not just that he was so often absent but that even when he was at home he wasn't really with us: he was on the phone, on the computer, in the messy little junk room which we grandly called his office.

Eventually I decided it would be easier not to have him around at all and sued for divorce. It didn't work out that well, actually. I know he's wonderful at getting justice for the underdog but he also got himself a very good divorce settlement. When he tells me that I should take on responsibility for Freda, I point out that this would mean giving up my job and that someone would have to pay the bills. I ask whether that would be him. He has paid maintenance for the girls, of course, but Ellie's stopped the moment she became eighteen and what he pays for Annie barely keeps her in designer trainers. *'God, Gina,'* he says, *'you know how much of my work is pro bono.'* I rest my case.

As I hear Ellie's car die outside, I go to the front door. She is striding up the front path carrying Freda on one arm and, ominously, a large bag in the other hand.

'Thanks so much, Ma. I think everything's here. I'll see you Sunday afternoon.'

'Sunday?'

She looks furiously at Annie, who is hovering uneasily behind me.

'Didn't you tell her?'

'Tell me what?'

'It's a party. Up in Manchester. I'll be able to see everyone. You don't mind do you?'

'A party? For the whole weekend?'

'Oh come on, Ma. You know how it is. Please. I must be allowed to have some fun - occasionally.'

She thrusts her double burden at me and runs off down the path, calling over her shoulder,

'I'll just get the buggy.'

She returns with the buggy, hands it to Annie, plonks a kiss on Freda's head, blows one at me and is off down the path again.

'You're not driving to Manchester in that, are you?'

'Sure.'

'Ellie –'

'It'll be fine, Ma.'

And she's off in a screech and a rattle. Freda starts to whimper. I thrust the bag at Annie, who looks resentful and remembers to limp as we trail indoors.

Annie sets out for the uncertain pleasures of an evening spent trying to look old enough to get into a pub; Freda is consoled with a chocolate biscuit and we sit down to watch *EastEnders*, which she seems to enjoy until she falls asleep. I carry her upstairs and put her to sleep in my girls' cot, which is now in Ellie's old room, then realise that I am covered in chocolate. I take a bath.

I read a lot of *Other People's Children* once I'm in bed. I can't switch out the light till I hear Annie come in. I know she shouldn't be out in the pubs at sixteen but it's what they all do. They know which ones will turn a blind eye and the concentration of teenagers in these drives older drinkers elsewhere. To comfort myself, I characterise these places in my mind as *junior pubs*. I live in a fool's paradise, I know. I have given her five pounds for a taxi home, as usual, and as usual she has tucked it into her bra. They don't take bags or coats with them: in their haphazard night life coats and bags get pinched the moment you put them down, apparently. So they set off into town nakedly exposed and I would be more fearful for her, except that when her girl friends – *the posse* - come to pick her up and they stride off, laughing, down the road together, they look terrifying. I know their confidence is skin deep, but I'm not sure they do, and I'm pretty sure the boys don't. So I hope for the best, and soon after eleven I hear a car stop outside.

From the shouted farewells, I guess the taxi is going on to drop off others, or she's got a lift, but I shan't see my five pounds again either way. She puts her head round my door, lit up like a firework, and says she's had an ace evening and what's all this about one of my students being killed? I promise to tell her in the morning (though she's the last person I'd divulge anything to) and I turn out my light.

It is when I am drifting off to sleep that the words on the board come to me again: *If I would kill him, I would be happier*. And I am puzzled because that's a German error, and that makes no sense at all.

6

SATURDAY: Investigation Day Three

Scott woke with Irina Boklova-Yilmaz in his head. Not because she was beautiful, he thought as he surfaced slowly to the knowledge that it was Saturday, certainly not that. She was one of the plainest women he had ever met. Most women in their twenties had something to recommend them but she seemed to fail on all counts: heavy build, pasty complexion, little piggy eyes and that weird red hair. She had sat opposite him, though, so composed, neither aggressive nor nervous, perfectly sure of herself. When she answered his questions, her voice was surprising: low and rich, authoritative. He was almost intimidated. He had asked, with some tact he thought, if she was related in any way to Ekrem Yilmaz and amusement had beamed in her small blue eyes.

'You think he was my husband? No. My husband was idiot but not so much idiot as Ekrem.'

She pronounced the name 'Ek*rem*', with the stress on the second syllable and it sounded to him more authentic that everyone else's '*Ek*rem'.

'And your husband is not related to Ekrem Yilmaz.'

'My *ex*-husband is name Direnç Yilmaz. Ekrem says – said – he knows my husband, that he is far cousin, but I think this is just wind-up.'

'I understand that you've had some trouble from your ex-husband, Mrs Yilmaz, and that's why you're here. Did Ekrem ever threaten to let your husband know where you are?'

'Don't please call me Mrs Yilmaz. I am Dr Boklova. My ex-husband is simply loser, actually. He has no money to travel to UK even he knows I am here. I met him when I was on holiday by Black Sea in 2003. We married soon. You call *whirlwind romance*. Was big mistake. He wanted me for Russian passport. He thought he could make big money in new Russia, but he was complete failure actually. Now he wants me because I am bread-earner. Now he is street seller or something of that. Sad man.'

And on the whole he believed her. So that was the end of that line. His talk to Clive Davies, the porter on duty on Wednesday night, hadn't been any more helpful. Yukiko Iwaki had handed the keys in to him at ten past ten – he had written it in his log. Yes, that was usual; they generally tidied up a bit after the library closed. He had remained in his booth until ten thirty, then had done his rounds, checking the security of the buildings. He was sure the library's emergency door had been closed; he always checked because people sometimes went out that way for a smoke and didn't close it properly when they came back. He always checked the main library doors and they had definitely been locked on Wednesday night, as had the door from the library office.

This was turning into a 'sealed room' mystery and Scott didn't like it one bit. The logical answer, of course, was that someone else beside Yilmaz had hidden in the library and that Yukiko Iwaki had stood and watched while he committed a bloody murder, then let him out and locked up after him. But it was such an improbable scenario. And how would the murderer have known that Yilmaz was going to be there? Only if he had made an assignation with him. And why would two men make an assignation in a library after hours? If Ekrem was dealing drugs, surely there were easier places to do it.

He rolled out of bed and then groaned as he remembered

43

that he had not shopped as he had intended to the previous evening and there was nothing for breakfast. Swearing, he pulled on a tracksuit and sprinted to the garage that he used as his corner shop. He bought orange juice, bacon and sliced bread but failed on ground coffee. After a couple of satisfyingly greasy bacon sandwiches, offset by the virtuous properties of the orange juice, he stacked his dirty crockery alongside the precarious heap on the draining board, emptied the laundry basket into the washing machine and, unshaven and still in his tracksuit, got into his car and headed for the station.

Marlbury was bright and busy with a hint of spring in the sunshine, though it was only February. As Scott took the ring road past the city walls he noticed the snowdrops and daffodils sprouting artfully around them – an imaginative piece of civic planting. He looked dispassionately at the town; he wasn't really a native. He'd been at secondary school here but before that he'd moved around, following his father, who was in the army. His father had retired while he was stationed at the barracks in Marlbury and decided to stay around there while David finished his schooling. When he'd left for university, his parents had moved out to the nearby coast; Scott had visited them there but had rarely gone into Marlbury. They were both dead now – they had been elderly parents with one late child.

When he'd been sent here as a DCI, he hadn't expected it to feel like a home-coming, but he had been surprised to find himself so detached. It had changed a lot, of course, transforming itself into a shopping Mecca for the surrounding area, but even the places he recognised seemed like stills from a familiar film – observed before but not experienced. He'd been greeted by one guy who recognised him from school; they'd shaken hands and said they must meet for a drink some time, but both knew they wouldn't. He could log onto Facebook and see who else was around, but he wouldn't do that either.

He'd bought a house on a new development near the

railway station, slickly finished and needing no work, even down to its paved courtyard garden. Most of his neighbours were around his age but they all had partners and families; he didn't fit into their social world. He didn't mind; he had a habit of self-sufficiency gained, he guessed, from all that moving around when he was young. He'd had no luck with women really: a relationship started at university which had drifted on through his twenties until she got tired of it and moved on; his thirties punctuated by a few unsatisfactory attempts to build something, mainly with work colleagues. To be honest, he didn't find women police officers very attractive on the whole; he admired them, thought they often did a great job, but they had a hard edge that he didn't care for. Outside work, he didn't want to be challenged; he wanted softness, someone who would smooth away his day. An old-fashioned woman, he supposed.

He found on his desk what he'd hoped to find: the autopsy results. They'd come in the previous evening while he'd been talking to people at the college. He scanned Lynne McAndrew's report: Yilmaz had been standing when he was killed. He had sustained crushed bones and internal organs; the single wound that had killed him had been a broken rib puncturing the left lung. There were shallow cuts or stab wounds on his right arm – possibly defence wounds - and on the right side of his face. (Did that mean he'd had a fight with someone before he was killed?). The body showed no signs of disease and blood tests showed nothing out of the ordinary, though his cholesterol level was high for a man of his age. HIV test was negative. There was no alcohol in his blood; he had smoked some cannabis not long before he died but not in a quantity that would have made him incapable of defending himself.

As he picked up the report to look through it again, he saw that there was another sheet beneath it. Jackpot! The preliminary forensics were in as well. He ran his eyes over it.

45

There was a mass of stuff, but the highlights had been helpfully bullet-pointed: fibres on the floor, some matching Yilmaz's clothing, others cotton in several colours, had gone for further analysis; blood and saliva matching Yilmaz's DNA; also semen matching Yilmaz found on the floor at the back of the bay (so not at the front where he was killed). Was that it, then? Did Yilmaz have sex with some guy in the library and then get killed by him? Another Turk? Did Yilmaz threaten to inform on him? None of that explained the locked doors. He needed to find out how tight security was on those keys. A lot of people handled them – different students every evening – so could Yilmaz's killer have got hold of one?

He scanned the rest of the report: other stuff had gone to the lab for analysis, including a couple of hairs that might be helpful, but people presumably walked in and out of that bay all the time, shedding hair, skin cells, snot and the leavings from their shoes. He turned back to the autopsy report. Those cuts on the right arm, what were they about? He visualised the scene: a man with his right arm up, protecting his face; another man with a knife – driving him into the bay? But once he'd driven him in, he'd have to leave him there while he went round to move the stack. What kept Yilmaz there? The answer came but his *eureka* moment was interrupted by a tap at the door and the arrival of Mark Tyler.

'I thought I'd find you here, boss. I've been working on the mobile records and there are some things I thought you'd like to see.'

'Beyond the call of duty, Mark, but thanks.' Unspoken was the recognition that this was Tyler's reparation for yesterday's clumsiness over Irina Boklova-Yilmaz. 'Before I look at those, take a look at these – autopsy and forensic results. See if I'm right but I think we have to be looking for two men.'

Hardly giving Tyler time to take in the reports, Scott explained.

'Yilmaz is in the bay when the stack starts to move in on

him. He protests, but nothing happens. He tries to get out, but someone is there with a knife, threatening, keeping him in there. As the stacks move in, Yilmaz turns side on, making himself a thinner target, pressing against the moving stack, but he's still desperate to slide out, only he's kept there by the guy with the knife, stabbing at his exposed right side. It answers your question when we first looked at the scene – why didn't he get out? He wasn't drunk, or drugged to any significant degree, and he was standing up when he was crushed. Someone else had to be keeping him in there.'

'So what's your scenario?'

'You saw the mention of his semen in the forensics? I think it must have been a blackmail attempt that went wrong. He's lured there for gay sex with one guy while the other one's there as a witness. He was an informer; maybe they wanted something to hold over him to keep him off their backs, but he wouldn't be threatened – maybe said he would expose them – so they ended up killing him.'

'The library's a funny place for it, isn't it?'

'People get their kicks in funny ways. You must have discovered that working in this job.'

'So, you're thinking they had a key?'

'That's the crux. Could anyone have got a key cut? I'll need to talk to the Social Science librarian on Monday and get an honest answer about their security arrangements.'

'Meanwhile, do you want to take a look at these? Our man was pretty busy in the month before he died, and the other students did quite a bit of talking on Wednesday night. Makes interesting reading.'

It was after five when Scott left the station and headed for the supermarket. Most of the fresh stuff would be gone but, to be honest, he rarely bought much of that anyway. Coffee, that was the really important thing. He surfed the fruit and veg aisles, picking up a few end-of-the-day bags, and moved on to the ready meals. It was when he reached the dairy aisle that he spotted Gina Gray. She was wheeling a loaded trolley and trying to distract a small baby who was sitting in her trolley and attempting to throw things out of it. As she set off again, he wheeled his trolley alongside hers.

'I thought it was only the chronically disorganised like me who left their shopping till this time,' he said.

She rolled her eyes heavenwards.

'This is my second trip today. The first had to be aborted – you don't want to know why. This is my granddaughter, Freda, by the way.'

The baby gazed at him appraisingly, sucking vigorously at a handful of pink cloth. He sought around for something appropriate to say and then gave up.

'Do you mind if I ask you something?'

'Go ahead.'

'How much do you know about your students' sexuality?' he asked.

She gave a hoot of laughter.

'They say supermarkets in the evenings are great places for singles to meet, but I'm not sure that's going to get you far as a chat-up line!'

He could feel himself blushing. Damn the woman. Well, he wasn't going to be deflected.

'Sorry, it's just – is it possible Ekrem Yilmaz was gay?

She'd stopped laughing at him, at any rate.

'I never thought he might be gay. He seemed quite hetero - pretty leery with the women in the class. They didn't like him a bit. I would say definitely not gay. Except it might be that given the culture he came from and the attitude to homosexuality – and given that he was working for the government - it's possible he could have been adopting deep protective cover.

'Did you ever see him around with women?'

She thought for a moment. 'No,' she said.

She reached for some yoghourts off a shelf and pushed on.

He trailed beside her. In the next aisle they nearly ran into Yukiko Iwaki and Christiane Becker, poring over jars of sauerkraut. She was all over them of course, and they were all over the baby, who grinned gummily at them.

'Christiane is such a cheat,' Yukiko told Gina Gray. 'We each have to make a typical national dish to take to an international evening, and she's *buying* a jar of sauerkraut!'

Christiane was laughing. 'I told Yukiko – no-one *makes* sauerkraut in Germany any more. It's a national dish you buy in the supermarket!'

Gina Gray laughed too, warmly, affectionately, not mockingly as she laughed at him.

'Quite right too. Life's too short for pickling cabbages. I love your coat, Yukiko. Is it new?'

He watched Yukiko as she ducked her head in acknowledgement of the compliment. It was true she looked good; the coat was short and a pale cream colour, and she was wearing a matching scarf and cap. She could have been on a fashion shoot. He, on the other hand, was becoming horribly conscious that he was still in his tracksuit, still unshaven, and probably hadn't cleaned his teeth that morning. The girls hadn't greeted him; was it possible they hadn't recognized him without his suit and tie?

Needing to make a getaway, he waved a hand vaguely at the three of them and hurried on to the checkout. As he unloaded, he felt a tap on his shoulder: she was there again, behind him, giving the once-over to his pile of ready meals.

'I see you're not into home cooking, DCI Scott,' she commented. 'You can't hope to keep your mind sharp if you live on rubbish, you know.'

For a moment he thought – hoped? – that she was going to invite him round for some home cooking, but she simply laughed and turned to unloading the smug fair-trade, organic contents of her own impeccable trolley.

7

SATURDAY: *First Person Plural*

Friday night is not without incident. Freda wakes several times and is inconsolable despite nappy changes, drinks of water, cuddles and songs. I feel it must be my fault. Ellie, when she was small, once told me *you're shouting with your face*, and it is possible that this is what I'm doing to Freda at 3.30 am. I take her into my bed and she falls asleep; I can't sleep, however, as I'm racked by waking dreams of rolling over on top of her and crushing her to death. Eventually I pick her up and carry her, still asleep, back to her cot. Then, as I am lowering her into it with infinite care, she wakes and resumes her screaming. And so it goes.

In the morning, Annie remains inert in her room and I haven't the energy to shout at her. I give Freda her breakfast, sluice down the kitchen afterwards, dress her, find her coat, hat, gloves, shoes and cuddly toy, and my wallet, shopping bag, keys and list, and strong-arm her into her buggy. She does that arching thing that they do to try and thwart me, but it's a bit half-hearted. She's exhausted too. Because it makes me feel better, I bang loudly on Annie's door before I leave, shouting,

'I'M JUST OFF TO SAINSBURY'S. I DON'T WANT TO FIND YOU STILL IN BED WHEN I GET BACK.'

Then I set off. Normally, I cycle to the supermarket and wheel the shopping back, slung onto the handlebars. As I can hardly sling Freda onto the handlebars, I walk today, pushing Freda. It's about a mile and the morning is alive with tantalising early sunshine. Marlbury is a nice place, though not as nice as it thinks it is. I've always thought it was pretty smug about itself, actually. I'm not really a native, of course; my washing up here was a consequence of my marriage, as so much else has been. My husband, Andrew, is Marlbury to the bone: his father and grandfather were solicitors here; his mother's father was once the mayor. Andrew, like his father, grandfather and brother, went to Marlbury Abbey School, which has a claim to being the oldest school in the country. He was Head Boy. I was always an interloper with my sloppy London ways.

At first, I found the absence of anonymity unbearable: Andrew couldn't walk down the street without being greeted, without stopping to chat. My head whirled with new names and faces and I yearned for the soulless metropolis. It got better, of course: I made my own friends – work colleagues and fellow mothers – and then Andrew and I divorced and a lot of people no longer bothered to stop and chat. Some even passed by on the other side.

As I walk through the town this morning, I try to visualise it through the eyes of the new season's tourists. The bulbs are out round the walls; the Abbey looms picturesquely from the end of the high street; all the major chains are represented in the shopping mall. This is middle England: comfortable and civilised, blinkered and self-satisfied.

Freda has fallen asleep by the time we reach Sainsbury's, but when I lift her out of her buggy and sit her in a trolley she wakes and immediately bursts into tears. She is inconsolable and I soon realise why: we have lost Piglet. Piglet once bore some resemblance to a Sheppard drawing. Though he is now little more than a small pinkish bag, distorted by months of vigorous sucking and tugging, he is the love of Freda's life. When we set out for our walk, Freda was clutching him; we have dropped him somewhere along the way. Though everything in me rebels, I know there is only one thing for it: I remove Freda from the trolley, strap her back in her buggy and set out to retrace our steps.

I have almost despaired of finding him when, two thirds of the way back, I spot a pinkish bloom in the War Memorial Garden which seems not to belong there. I sprint across the grass, in contravention of the many signs forbidding me to, and snatch him up, realising as I do so that I can't possibly hand him back to Freda, whose wailing is reaching new heights of passion. It has rained in the night, he is covered in mud and she will shove him straight into her mouth. I stuff him into my pocket and head for home at an ungainly run, scattering pedestrians as I go.

Back home, I recklessly ply Freda with chocolate biscuits and plunge Piglet into hot soapy water. Now I have to get him dry. I don't own a tumble drier – I never have – it's my puny contribution to stemming global warming and I've always been irritatingly priggish about it, I expect. Today, I wouldn't, quite frankly, give a toss about global warming if I could just get this soggy little bundle dry and stop my grandchild from screaming at me. I wring the water out of him with the savagery of one murdering a chicken, stick him on a radiator and turn the heating up to sauna temperature.

From here on in things begin to improve: Annie emerges and plays *incy wincy spider* with Freda; I have a cup of coffee and read The Guardian; Piglet dries; we have lunch; Freda falls asleep, exhausted. It is, therefore, nearly four thirty when we set out for the second time on the trip to Sainsbury's.

All the best stuff has gone, of course, by the time we get there, and I am forced to buy the expensive stuff – fair trade and organic – which is all that is left. As I make my way round to the dairy aisle, I see David Scott. I'm not sure it's him at first because he looks so unlike his professional self. He's wearing a track suit and trainers, none too clean, and sporting designer stubble and unbrushed hair. He immediately starts talking to me about sex – well the sexuality of my students, actually, so it's not that much fun. He thinks Ekrem might have been gay, which is an interesting idea. Is it possible that all that sleaziness with the girls was overcompensation?

We meet Christiane and Yukiko doing their shopping. A fine style contrast they present: Christiane is in a sensible padded anorak and a woolly hat, while Yukiko is in a light spring coat (too thin really for today's cold wind) and Burberry accessories. I'm not sure if they recognise DCI Scott in grunge mode – they certainly don't acknowledge him. His trolley screams *single man*: milk, cereal, strong Italian coffee, pizzas, shepherd's pie, bangers-and-mash-for-one and a twelve pack of Foster's. I feel a pang of envy for the singleness of it, for the please-myself solitude it betokens, but as I start my walk back home, pushing my laden buggy, I rather wish I'd invited him back for supper.

8

SUNDAY: Investigation Day Four

Waking in the insistent light of a bright, blowy morning, Scott registered *Sunday* and pulled a pillow over his head, not so much because he would enjoy the luxury of sleeping in but because he couldn't imagine what he was going to do with his day. He'd spent hours mulling over the students' phone records the day before and he had questions to ask, but that would have to wait till tomorrow, when he'd take Tyler with him. And he couldn't talk to the librarian till tomorrow. So what to do today?

Suddenly, propelled by a kind of fury, he was out of bed and down the stairs. Barefoot, in his boxers, he switched the radio on loud and tackled the mess in the kitchen: he ran bowls of scalding water, created mountains of detergent foam, scrubbed, sloshed and dried until an orderly heap of clean crockery and cutlery lay on the kitchen counter. A couple of saucepans, victims of his errant attempts at cooking, he put to soak, though he knew this was only a preliminary to throwing them away. Then he hauled out the wet washing from the machine and stuffed it into the tumble drier.

He surveyed the kitchen: better, certainly, but the floor was dirty and the cooker top stained. The sitting room, when he went into it, was tidyish (he didn't spend enough time there to make it untidy) but dusty and unwelcoming. He could tackle this too. Or he could not. He picked up the Yellow Pages and checked 'Domestic Cleaning Services', found 'We Clean 4 U' (*fully insured – references guaranteed*), phoned the number and left a message. He made coffee and toast and ate and drank on the move as he threw yesterday's tracksuit into the washing machine, shaved and showered and dressed in sweater and jeans. It was now ten thirty and the day loomed ahead.

Half an hour later he was driving into Dungate, the small, grey seaside town where his parents had spent their retirement. When he'd got in the car, he'd had unspecified thoughts of a walk by the sea, and he'd somehow ended up here, cruising past his parents' bungalow, now rendered unrecognizable by the addition of a huge conservatory bolted onto the front, obliterating his father's symmetrical flowerbeds. He drove down to the sea wall and parked.

The wind was furious here, fighting with him as he opened the car door. The wall offered a wide walkway, stretching for miles along the coast. On his right was a continuous line of beach huts, three or four deep, lovingly painted and slightly fantastical in their decoration; on the left was a steep drop to the pebbled beach with steps down at intervals. He set off at a brisk walk. At times like these, he wished he had a dog with him. Perhaps he should get a dog. It might be good for him, make him take more exercise. And it might be good to have something there to greet him when he got home. With the hours he worked? Who was he kidding? Anything or anyone who waited for him to get home would be so pissed off by the time he arrived it wouldn't be worth it.

He broke into a jog. The wind came almost directly off the sea and it was hard to steer a straight course. One or two of the beach huts had been opened up and their owners were sitting outside them, swathed in coats and rugs, drinking from thermoses. They were elderly couples and family groups mainly. No-one sat alone. He saw himself through their eyes, a lone figure in their landscape, just passing through. After a while, he slowed to a walk again and allowed his mind to slow too, to roam where it would until it settled, uncomfortably, on Gina Gray.

Was it just because she had been his teacher? Did teachers always seem like that: so settled, so secure, so permanent? She had made him feel so impermanent somehow, yesterday in the supermarket, with her granddaughter and her trolley full of real food, smiling acknowledgements at people as she went round. He imagined her today, cooking Sunday lunch for the family: husband, children, grandchildren. There were probably dogs and cats too. He wouldn't be surprised if lonely foreign students found their way to her table. She was certainly pally enough with the girls; he could see her laughing and chatting with those two yesterday, while they totally ignored him.

He really could do with her help in this case. It was difficult interviewing those students. They seemed to understand English pretty well but they expressed themselves oddly and he couldn't tell if that was just a problem with the language or if they were hiding things. Usually he prided himself on being pretty acute about the way people answered his questions: he could spot evasion and unwillingness as well as fabrication and guilt. With these students it was different. He'd had a sense with nearly all of them that they could have told him more, that he was being offered polite stonewalling. If he felt certain he could trust her, he'd ask Gina Gray to sit in on the interviews second time round, but he wasn't sure that he could trust her. There was something about her manner: a kind of – skittishness was the word that came to his mind, as though you couldn't be sure what direction she might suddenly go off in. And she found everything so bloody funny, him included.

He sat down on a bollard and ate the cheese sandwich he'd brought with him. He could have had lunch in a pub, but he didn't want to, didn't want to be a sad man eating and drinking alone among the cheerful family groups out for Sunday lunch. He ate his apple as he walked back, thinking about those mobile phone records. How connected they all were, those students: Yilmaz and his Turkish and Russian friends; the Iranians and their calls home; the girls all phoning each other on Wednesday evening; Desirée phoning Denis from the girls' night out; half the class, including Yilmaz, calling the Turkish girl when she was off sick. Such interdependence: how was he to cut through it? What did he understand about it? He felt for his mobile in his pocket. Tomorrow, it would be ringing again. Tomorrow he'd get back to real life.

9

MONDAY: *Present Indicative*

I don't hate Mondays as a rule; I like my job and find it more restful, generally, than being at home. Today though, I am resentful because I lost my weekend. Don't misjudge me, please. I'm not a monster: I love my granddaughter and would murder with my bare hands anyone who tried to harm her. I do need time to myself, though. When my own children were small, I used to shut myself in the loo for a bit of solitude, but they would come battering at the door, demanding to be let in, threatening to *poo here on the floor* if I didn't admit them. So this morning I'm a touch frazzled.

I meet the 2-year Masters class at ten o'clock. We are in Seminar Room 2 on Mondays and instead of the conference table arrangement there are rows of chairs with little flip-over writing boards attached to one arm. They're fairly impossible to write much on, so we work together on the board. Laurent is missing. No-one has seen him since Friday. Denis and Desirée, who share a flat with him, knocked on his door this morning but got no reply. He didn't say he was going away for the weekend. I wouldn't normally be worried: Laurent is never very good at Mondays. Today, though, a niggle of anxiety is at work. I shall ring David Scott as soon as this class is over.

We do the disappearing sentence exercise. This is syntax practice. It's about putting together and pulling apart complex sentences. It's also a game. What happens is that we build up a complex sentence on the board. Each person takes a turn at adding one, two, or three words to a sentence (they may also add a comma instead of a word). The aim is to make the sentence as long as possible: everyone tries not to be the person to add the last word. We also try to be a little fantastic. *Nothing trite*, I urge them, *nothing banal*. When we've got our sentence, then we dismantle it: we take turns at removing one, two or three words, but we have to do it so that the sentence still makes sense at every stage. We go on until we have the irreducible minimum, the shortest sentence possible. *Jesus wept* is our model. So this is how it goes today (you may think this won't be interesting, but trust me, it will – what's about to happen I can only compare, sceptic though I am, to an unnerving Ouija board experience).

In this seminar room, with its rows of chairs, the students arrange themselves differently, the genders slightly more mixed up. Picture the scene with me. From left to right in the first row in front of me are Ceren, Christiane, Yukiko and Irina, and next to Irina is Valery, who has trouble with grammar and hopes Irina will help him. In the row behind, left to right, sit Desirée and Denis, the Turks, Asil and Ahmet, then the Iranians, Atash and Farid. To give you the whole picture, the door is to my right and there is a window looking out to the corridor in the right-hand wall. The whiteboard is, of course, behind me. Having given you the stage directions, for ease and for drama I shall recount to you what follows playscript style. The script goes thus:

CEREN: My father
CHRISTIANE: My *dear* father
(*She has done this before and knows the ropes*).
YUKIKO: Add comma, then 'who worked'
IRINA: In circus
(*Laughter*)
GINA GRAY: In what, Irina?

IRINA: In *the* circus
VALERY: As *the* man
                (*Applause. Valery says something to Irina in Russian*)
FARID: On the – swing?
GINA GRAY: Not *swing*. Does anyone know what it's called?
DESIREE: Trapèze
GINA GRAY: Well, *trapeze*, yes. What was that, Irina?
IRINA: It is same word in Russian. I am explaining Valery.
GINA GRAY: Well, please speak English, you two. Atash, what next?
ATASH: I can add, *daring* man?
GINA GRAY: Excellent, yes. So, we've got *My dear father, who worked in the circus as the daring man on the trapeze*. Ahmet, what next?
AHMET: Comma
GINA GRAY: Comma. Asil?
ASIL: Enjoyed
DENIS: Watching
DESIREE: The happy faces
CEREN: Of the children
CHRISTIANE: In the audience
YUKIKO: So
IRINA: Much that
VALERY: One day
FARID: He looked down
ATASH: For too long
AHMET: And slipped
                (*cries of mock horror*)
ASIL: Off
                (*laughter*)
DENIS: And
DESIREE: Fell
CEREN: Missed the net
GINA GRAY: We'd need 'and missed', but we've got a lot of *and*s. How else can we do it, Christiane?

CHRISTIANE:Comma, then *missing the net*

GINA GRAY: Good. What sort of net. Does anyone know what it's called?

DENIS: Security net

GINA GRAY: Not security, but safety. So, we've got, *My dear father, who worked in the circus as the daring man on the trapeze, enjoyed watching the happy faces of the children in the audience so much that one day he looked down for too long and slipped off and fell, missing the safety net.* Yukiko, can you add any more?

YUKIKO: Comma, and sadly

IRINA: Was crushed

VALERY: To death

FARID: On the ground

So there we have it and for brevity's sake I shall summarise for you how we dismantle it. All the adjectives and adverbs go first so, on the board, we have:

My father, who worked in the circus as the man on the trapeze, enjoyed watching the faces of the children in the audience so much that one day he looked down for too long and slipped off and fell, missing the net, and was crushed to death on the ground.

Then Desirée takes out *in the circus,* Ceren *the faces of,* Christiane *one day,* Yukiko *for too long,* Irina *and slipped off* and Valery *missing the net.* We pause to look at our sentence now:

My father, who worked as the man on the trapeze, enjoyed watching the children in the audience so much that he looked down and fell and was crushed to death on the ground.

Now Farid takes out *on the ground,* Atash *who worked as,* Ahmet *the children in,* Asil *down,* Denis *looked and,* Desirée *to death.*

My father, the man on the trapeze, enjoyed watching the audience so much that he fell and was crushed.

So we're back to the front row again and Ceren takes out *my father* and the comma, Christiane *on the trapeze,* Yukiko *watching,* and Irina *fell and.* As I'm rubbing this off, I hear her say something to Valery in Russian and I turn with my rhetorical *What's the first rule in an English language classroom, Irina?* on my lips - and I only just restrain myself from screaming, though even so I know my hand goes to my mouth in an absurdly dramatic gesture.

What I see, as I turn round, are Irina and Valery with their heads together, sharing a joke, and beyond them, through the window out into the corridor, a man's face looking in – Ekrem's face. He is watching Irina and Valery, and I'm aware that my legs feel very odd. I wonder, in an abstract sort of way, whether I may be going to faint, but then his eyes meet mine and I realise that he's not Ekrem – he's not even very like Ekrem. He is a Turk though, I think, and there's something about his face, so that for a moment there I really thought I'd seen a ghost.

He disappears from view, not hastily or guiltily, but quite casually, and I turn back to my class who are looking at me and my (presumably) stricken face in some alarm. I know how Macbeth felt when the ghost of Banquo turned up at his party and no-one else seemed to notice. (Macbeth had ordered Banquo to be murdered, of course; I wouldn't want you to think that this is a clue that I am the murderer. This isn't *The Murder of Roger Ackroyd* with a killer-narrator. I tell you the story as it happened. I play no tricks on you).

I admonish Irina and Valery, who must wonder why their peccadillo has caused me so much distress, especially as my voice, I find, is by no means steady. Then I turn back to the sentence on the board.

The man enjoyed the audience so much that he was crushed

I've no idea whose turn it is so I call at random on Desirée, who takes out *the audience*.

Denis protests, 'Surely *enjoyed* must have an object. It's a transitive verb.'

I overrule, 'But it's got an object now, Denis, hasn't it? *The man enjoyed so much.* Before, *so much* was adverbial – he enjoyed *to such an extent*. Now *so much* means *so many things*, so it becomes the object.'

This is complicated and I've probably lost several of them, but they are happy to believe me. *Trust me, I'm an English teacher*. And then, in quick succession, it is done. Ceren (who hasn't quite got the point about *so much*) takes out *much* and I allow it, then Christiane takes out *that* and Yukiko *enjoyed so*. And there it is. Why the hell didn't I see this coming? Our sentence sits there on the board and we all gaze at it:

The man was crushed.

There is a silence. I look at them and they don't look at me. Atash and Farid exchange a look; Desirée twists a lock of shiny brown hair round a finger; Denis inspects his shirt cuffs. In the front row, only Ceren stares at the board. Christiane writes something in a notebook; Yukiko has withdrawn into some private, interior space and is focusing on a point on the floor; Irina is putting away her pen and notebook; Valery has a hand over his mouth, but I think he is smiling. Then Asil – bless him - asks,

'We can't say just, *The man crushed*?'

So now I can go back into teacher mode and explain how *crushed* would need an object. I ask, for good measure, what the sentence would mean if we removed the initial *The* to leave *Man was crushed*, and Farid tells me that it would mean mankind in general. I, because I can't resist it, ask if that would include womankind. He says it would, and I even see the glimmer of a smile deep in the forest of his beard. I find that I can, quite casually now, wipe the sentence off the board, and the waters close once again over Ekrem's head.

At coffee time, standing outside the SCR with my cigarette, I fish out the card David Scott gave me on Friday and use my mobile to ring his. He is, it turns out, on the campus. I tell him about Laurent and he says he'll meet me in the SCR. A second assignation: people will start talking. I hope.

He looks a lot better than he did on Saturday evening - he's

63

clean and wearing another good suit – but he looks stressed. I get him a coffee, black with sugar, we retire to our corner nook and he says, 'Bloody keys!'

It turns out that he has a brilliant theory about Ekrem's murder (he doesn't specify what it is) but it depends on someone having got hold of a key to the library. He has spent the best part of the morning talking to the Social Science librarian, the security staff and anyone else he can think of but he's been assured that 1) no key to the library has gone missing in the past three years and 2) the library keys can't be copied: because they are external keys (the library office key also opens the front door to the Social Science block) they are made so they can't be copied. No key-cutter would be able to produce a copy. So Yukiko was the only holder of a key that night and at five feet and seven stone she can't be the murderer.

'Unless the porter dunnit,' I suggest.

'I have thought of that, obviously,' he says, and I detect a bit of sarcasm there, 'but Clive Davies has worked for the college for over thirty years, has never been in trouble and has no criminal record of any kind.'

'There's always a first time. Perhaps it was a *crime passionnel* – especially given what you were telling me in Sainsbury's on Saturday.'

'This has to have been planned, and there have to have been two of them.'

Though I try to look casual, he sees my ears prick up and I think he's going to clam up on me but he says,

'We've got Yilmaz's mobile records: there's no sign of Davies there but Amiel and Longueville are all over them.'

'Really?' I am genuinely surprised. 'I didn't think they were friends. I never saw them speak to each other.'

'He was definitely supplying Amiel with drugs – the lad finally admitted it – and I'm prepared to bet he was supplying Longueville with some recreational stuff as well.'

'That's why you talked to them again on Friday'

'Yes. Amiel was quite helpful once I put the pressure on. Longueville played the little lawyer and wanted to know what evidence we'd got against him.'

'The fact that Laurent was helpful makes me worried now that he's disappeared.'

'I've got a couple of men on their way to his flat now. I'm just heading over there myself. It's in somewhere called Beechwood, if you can tell me where that is.'

'I'll come with you and show you if you like. I'm not busy.' I see him hesitate so I add, 'I can stay in the car.'

We get into his blue Peugeot. It's clean and tidy without appearing to be the love of his life, of which I approve. Beechwood Village, as it's officially known, is on the edge of the campus. It's designed to look villagey so the flats are disguised as houses, each with a front path and a little porch. There are no gardens, though. They'd soon run rampant left to students' care. The police car is already there when we arrive and Scott seems not to notice when I follow him into the building. The flat, which Laurent shares with Denis, Desirée and a quiet Danish mathematician, is on the ground floor. There is a central living-room-cum-kitchen with doors leading off it and the door of what must be Laurent's room stands open. As a man emerges from it, I sit down on a sofa and try to blend myself into the background.

'He's not here, sir.'

'Was the door unlocked?'

'We had to force it, sir.'

Scott goes inside and I dare not follow, so I concentrate on trying to hear anything he says. I hear 'struggle'. Was that 'signs of' or 'no signs of'? I hear a lot of moving around, drawers being opened and closed, a window being opened, and then the underling emerges with some stuff in a bag and Scott follows him out.

'Get that lot straight to the lab.'

He takes a look round the living room and kitchen and I'm interested to watch a professional at work, to see where he looks first, where the obvious hiding places are. (I'll pass on a tip: if you've got anything incriminating, never hide it in the bread bin or the freezer). He says nothing as we drive back to the main campus, so I venture an indirect approach.

'Are you allowed to take things away from someone's room like that, without a search warrant?'

He's wondering whether to bother answering, but he says, eventually, 'He was reported by you as a missing person; we're looking for anything that will help us find him. What was taken away was possible evidence of criminal activity.'

'A weapon you mean? Or blood'

He sighs, 'No.'

'Drugs then?'

He says nothing. I am beginning to get tired of this.

'So do you have any more idea where he is than I would have if I'd gone in and looked round his room?'

He brings the car to a stop outside the Student Union building and without looking at me he says, 'Amiel's wallet and phone aren't there. That means we can check for credit card transactions and cash withdrawals and monitor his phone activity. We've still got his passport, so he won't be leaving the country. It shouldn't be difficult to locate him.'

'Alive or dead?'

'We've no reason to suppose he's dead.'

'Except that he was very helpful to you about Ekrem Yilmaz's drug-dealing activities and Ekrem Yilmaz has been brutally murdered.'

He opens his door and before he can come round and usher me out of my side, I get out myself. I smile breezily at him across the bonnet.

'Well, DCI Scott, I'm sure you'll keep me informed of progress. If he hasn't turned up by tomorrow, I shall have to phone his mother and I'd like to have something to tell her.'

I think he's going to get back into the car without replying, but instead he moves towards me and says, 'Talking of phoning, maybe you can tell me something. The girls – women - in your class all made mobile calls to each other on Wednesday evening, though they say they spent the evening together here at the Union. Desirée Bonfort, Christiane Becker, Ceren Vural and Irina Boklova all made calls to one another in the early evening and Yukiko Iwaki called Christiane Becker just before ten, though she claims that she met up with them shortly afterwards.'

I pat his arm in what I know is an irritatingly patronising manner.

'You've never been a young woman DCI Scott. The early calls were to discuss what they were wearing and the optimum arrival time. Yukiko called to say she was coming over. Women like to communicate. We think it makes the world go round.'

As I walk across to my office I wonder why I feel the need to be so arsey with him and I find I can think of several reasons:

1.   I have a problem with men in general (due in no small part to my experience of marriage) and with men in authority in particular.

2.   I feel a need to keep prodding to make sure that David Scott, whom I remember as a schoolboy, is really a senior policeman.

3.   (Paradoxically when taken with 2) it is just possible that I fancy him.

10

TUESDAY: Investigation Day Six

They brought Denis de Longueville into the station for questioning. If he wanted to play it by the book, then he could see how he liked it. At first he wanted to call a lawyer in London - *a friend of my father* - but when he was told that they would keep him at the station till his lawyer arrived, he agreed to the prompt arrival of the duty solicitor. Emma Bright was small, sharp-faced, young and assertive. Scott had dealt with her before but he'd never seen her so fluttered by a client. De Longueville strolled in wearing a blazer and an open-necked white shirt. His air of disdain and his immaculate tailoring seemed to stir Ms Bright to even greater efforts than usual in the defence of her client's civil liberties.

Her client, in spite of his air of *hauteur*, was palpably nervous to start with. Sweaty palms, Scott thought, but he watched him relax visibly as he saw where the line of questioning was going. What had he been expecting? Scott wondered. Was he asking the wrong questions? He was interested in the drug-dealing as the most promising line open at the moment. Had de Longueville ever bought drugs from Ekrem Yilmaz? Ms Bright replied that her client was not obliged to answer that question. Did he ever use drugs, smoke a bit of cannabis, for example? Her client was not obliged to answer that either. Did he know of anyone else who bought drugs from Yilmaz? Her client preferred to remain silent.

Scott tried a different approach: he described the manner of Yilmaz's death in graphic detail and had the satisfaction of seeing de Longueville's pretty, self-satisfied face turn a shade paler; he asked him, as a future lawyer, if he didn't think it right that the police should make every effort to find Yilmaz's killer or killers. Did he not, Scott asked, think it was his duty to give the police every possible assistance?

Ms Bright requested a conference with her client and eventually came back with a deal. Her client, she said, intended to have a career as an international lawyer. Of course, he wished to give the police all the help he could but he was understandably anxious not to prejudice his future career by acquiring any sort of criminal record. She had advised him that his own personal behaviour could not be deemed relevant to the case under investigation, but he was prepared, in the spirit of civic duty, to name some of Ekrem Yilmaz's associates, without any implication that they had been involved in criminal activity.

Scott had to be content with that. He knew that Yilmaz could have tried blackmailing de Longueville and he put that possibility to him, but the Frenchman shrugged it off with the rejoinder that he thought his word on anything would have more credibility that Yilmaz's. Although Scott hated his smug tone and would have liked to wipe the smile off his face somehow, he knew that what he said was true, and he judged him to be a man who would get himself out of trouble by bluff, guile and pulling strings rather than by anything as strenuous as a violent murder.

He'd called a team meeting for Wednesday morning. He needed to be able to give them a strong line of enquiry; at the moment they were going in too many directions at once. He got into his car and drove fast round to the college. He tracked down Clive Davies on his tea break but got nothing more than he had from the first interview with him. Davies was relaxed and eager to help if he could but he offered nothing Scott wanted. Here was the only man with the obvious opportunity to kill Yilmaz and he appeared to have zero motive. He didn't feature in Yilmaz's phone records or in de Longueville's list of Yilmaz's contacts; he was happily married, a model citizen and had never been to Turkey.

Yukiko Iwaki was also anxious to be helpful: she came into Gina Gray's office looking as neat and trim as usual, this time in a little Black Watch tartan skirt, black tights and a green sweater. *A little doll*, he thought. She made a small ducking movement of her head, a sort of residual bow, as he greeted her, and sat down tidily, knees together, on the edge of a chair. He took her again through the events of Wednesday night; she answered calmly and precisely without hesitation or uncertainty, changing nothing until he asked her, as he had before, whether she liked Ekrem Yilmaz. The previous time, he noted, she had simply said *Not so much, really*; this time she looked directly at him and said, 'He passed away, so we should not speak badly about him, but I think nobody is sorry that he died.'

As she left the room and he was scanning his notes, he spotted something he had circled. He jumped up and called after her,

'Yukiko.'

He followed her down the corridor.

'You closed the library doors just before ten but you didn't hand in the keys till ten past ten. What were you doing in those ten minutes?'

He didn't really expect an interesting answer. *Clearing up*, he thought, or *putting books away*, but she gave a little trill of laughter and put her hand to her mouth in embarrassment.

'I was changing my clothes, in the toilet.'

'Why did you change?'

'To go to the Student Union.'

'And you couldn't go in the clothes you were wearing?

She giggled again.

'I was wearing library clothes. They weren't dancing clothes, you see.'

'I see.'

And suddenly he did see: not everything, but a glimmer of light.

'Yukiko, if the stacks were moved together while you were in the toilet, do you think you would have heard them?'

She was looking at him, wide-eyed with surprise for a moment, then she shook her head.

'Maybe not. I always close the two office doors, and the water was running some of the time. And I think maybe I was singing a little bit too.'

Again, her hand went to her mouth.

'So you might not have heard someone going past the toilet door and out into the foyer?'

'Aah. Maybe not.'

'One last thing. Do you usually go straight out by the office door after you've locked the main door?'

'Oh no. Usually, I make it tidy We don't re-shelve the books. That's the librarians' job. But the students leave a lot of books on the tables and I pile them up tidily. I'm afraid I didn't do that on Wednesday. I left a mess.'

As he drove back to the station, his spirits, which had soared at the glimpse of a possible solution, started spiralling downward again. It wasn't really such a clever solution; it left a hell of a lot of things unexplained. For one thing, there was the sex: there might have been time for Yilmaz to be killed in those ten minutes, but not for him to have sex first. And then wouldn't the porter have noticed two men coming out of the office exit? He hadn't asked Clive Davies about anything that happened before Yukiko handed the keys in, but wouldn't he have mentioned two men coming out just before she did?

He called Clive Davies on his work number and left a message for him to call back urgently. He decided to bring the Turks in for questioning: Ahmed Kurtal, Asil Yurekli, Ceren

Vural, and five others who featured both in Yilmaz's phone records and in de Longueville's list. He was tired of getting nowhere, sick of being stonewalled. These people would be scared by a police station; it was time to play tough.

11

TUESDAY: *Comparative Forms*

Nine a.m. I am in my office and I have to call Laurent's mother. I can find no excuse for putting it off any longer. I have spoken to her once before. When we first realised that Laurent had a drug problem, back last October, I summoned him and told him he would have to go home. Simple. Easy. We have a *no drugs* policy. Out. Twenty minutes later, I got a panicky call from Gillian in the office.

'There's a woman on the phone, speaking French. I think she wants you.'

Mme Amiel did want me and she was indeed speaking French, very fast and with a great deal of sobbing. Since she also repeated herself a lot, I got the drift: an absent father; her daughter such a good girl, never any trouble; Laurent a good boy really but in bad company; England her last hope et cetera. Cravenly, pusillanimously I gave in, stipulating only, in my crude French, 'Laurent doit avoir l'assistance d'un conseiller de drogues, Mme Amiel.'

She agreed eagerly: the best, no matter what it cost. *Le meilleur, n'importe combien il coûte.*

So of course I'm really looking forward to talking to her again and explaining, in French, that we appear to have lost her son, who has now been missing for four days. I make some preliminary notes - useful phrases, an opening gambit – then I take a deep breath and pick up the phone. I present the conversation to you verbatim here for those who can really speak French and might enjoy the pleasure of critiquing my attempts, but I also give you a translation which, I feel, successfully conveys the extreme banality of our conversation. The translation, in fact, reads exactly like one of those model conversations one finds in English Language textbooks, which bear no relation to real life as we know it.

'Mme Amiel? Ici c'est Mme Gray de Marlbury College. Je regrette que je dois vous raconter des mauvaises nouvelles.'

(*Madame Amiel? This is Mrs Gray from Marlbury College. I'm afraid I have to tell you some bad news*)

'Mon Dieu! Mon fils! Qu'est-ce qui est arrivé?'

(*My God! My son! What has happened?*)

'J'ai peur que Laurent a disparu, madame.'

(*I'm afraid Laurent has disappeared, madame*)

'Disparu? Laurent a disparu?'

(*Disappeared? Laurent has disappeared?*)

'Oui madame. Personne le n'a pas vu depuis vendredi soir.'

(*Yes, madame. No-one has seen him since Friday evening*)

'Ah mon dieu! Que vais-je faire?'

(*Oh My God! What am I going to do?*)

'Ne vous dérangez pas, madame. La police le cherche à ce moment, Madame Amiel, et nous esperons qu'ils le trouveront bientôt.'

(*Don't upset yourself, madame. The police are looking for him at this moment and we hope they will find him soon.*)

'Ah mon pauvre fils, mon pauvre petit Laurent!'

(*Ah my poor son, my poor little Laurent*)

'Je vous informererai aussitôt que j'ai plus de nouvelles.'

(*I will inform you as soon as I have more news.*)

'Merci, merci. Ah Mon Dieu, Mon Dieu.'

(*Thank you, thank you. Oh My God, My God*)

'Au revoir, madame.'

(*Good-bye, madame*)

I replace the receiver, put my head down on my desk and

whimper for a bit. Then I go out for a cigarette. What do I really think about Laurent's disappearance? I ask myself this as I puff my way round the outside of the building. Do I really think he might be dead or do I think he's down in London getting wasted on his mother's money? DCI Scott will know by now whether he's used his bank cards since he went missing, but is he going to tell me? I may need to bully him a bit. He thinks I'm a nosey old cow, I know, but I am after all responsible for Laurent - in a way. This isn't just idle curiosity; I've told his mother I'll let her know any news. I think of phoning him but an unusually ruffled Desirée has already been to my office this morning to tell me that Denis has been taken to the police station for questioning, so Scotty is presumably busy stringing him up by his thumbs at this moment. I'll get him later though. He shan't escape.

I teach for the rest of the morning: I listen to a recording of train announcements with a bewildered elementary class and I don't let them in on the secret that native speakers generally can't make head or tail of them either; I read *The Quiet American* with an advanced class taking a literature option and I lose the will to live with a foundation year Economics group giving talks on supply and demand. As I return to my office at lunch time, Gillian comes out of the office, flapping a telephone message at me: the Principal would like to see me as soon as I have a moment.

I wouldn't want you to get the impression that I'm in the habit of popping into the Principal's office for a chat. I have, in fact, never had a chat with him of any kind. He chaired the awesome appointment panel which interviewed me for my job and when he sees me around the college he smiles vaguely at me; he knows he should know who I am but can't quite remember. So, always up for a new experience, I comb my hair, put on some lipstick and head across to Norman Street's office.

His secretary, obviously primed for my possible arrival,

ushers me straight in and he comes round his desk to offer me a hearty handshake. His stock in trade is being the bluff Yorkshire man and I expect he thinks of himself as *good with people*, which he probably could be if he were a bit more interested in them and a bit less interested in money. There used to be a cartoon character on children's television with a face like a cash register and £ signs spinning in his eyes; I always expect our Principal's face to do that. Money is what is exercising him this afternoon, though he goes through the niceties over Ekrem and we agree with one another that his death is a terrible thing to have happened and share the hope that the police will get to the bottom of it soon. Then he gets down to it.

'I don't need to tell you, Gina –'

Gina? Since when have we been on those terms?

'– how important our overseas student recruitment is to college finances.'

I smile noncommittally.

'And we do appreciate what a crucial role the ELTD plays in both recruitment and retention.'

Oh good. So crucial that he's going to stop paying us peanuts?

'But an event like this, you know, could seriously knock our overseas recruitment. People understandably get anxious and ....'

I let him witter on in this vein for a bit and when he finally peters out I say,

'If it's any comfort, I think we shall find, when the police have gathered all their evidence, that Ekrem was a pretty unsavoury character and probably involved in criminal activities. The fact that someone like him has been killed shouldn't make parents feel that the UK is a dangerous place in general to study in.'

'Ah.'

His brow furrows and he shifts in his chair. He is not as comforted by my words as I expect.

'I wonder, you see,' he continues, 'whether the police may be overreacting.'

'Overreacting? To the murder of a student?'

'No - to the possibility that there may be some criminal activity behind it.'

'Well murder is a criminal activity, isn't it?'

He gives me a hard look and I realise that, though his eyes don't actually spin £ signs, they are quite scarily sharp.

'I'm sure you know what I mean, Gina. This chap Yilmaz was an employee of the Turkish government, and so are several of the other Turks we have here. I gather that two of them have been questioned by the police already. The Turkish government is very unhappy about that. I've had their Education Minister on to me personally this morning: apparently, one of the students telephoned his office complaining about the aggressive interrogation of his wife.'

'Aggressive interrogation? Compared with the methods the Turkish police use? Well, I think you'll find the students and their wives have still got all their fingernails.'

He clenches and unclenches a hairy fist. Possibly he would like to slap me. I can see this interview isn't going as he hoped it would. Suddenly he bares his teeth in an approximation to a smile and says,'I'm sorry. You must be missing your lunch. I'll get Janet to bring us some coffee and sandwiches.'

He strides to the door, issues some instructions and then ushers me down to the other end of the room where, he assures me, we shall be *more comfortable*, though I was actually quite comfortable where I was. This isn't so good. It's difficult for a small woman to be assertive from the depths of an easy chair: sit forward and you look ill at ease; sit back and your feet don't touch the ground. He makes small talk – the latest building development – and reflects on how pleasant it would be for me and my staff to have a purpose-built language unit to work in. I begin to lose my grip on the situation. Am I about to be offered a bribe of some sort? To do what?

Lunch arrives and I have not been served such a daintily presented sandwich lunch since the days when my husband, Andrew, inveigled me into joining the Board of Visitors at the prison. There, we used to get lunch in the Governor's office: sandwiches - minus crusts – served on rose-patterned china on a tray with an embroidered cloth, carried in by a 'trusty' in a vest with tattoos down both arms. Today, we don't have the tray cloth, and Janet, of course, doesn't have the tattoos, but the sandwiches look sumptuous. We dive in and as he deals with the mayonnaise running down his chin, Norman Street says, 'I try to get over to the SCR for lunch – it's a good time to have a chat to folk – but I often end up eating at my desk, I'm afraid. You eat in the SCR often, do you?'

As my mouth is full of prawns at that moment, I waggle my head ambiguously.

'I notice you've been having lunch with Detective Chief Inspector Scott. Friend of yours, is he?'

'No,' I reply blandly.

'I thought perhaps -'

'No.'

Oh go on, Gina. Tell him.

'He's a former student of mine, actually.'

'Oh, I see.' He gives an odd laugh. 'I must say, you don't look old enough. Ah, well, mm...'

He eats in silence, thinking hard, I would say, then he wipes his mouth, puts down his napkin and says,

'The thing is, Gina, I was wondering if you and this chap Scott might be close.'

'Close?'

'Yes. I thought you might have some influence with him.'

'Influence?'

'I don't want to interfere – seem to be uncooperative – but if you know him could you perhaps get him to steer clear?'

'Steer clear?'

'Yes. Of the Turks. Pursue other avenues.'

'Other avenues?'

I can keep this up for hours.

'Well he keeps saying they're pursuing several avenues of enquiry. Can't he pursue one of the others for a bit and lay off the Turks?'

'I imagine DCI Scott will go down whichever avenue he thinks will lead most directly to Ekrem's killer. We wouldn't want him to do anything else, would we, Norman?'

I get another of those sharp looks.

'Gina, I think we need to understand one another. The link we have with the Turkish government is crucial to our operation and to your department. Your job and those of your staff are highly sensitive to any downturn in overseas student numbers. At the moment, the Turkish government sends us an average of fifteen students a year. £150,000 in fees – just about the salary bill for your department. In our conversation this morning, the Minister of Education made it clear that unless their students are protected from police harassment, they will order them all home and will terminate their contract with us. So, what have you got to say now?'

I have so many things to say that it's difficult to marshal them all at once. They may not come out in the perfect order, but I tick them off on my fingers.

'Well, first I'd say that the ELTD pays for itself over and over again, though we don't see the benefits of the money we make for the college, and it would be grossly unfair to penalise us if overseas student numbers took a temporary dip. And anyway you'd simply be killing the golden goose. Secondly, the Turkish government can't take their students home if they're part of a police investigation – they'd be stopped at Heathrow. Thirdly, if we lose the Turks, we'll have to find some more students from somewhere else. Fourthly, David Scott is a good policeman who's not going to throw up a murder case and risk his career just to keep us happy. And lastly – no, please let me finish – there is such a thing as justice and the rule of law, whatever the Turkish government may think. *This is the English not the Turkish court –*

'What?'

I pick up the coffee pot.

'Henry IV Part Two. The new king, Henry V, assures the court that he's not going to be a despot and that under him England will be ruled fairly and justly. Turkey was a byword for corruption at the end of the sixteenth century. Can I give you some more coffee?'

He brushes the coffee aside, gets up and paces about, looking out of his picture window. His is the only office on the campus that still has a view.

'I'm sorry you're taking this attitude, Gina. I can only say that there will be repercussions, especially as I gather you've lost another student now.'

'Well, I didn't lose him personally. I mean, it wasn't like letting a dog off its lead and then having it run off. He's –'

'Do you really think this is something to be flippant about?'

I stand up, brushing down sandwich crumbs.

'No. No I don't. I take finding Laurent very seriously, as I do finding Ekrem's killer. Which is why I intend to give DCI Scott every possible assistance. Thank you for lunch.'

And I'm out of there fast before I find myself offering my resignation.

12

WEDNESDAY: Investigation Day Seven

Scott was in the Incident Room long before anyone else. He'd not slept well: the need to give a clear message to the team had made his mind churn with confusion. He couldn't get a proper foothold yet; every step so far had opened up alternative routes. In the darkest reaches of the night he'd got up and made some notes but now they looked like nonsense, the product of a waking dream. He found a fresh sheet on the flip chart and started to write. There were three aspects of Ekrem Yilmaz's sordid life that might have got him killed and differentiating them would be a good start. There was the drug dealing, there was the informing and there was the sex. On the sex he had some good news from forensics, at least enough to make his theory of the ten-minute murder still a goer – and Clive Davies had thrown him a life-line too; on the drugs he'd got something and nothing from his interviews with the guys Denis had named; on the informing he had got somewhere, eventually, once fear of police interrogation began to bite. He had interviewed Ahmet Kurtal and Asil Yurekli for a second time and then three other Turks who featured both in Yilmaz's phone records and on de Longueville's list of customers for Yilmaz's drug supplies. These three were younger men, in the UK without wives or children. He couldn't crack any of them on the drugs but two of them looked in a bad way: they'd lost their supplier, he reckoned, and hadn't yet found an alternative. Which made it unlikely that they'd killed Yilmaz, of course – who would want to cut off the supply of golden eggs? On the informing, Yurekli had broken first, in a wail of outrage:

'It is hard for us make life in UK. There is my wife very sad. English people have suspect us because we Muslims. She is being lonely and needing make friend. The children doing fine. Making friend, learning good English than me. But my wife speaking only little English. Then some mother from school inviting her to home, she very happy with this and making new friend – many friend, other mother. I was being proud to her, approving she go. All very good. Then there is Ekrem coming to me and saying this not good. These people not being good. One mother not marry to father. Not moral people. He must be informing to Education Department in Turkey unless she is stopping. Now she is being sad again and wanting take children, going back to Turkey. This is all being Ekrem's fault. There is bad man.'

Armed with this, he had been able to tackle Kurtal and the stories had begun to pour out – not just of their own persecution but of others too. Often it was the wives who had been Yilmaz's target: one had been prevented from joining the school PTA, another had been stopped from working in a charity shop, another threatened because she swam at the local pool. He felt the men's fury, their damaged pride, their gut loathing of this man who spied on and threatened their stressed and lonely wives. Would it have been enough to drive them to murder? Two men, he thought, had done it, and here were two – friends and fellow sufferers, humiliated and harassed, desperate to protect their wives and hold their families together. Was it enough?

He had just finished writing up his flip chart headings when the team started trickling in. Paula Powell came first. She greeted him cheerfully. He had to say this for Powell: she might be a pain in the arse sometimes with her pc stuff on sexism, but she was cheerful with it. Nice smile. Pretty altogether. She looked around the room.

'Dirty slobs,' she said, picking up empty plastic coffee cups and slinging them in a bin.

'I thought you'd expect them to clear up their own mess, not leave it to the only woman in the team, Paula.'

'I'd be expecting forever, wouldn't I, boss? They don't even notice the mess. I'm the only one who minds it, so I get to clear it up.'

'Is it like that at home too?'

'I live on my own, and that's the way I like it. I make my own mess and I clear it up. You won't see me running round after a man.'

Boxer and Kerr caught her last words as they came into the room.

'What's that, Paula?' asked Boxer. 'You never run after a man? That's not what I heard.'

He sniggered and Kerr joined in. Powell smiled sweetly.

'Well hearing is all you'll do, Steve. You won't find me running after you. I never could stand a man with a beer belly.'

'Whoo,' carolled Kerr, shifting adroitly to the winning side. 'You go girl!'

Scott cut them off as the rest of the team came into the room.

'Enough, people! Keep this for playtime will you? This is a murder inquiry.'

As they settled, he went on,

'First of all, what have we got on Laurent Amiel? Any phone activity? Any withdrawals on the credit card?'

Kerr answered. 'Last calls on his mobile were made on Friday. Two short ones, both to other students.'

'And?'

'And we checked them out. Both say it was just social stuff.'

'Nationality?'

'One Turkish, one French.'

'Check those numbers against Yilmaz's calls, will you? And with de Longueville's list of Yilmaz's customers?'

'Have done.' Kerr flushed with self-satisfaction. 'The Turk is on both. The French guy is on de Longueville's list.'

'So, we can assume he was after drugs. He'd lost his supplier and was checking to see if anyone had found a new one.'

'Seems like he thought he'd found one. Friday afternoon he cleared his current account. Just over £400. But that's all. No credit card activity.'

'So what do we think the possibilities are?'

'The new supplier didn't like him.'

'He bought crap stuff and it's killed him'

'We've checked all the hospitals, I assume?'

'Yep. Several O.D.s but none French-speaking.'

'All right. We'll need to step up the search. Bring in the two he spoke to on Friday. Let's see what we can get out of them.'

He turned to his first sheet on the flip chart.

'Let's move on to Yilmaz. Drug dealing, informing, sex. Any one of these may have got him killed. I'll start with the sex.'

He rode the inevitable snigger without comment.

'Yilmaz's semen was found on the floor near where he died. Our first hypothesis had to be that he was killed by whoever he had sex with. However, the forensic results show that the semen had been there at least twenty-four hours when Yilmaz died, and the autopsy showed that he hadn't had sex immediately before his death.'

'So what was his spunk doing there then, sir?'

'We don't know, but we can assume that he was in the habit of spending time in that part of the library. The SOCOs are still in. going over the rest of the place.'

He paused and flipped to a page which was headed 'Opportunity: Ten Minutes'.

'The fact that Yilmaz didn't have sex gives us a possible modus for the killers. Bear in mind, the duty porter says the library doors were all locked when he checked them at about ten thirty, and they were locked in the morning when the librarian came in. It doesn't seem possible that anyone could have got hold of a key: they're security protected and can't be copied. But the girl on duty in the library that night, Yukiko Iwaki, cleared the students out and locked the main door just before ten, then spent ten minutes in the staff cloakroom getting ready for a night out. There's the library office and a corridor between the library and the cloakroom. If she went to the toilet there'd have been four closed doors between her and whatever was going on in the library. She didn't go back into the library – just went out of the staff exit and locked the door.'

'So you think the killer got in and out through the staff door, sir?'

'Killers plural, almost certainly. But I'll get onto that in a minute. I think they may have been in the library already. Yilmaz was seen there earlier and they could have been there too. There are plenty of places to hide in among those stacks and the girl on duty wouldn't have thought she needed to go round looking for people who might want to spend the night in there. But they would have had to go out by the staff door and that raises two problems. One, they'd have gone right past the cloakroom door and you'd expect Iwaki to hear them and two, the porter in the foyer would have seen them come out that way. On number one, Iwaki says she had water running some of the time and she was singing to herself – getting geared up for her evening; on two, Clive Davies, the porter, took a phone call at ten o'clock. It was a query from someone who'd booked rooms on the campus for a conference and he had to check things on the computer. It was quite complicated stuff about disabled access, he says, and he was fully occupied. He might not have noticed people leaving by the library door.'

There was a silence. Mark Tyler raised a hand.

'That's a lot of coincidence, isn't it sir. How could they know the girl would conveniently go and shut herself in the cloakroom? And how would they know the porter would get a phone call?'

'The phone call could have been a set-up,' Paula Powell suggested.

'Yes, it could. Get the number and check it out will you? As for Iwaki, I'd guess the killers expected to have to deal with her – hit her over the head, tie her up, whatever. Maybe she was just lucky – in a hurry to get off, straight into the cloakroom, so they decided not to bother with her. She's a tiny little girl – they could have dealt with her any time they needed to.'

'It's only guesswork at the moment though, isn't it, sir?'

'Yes, it is. It's a best guess for the moment, but we don't have anything better. All those locked doors cut down our options.'

'You said killers plural, sir. Why's that?' Kerr asked.

'We've tried rolling those stacks. They can't be rolled together so fast that Yilmaz couldn't have got out. He wasn't drunk or drugged, so someone else kept him in there. The pathologist found cuts on his right arm and the right side of his face. Someone kept him in there at knife point.'

Powell chipped in again.

'So if the phone call was a set-up, we're talking about three people involved.'

'Yes. But there's no shortage of people who were glad to see the back of him. His informing activities had seriously riled the other Turks. He'd been spying on their wives and that really got to them. And then there's his dealing.'

'Can I say something on that, sir?'

'Boxer?'

'When I put Yilmaz through the computer, I found he's got form. He was prosecuted for dealing in Turkey in 2003.

Another guy was tried with him – a Russian, name of Mikhail Belenki. They were both acquitted. The judge ruled some of the evidence inadmissible. The thing is –' Boxer was almost stammering with excitement, 'thing is, I checked out Valery Tarasov's father – the guy who's supposed to have been killed in a mafia revenge shooting. Anton Tarasov was a witness in a big drugs trial in Russia in 2006 – and one of the defendants was Mikhail Belenki.'

Scott let out a long whistle of surprise.

'Were they convicted?'

'Yes. And got hefty sentences.'

'So that might have been what got Anton Tarasov killed – and who knows how Yilmaz might have been involved. If he was working with Belenki but managed not to get caught, one of Belenki's associates could have been out to get him too. Well, that's great work, Steve. Complicates things, of course, but gives us a new line. A more convincing one than the Turks, to be honest. They've never looked like killers to me.'

Paula Powell chipped in. 'Their alibis are pretty solid. I know it's only their wives' word, but their stories tallied – what they ate, what time the kids went to bed, what they watched on TV. I didn't think they were lying.'

'Boxer, see if you can get any more on Belenki, will you? And any link you can find between Tarasov and Yilmaz.'

'It's an odd coincidence, isn't it?' one of the DCs asked. 'Tarasov's son being at the same college here as Yilmaz?'

'Not necessarily. If Yilmaz and Tarasov knew they were in danger and Yilmaz managed to get himself sent over here, he could have suggested to Tarasov that this would be a good safe place to send his son to. May even have said he'd keep an eye on him.'

'Do you think he's in danger too then, sir?'

'I think I need to talk to him. Find out if he thinks he is.'

He paused, trying to slot this new information into place.

'Let's get back to the murder itself. Did anyone see anything around the library? What did we get off the witness statements?'

Paula Powell brandished a thick handful of papers. 'Nobody saw anything. If these guys were hiding out in the library, no-one saw them. The boys obviously don't like the women only night at the Union – several complained about being chivvied out on the dot when the library closed because the woman on duty was obviously eager to be off. It really riles them, poor little lads.'

'OK. I'll take a look at them myself. There may be something we can follow up. Get back to me over that phone call to the porter will you, Steve? Simon and Paula, bring in Amiel's phone contacts.'

His mobile rang and he checked the caller ID. Gina Gray.

'I ought to take this,' he said. 'I think we're done here.'

Outside the room, he made contact.

'Mrs Gray?'

'DCI Scott.'

'How can I help you?'

'I'm sending a photo to your phone. I've just taken it. Another message on the classroom board. If you asked me, I'd say it was written by a Turk. I need to clean my board but I think you should see it. Any news on Laurent?"

'No phone calls and no credit card activity since Friday.'

'Serious then. No crumb of comfort for Mme Amiel?'

'We haven't found a body.'

'Oh that's all right then. Nothing to worry about.'

'We've got some leads.'

'I'm sending the photo. Let me know when you get it. Oh – and I've captured the board pen, for fingerprints.'

A minute later the photo came through. Scott looked at his screen in puzzlement and read,

IF THE MAN WASN'T BEING A DRUG ADDICT,
HE WASN'T DISSAPPEARING

He sighed and called her back.

13

WEDNESDAY: *Semantic Fields*

I start the day with the weekly staff meeting. I called a quick meeting as soon as we got the news about Ekrem, just so we all knew what there was to know, and we've mulled over scenarios and speculated over Laurent's disappearance at odd moments over coffee. Iris Cooper, who obsesses over exam results, thinks we should write to the exam board explaining the trauma the students have suffered – including those in other classes; Tessa Lavender thinks Yukiko is badly affected and worries that she's not eating; I'm worried about Ceren, who still seems pale and tearful; Malcolm Burns thinks the other Turks have got demotivated; Jenny Marsh is frantic to get back into the library because she's working part-time for a PhD in Sociolinguistics.

This is our regular meeting, however, and we have department matters to discuss. I go down to the office to photocopy papers and look in on Seminar Room 5, where we're having the meeting, to drop them off. I'm irritated to see that the board hasn't been cleaned, and then I read what's on it:

IF THE MAN WASN'T BEING A DRUG ADDICT,
HE WASN'T DISSAPPEARING

Not my own handwriting this time, but neat block capitals so regular as to be bereft of individuality. I don't know who wrote it but the syntax looks distinctly Turkish: the spelling error could be anyone's, but it's Turks who have trouble distinguishing between the progressive form – 'was disappearing' – and the simple – 'disappeared', and they use the past tense in the main clause of unreal conditions. I look at it. This is about Laurent. Does that mean there's a definite connection between his disappearance and Ekrem's death? And why am I being sent these messages? What am I expected to do with them? I suppress a niggle of fear. I need to show this to David Scott: it's evidence of a sort and it might encourage him to step up the search for Laurent. But I don't want it sitting on the board here all through our meeting because it will derail us and there are decisions we have to make. I shall take a photo of it on my phone. Annie does this all the time - if you're out with her you find her brandishing her phone at anything she sees that amuses her – and she has shown me how to do it. I can manage the technology.

I take the picture and it shows up clearly on my screen. I have a qualm, though, as I go to rub the message off the board. I worry that I'm destroying evidence, so I do two things: I pick up the black board pen lying on the desk, holding it with my skirt to avoid leaving prints (though my prints must be all over it, actually, as I use it every day) and I slip it into one of my plastic document wallets, feeling rather thrillingly professional; then I fish out David Scott's card and phone him. I don't want to rub this off till he has seen it, so I'm going to send it to him. Technological wizardry – I hope he's impressed.

Once I'm sure he's got the picture I clean the board and manage to launch us into the business of the meeting without getting bogged down in the Ekrem drama. We make final decisions on entries for Cambridge Proficiency and First Certificate exams; we agree on recommendations about progression to academic courses; we sketch out staffing for summer courses. Then there's the issue of the budget surplus – all two hundred pounds of it. We have to spend all this year's allocation before April 1st or return it, so we've only a couple of weeks to spend our surplus and, inevitably, everyone has a different priority. After half an hour we decide on beefing up the books for the summer courses and go for coffee.

Over coffee I field questions about Laurent. We all, except Iris, teach this class: Jenny takes them for Listening, Tessa for Speaking, Malcolm for Reading; I, as you know, do Grammar and Writing. We all know that Laurent is pretty feckless but he's never stayed away from classes for more than a day or two. We're all worried and we all wish the police would show more sign of being worried. I report on my information from DCI Scott and we're discussing its implications when Gillian from the office comes into the SCR to tell me that Mme Amiel and her daughter are here to see me.

Mme Amiel is bronzed and glossy but her face has a defensive, downward cast that speaks of disappointment and mistrust. She is smartly trouser-suited and her shoes and bag look dauntingly expensive. She looks round my office with distaste and a little perplexity. Maybe she's not used to the academic world – or to the world of work in general. Her daughter, Claudette, on the other hand, seems quite at home. She is in designer jeans and a jacket of soft, golden suede. She is, I've already learnt, a student at the University of Lausanne, where she is getting excellent grades. Her mother has expatiated on the contrast between her and her brother at some length and I gather that she has always been a paragon of virtue, and proof that Mme Laurent *n'est pas une mauvaise mère*. Claudette has been brought along as translator, as her English is *superb* (her mother again). I have not had the chance to judge as yet since modesty is obviously among her many virtues and she has not been translating her mother's eulogies on herself.

Still, I am relieved that she's here: my French really isn't up to the kind of conversation I see we're going to have. This is how it goes: Mme Amiel produces a torrent of French, of which I sort of get the gist, then Claudette gives me a précis in English, I reply as succinctly as I can and Claudette appears to expand my answer into discursive French. Mme Amiel does not hold back: from the start a handkerchief is produced and she weeps mascaraed tears.

'My mother,' says the admirable Claudette when her mother pauses for breath, 'thinks that the police are not concerned because Laurent is a foreigner. She thinks that if he were a British boy, they would have done more. My mother has read many accounts of the murders of foreign students in Britain. She thinks it is a very dangerous place for foreigners.'

Wham! I gather my forces, wishing I had some statistics to counter Mme Amiel's assertions about the slaughter of the foreign innocents. It is true there have been some high-profile murders of foreign students, but are they really a high-risk group? As a devoted listener to Radio 4, I know that there are about 800 murders a year in this country; that two women a week, on average, are killed by their partners and that at least one child a week is killed by a parent. I'm not good at remembering numbers but these stick in my mind. I'm not sure that being a foreign student is as dangerous as all that. I hope not because we in the English language business trade on the UK being a safe place – it's how we're able to beat off competition from the US.

'Please tell your mother,' I say to Claudette, 'that the police here take the disappearance of a foreigner just as seriously as they do that of a British citizen, but Laurent is an adult and responsible for himself. We are not talking about the disappearance of a child here.'

Claudette turns to relay this to her mother, but I hold my hand up (rather imperiously, I realise).

'The police have evidence which suggests that Laurent may have been planning to go away. He withdrew all the money from his bank account on Friday afternoon.'

Mme Amiel's response is further tears and gestures of despair. I give up the attempt to comprehend and wait for enlightenment from Claudette.

'My mother,' she explains, 'is concerned that Laurent may be on his way back to Switzerland. Perhaps he is there and we are here.'

I can help with this at least.

'Impossible. Laurent hasn't got his passport with him.'

This quietens Mme Amiel, as well it might. Mind you, the Amiels don't yet know about the disturbing phone silence, and I'm not going to tell them unless I'm pushed. A job for DCI Scott, I reckon. We all sit for a moment in silence, contemplating individually the possible intentions of Laurent in emptying his bank account and disappearing from view. Coercion? Trouble with drug pushers driving him underground? A weekend binge gone wrong? The Amiels start a muttered conversation, clearly not designed to be relayed to me. Time to bring this to a close, I think. Treacherously, I say to Claudette, 'I think you should talk to the policeman in charge of the case, Detective Chief Inspector Scott. I'm sure he will be able to give you more help than I can. I have his card here.'

I call a taxi for them and with a few more tears on Mme Amiel's part and expressions of sympathy on mine, I am soon able to usher them out of the room. Should I warn David Scott that they're on their way? On the whole, I think not. It is his job, after all.

At lunch time, a quartet from the college chamber music group is playing Beethoven in the Concert Room. The room is actually a former chapel and, godless though I am, I love its aura of calm and longevity. These lunchtime concerts are always well-attended – not surprisingly as they're free for a start. More than that, though, there is something wonderful about escaping from the middle of a mundane day to allow glorious music to flow over you, even if it is only for a strictly limited forty-five minutes. Most of the members of my department go from time to time. I sit near the front, well to one side. It's not the best position acoustically but I hope to avoid having anyone I know sitting next to me. *I vant to be alone.*

They are playing the third Razumovsky quartet and Christiane is the violist. I have heard her play before; she plays, as she does everything, with gravity and grace. As they embark, delicately, on the tentative *pianissimo* opening, I am assailed by an unfamiliar emotion: envy. Envy isn't one of my sins, really; I've always thought it was a waste of time. Anger, pride and sloth, with occasional outbreaks of lust and gluttony, I will admit to, but envy and avarice I disclaim. Now though, just for a moment, as the music seeps into me and I watch Christiane's intent face, a whispering voice in my head asks, *Why can't I have a daughter like that, so sane, so competent, so certain?* I hope you appreciate by now that I love my daughters dearly; I would (and do) defend them savagely against anyone who criticises them. I'm not blind to their faults, though, any more than I'm blind to my own, and what I think most of all, as I watch Christiane, is what a relief it must be to have a daughter like that because you wouldn't have to worry about her; you would know that she would cope with the world, that she would be all right.

I banish such fruitless thoughts and let the music do its work through to its dazzling, frenzied finale. I walk back with the melodies still dancing in my head and my thoughts go back to Christiane: how amazing the resilience of German culture; how extraordinary to recover from the horror, shame and humiliation of Nazism, holocaust and defeat to be producing thoughtful, civilised, humane young women like her. Was it owning Beethoven and Brahms, Schiller and Goethe, that enabled them to do it, I wonder (I omit Wagner as he spoils my thesis). As I climb the stairs to my office I wonder whether Shakespeare will save us. On the whole, I'm inclined to think he will.

At four o'clock in the afternoon, I arrive in Seminar Room 5 to teach what I've come to think of as Ekrem's class. It is a week since we sat here and worked on conditional sentences; is that why I got the message about Laurent today? I start with a little t.l.c.. First I congratulate Christiane on her performance and she turns a bit pink and thanks me, unsmiling as musicians always are. However thunderous the applause, they stand and receive it straight-faced, as though it is the music and not they that is being approved.

Then I turn to Denis.

'Denis!' I cry cheerfully. 'Back in one piece from interrogation, I see.'

Denis gives his customary smirk.

'I employed my legal rights,' he says airily. 'I claimed the protection of the law.'

I love the way the French always call the law *'the low'*, but it's my duty to correct him:

'The *law*, Denis. Imagine it's spelt l o r.'

Then I turn to Yukiko.

'And Yukiko? You're obviously a dangerous criminal. How did you get on with Chief Inspector Scott?'

Yukiko colours and puts her hand to her mouth, with that special suppressing gesture that Japanese women use, before she says, 'I think Chief Inspector Scott is more gentle than Japanese police. And he is rather handsome.'

'I see. Well, you obviously got the better of him too, in your way. You're a dark horse, Yukiko.'

'What is *dark horse*?' Irina asks.

'Someone who has hidden abilities or who is not what they seem.'

The class regards Yukiko for a moment, as if trying to see into her hidden depths, and she droops her head under their scrutiny. I turn to work.

Since a lot of the students are studying law or law-related subjects, I've taken a section on legal vocabulary from *Advanced Vocabulary for Academic English*. We launch into an exercise on verb-noun collocations (commit a crime, try a case, stand trial, give evidence/ testimony, make a statement, take the witness stand, hand down a verdict, pronounce sentence et cetera). I sense a lack of interest in this exercise, though they plod through it dutifully, and as we finish I have doubts about taking them on to more of the same. I'm about to opt for a game of legal hangman when Denis raises a hand.

'Over the page here is an interesting exercise, I think. There are some *faux amis* that are useful for us.'

Faux amis, or false friends, are words which are similar in two languages but actually have different meanings. French and English have a lot of them: in French, for instance *passer un examen* means to take, not to pass, an exam; a *librairie* is a bookshop and *important* means 'extensive'.

'Assassinate', continues Denis, 'is not the same as *assassiner*, I think.'

I turn the page and find there is a chart of words to do with killing. They all seem eager to do this: no-one seems to feel that it is a tasteless topic to pursue only a week after one of their classmates has been killed and it involves ticking boxes, which always goes down well. I surrender and it all gets quite philosophical. We discuss why it is not possible to murder an animal, even when the killing is illegal; we conclude that when one criminal is murdered by another he is murdered as a person, not as a criminal; we debate whether the execution of a criminal must always be legitimised by the state; we compare *slaughter* and *butcher*, with their Germanic and French roots respectively, and decide that *slaughter* implies large numbers of victims while an individual may be butchered; I confirm that *assassinate* always involves a public figure, whereas *assassiner* can mean simply *kill*, and I expatiate on the epic implications of using *slay* (one may slay a dragon but not a cat, a knight but not a burglar).

In the end our chart looks like this:

	Germs	Animal	Person	Criminal	Public figure	Large numbers
Kill	X	X	X	X	X	X
Slay		X	X			X
Destroy	X	X				
Execute				X		
Murder			X		X	X
Exterminate						X
Slaughter		X				X
Butcher		X	X			X
Massacre						X
Assassinate					X	

As there is more than one way to kill a cat, so there are multiple ways of killing one's fellow humans. In large numbers we may slay, exterminate, slaughter, butcher or massacre them; individually, we may murder, butcher, assassinate or execute them. In discovering this we have ourselves killed the time. I send them home and I clean the board.

Back in my office, I find David Scott waiting for me. I find this annoying: I lock my door when I'm out of the office but he must have come in through the communicating door with 'his' office – the one I had to promise to keep locked. What has he been doing? Has he been at my computer? I make a pantomime of my exaggerated surprise.

'Help! An intruder!'

He looks a bit sheepish.

'Sorry. It got a bit claustrophobic in there.' He indicates the inner office. 'There isn't a window.'

'A perfect venue for harassing innocent students, then. Could you not find anyone to terrorise this afternoon?'

'Has anyone complained about being harassed?'

'Complaints have been made at the highest level, I gather. Innocent Turkish ladies have been terrorised by our brutal Marlbury police.'

He shakes his head in disbelief.

'Talking of Turks,' he says, 'you think that message this morning was written by a Turk?'

'Almost certainly.'

'And you've got the pen they used?'

I fetch the black board pen in its plastic wallet and I say, 'Of course lots of people will have used it - not just staff. We quite often call students up to write on the board.'

'And other classes use that room besides the two-year Master's class?'

'I'm afraid so.'

'So how many students, roughly, would you say could have handled that pen?'

I calculate. 'I replaced it last week because the old one was running out of ink, but there will have been four days of classes in there. In theory, it could be as many as a hundred,' I say.

He gives a snort of laughter.

'Well,' he says, 'since it's not a murder weapon, I don't think we'll go down the path of fingerprinting every foreign student in the place for the sake of identifying the phantom writer.'

He really doesn't think the message is significant, I can tell. I do, though. I feel sure that someone is trying to tell me something.

'I'm sure you know best,' I say, and my tone sounds absurdly sulky.

In revenge, I ask if he got on well with Mme and Mlle Amiel and he gives that shake of the head again. It's a bit like the shake my cat gives herself when she falls off a fence. He's a bit stunned, I think.

'So where to now with the Laurent inquiry?' I ask.

''I need the name of his drugs counsellor. I assume you know it?'

'I do. But I'm not sure it'll help. Isn't there patient confidentiality to consider?'

'If you could just give me the name and leave the other problems to me?'

I am put in my place. I give him the name and address.

'Barry Hughes, twenty-seven More Street. He's a neighbour of mine, actually,' I say. 'A lovely chap. He sounds like Neil Kinnock.'

'Well, that'll be reassuring.' He takes my piece of paper and glances at it. 'I'll see him in the morning. And if you're right about that message on your board, I'd better talk to your bloody Turks again.'

14

THURSDAY: Investigation Day Eight

More Street turned out to be much the kind of road Scott had imagined. *He's a neighbour of mine*, she had said, and as Scott drove slowly along, surveying the houses, looking for number twenty-seven, he could imagine her in any of them. Solid Victorian semis, they sat behind small front gardens, mostly slightly unkempt. Their windows were spattered with posters and flyers advertising concerts, plays, meetings and charity events; at eight forty-five in the morning, mothers – and the occasional father – were cycling off to playgroups with toddlers strapped in behind them, or ushering groups of older children down the road for the walk to school – no gas-guzzling school runs from this street.

He wondered which was Gina Gray's house but it really didn't matter; they would all be much the same. He knew what the insides of these places would be like: no three-piece suites, no polished surfaces, no fitted carpets. There would be sanded floors and stripped pine, junk shop finds and ethnic rugs – that deceptively casual look that belied the care with which it had been, apparently, thrown together. There would be plenty of teachers here, and social workers, and journalists, and musicians, all smug together in their worthiness. He'd bet plenty of *Guardians* hit the morning doormats in More Street. Oh yes, Gina Gray would be quite at home here.

At number twenty-seven the front garden had been paved,

with a couple of terra cotta pots as its only ornament. Scott rang the bell, heard the sound of rapid feet on the stairs and found himself overwhelmed by the force of the man who opened the door. Barry Hughes did indeed have the honeyed Welsh tones of Neil Kinnock but there the similarity ended: he was tall, with the build of a rugby player and a head of vigorous black curls. He grinned broadly, crunched Scott's hand in an awesome clasp and propelled him into his consulting room at the back of the house. Scott knew enough not to expect a couch but he did wonder, as he looked around, exactly how counselling sessions took place. At first glance the room was simply a small sitting room, with easy chairs arranged round a coffee table. There was a filing cabinet, though, and a wall of books – the tools of the trade.

Hughes waved him to a chair and offered coffee or orange juice. Scott opted for coffee, though he was well wired on Lavazza already; Hughes disappeared and returned with a mug of coffee for Scott and a glass of orange juice for himself. He sat down opposite Scott and leaned back, one leg crossed high over the other. He was wearing tracksuit bottoms and a T-shirt and looked as though he might be just back from a run; he exuded good health and well-being. Scott, imprisoned in his work suit, felt flabby and jaded by comparison. Time to square up, he told himself, or this genial shrink would be running rings. He set down his mug, sat forward and looked Hughes in the eye.

'Mr Hughes, we are extremely concerned about the disappearance of Laurent Amiel and finding him is a high priority. I know you have your professional ethics but I have to warn you that if you obstruct our investigation by hiding behind patient confidentiality I shall be quite prepared to –'

'Whoa, whoa!' Hughes rocked back in his seat and put up two protesting hands. 'Did I say I wouldn't co-operate? I'm in the dark here. I didn't even know the guy was missing until you phoned yesterday.'

'When did you last see him?'

'Monday last week.'

'And were you expecting to see him this week?'

'No. We meet once a fortnight.'

'What did you talk about at your last session?'

'See, now that's where we get ourselves into difficulties. I can't tell you anything he said to me – that *is* covered by client confidentiality. Client, by the way, not patient. I'm not a doctor.'

He drained his orange juice and leaned forward.

'Ground rules, OK? First thing, would you mind turning your mobile off? I ask all my clients to do that, and I guarantee I won't be taking any phone calls myself. We'll have a better conversation without interruptions. Second thing, I won't tell you anything that could incriminate my client and I won't tell you anything he said to me, but you know already that he has a drug problem and I acknowledge that it hasn't gone away. And if you tell me what you know about his disappearance – if that's what it is – I'll tell you what I think he's likely to have done, given what I've learnt about him over the past weeks. All right?'

There we are, thought Scott, *running rings*.

Aloud he said, 'OK'.

It was very warm in the room; the sun was hot through the big window behind him. He took off his jacket, turned off the mobile in its pocket and loosened his tie.

'Laurent Amiel was last seen on Friday afternoon. He didn't tell his flatmates he was going away. He's emptied his bank account. He hasn't used his mobile phone – it's switched off – and he hasn't used his credit cards. He hasn't made contact with his family – his mother and sister have come over.'

Barry Hughes smiled.

'Ah, the mother and sister, yes. I hope I get a chance to meet them.'

He was thinking hard, though, Scott could see, and after a moment he said, 'The thing you have to know about Larry –'

'Larry?' Scott queried.

'He likes to be called Larry here. He thinks it's cool.'

And nobody thought to tell us that, Scott fumed privately. *Nobody thought it might help our search if we knew what people called the guy.*

Hughes continued, 'What you have to know about him is that he's pretty bright. He's idle and he's screwed up but he's on the ball. He'll know that he can be traced through his credit card – that's why he drew the cash. And that's why the phone's switched off. Might be worth finding out if he bought himself another phone before he went missing.'

'You think deliberately disappearing is something he'd be likely to do?'

'Oh yes. If things got tough, that's what he'd do.'

'And had things got tough for him?'

Hughes smiled again. 'You tell me,' he rumbled. 'I think there are a few things you haven't told me. Like why you're so worried that a student has dropped out of his life for a bit.'

'There's a lot I can't tell you, I'm afraid. It's –'

'Client confidentiality, is it?'

'No.' Scott could feel himself blushing. 'It's a murder investigation and we can't be loose with information.'

'Murder? Oh, I see. You think Larry's disappearing is connected with this murder they've had at the College? Well, Larry's not a murderer. I can tell you that for nothing.'

'We didn't think he was. But it's possible that he's in danger from whoever killed the Turkish student.'

'Why would you think that?'

'I can't say, but can you answer me this: if Amiel's supply of drugs was cut off, would he be likely to put himself in danger to get hold of some from another source?'

'This Turkish guy was Larry's supplier?'

'I can't say.'

'Of course you can't. So it turns out, Chief Inspector Scott, that there's more you can't say than I can't say.'

'And the answer to my question? Would he be likely to put himself in danger?'

'Any addict will do that. Danger means nothing to an addict in need of a fix.'

'And Amiel is an addict?'

'I can't say.'

He grinned amicably. *Enough,* Scott thought. He'd got what he came for. He wasn't staying to play games. He thanked him and left.

He took DS Kerr with him to Marlbury College to talk to Valery Tarasov. At the English Language Teaching Office he enquired where Tarasov would be and was told that he would be coming out of a Listening class in Seminar Room 2 shortly. He left Kerr in Gina Gray's inner office and walked along to the seminar room, intending to catch Tarasov before he left. He found a man outside the room, apparently also waiting. He was looking intently through the glass panel in the door, watching the class inside, but as Scott approached he moved rapidly away. A foreigner of some sort, Scott thought, though he'd only caught a glimpse of his face. Greek perhaps, or Turkish. The door opened and the class started to trickle out. Tarasov emerged among the last, chatting to Irina Boklova. They both looked with distaste at Scott.

'I'd like another word, please, Mr Tarasov,' Scott said, 'about your father's business interests.'

Tarasov hardly acknowledged that Scott has spoken to him. Instead he turned to Irina and said something in Russian. As she started to reply, Scott cut in, 'Right away, please. Either here or at the Police Station. Your choice.'

As he locked eyes with Tarasov, he saw Irina give him a little push and mutter something to him. Tarasov shrugged.

'Fine,' he said.

In the windowless office, Tarasov sprawled in a chair, but his apparent nonchalance was undermined by the nervous movements of his eyes and hands. Scott didn't allow him to get comfortable. As Kerr drew a chair up close to the Russian, he leaned across the desk towards him.

'We know about your father's criminal activities, Valery. And we know about his connections with Yilmaz. It's a pity you didn't think to tell us about them yourself.'

Tarasov flushed but he maintained his insolent sprawl.

'Why I tell you?' he demanded.

'Because your father was murdered and now Yilmaz has been killed. Aren't you worried that you might be next?'

'Why I worry? My father's business not my business. I am student only. I study only.'

Simon Kerr intervened, drawing out a sheaf of mobile phone records from a file.

'I don't think so, Valery. Not judging by the calls you've been making back to Russia. Hours and hours of them. Cost you a fortune.'

'To my family, my mother I call.'

'Twice, Valery, in the last month you called your mum. Four minutes, five minutes. What about all these others? To your aunts and uncles were they?'

Tarasov stopped lounging and sat forward, hunched in his chair.

'I must arrange my father's affairs. I must fix. I am man of family now. My mother can't fix all these things.'

'Are you trying to run your father's business from here, Valery?' Scott asked.

'No, no I just fix. I pay who needs paid. I arrange.'

'And you're not afraid that whoever killed your father will try to kill you?'

'I know why my father killed. There is no danger for me. This is UK. Is safe for me here.'

'It wasn't safe for Yilmaz, though, was it?' Kerr asked.

'Was for drugs. For drugs they killed him.'

'Really?' Scott stood up and came round the desk to stand over him. 'Do you know who killed him then?'

Tarasov raised a protective arm as if to ward off a blow. Had he had dealings with the Russian police, Scott wondered.

'I guess,' Tarasov protested. 'I know he deals drugs – everyone knows this. I guess this reason for his death.'

'Do you do drugs, Valery? I can send my officer here to search your room right now, so you might as well tell me.'

'I don't. I don't do. I am good Russian.' He attempted a smile. 'Vodka and whisky only I do.'

'So you feel quite safe do you?'

'Yes. I am safe here. I am UK student. I work hard. I am safe, isn't it?'

As they walked back to the car, Scott took out his phone to call the station: he was anxious to know about the call to the porter on the night of the murder and he had been expecting to hear from Boxer. As he opened the phone, though, he realised that it was switched off. It had been off ever since Barry Hughes had asked him to turn it off that morning. He turned it on. *3 missed calls.* Damn! There was also a text message from Gina Gray. He opened it and read:

Have u heard? Turks going home
2day. Orders of turkish govt.
Can they do that? Have another
board message 4 u. Hope barry
was help. gg
Sender:
Gina Gray

DS Simon Kerr was startled out of his usual poise when Scott jumped into the car and revved off in a flurry of gravel before he had even managed to close his door.

15

THURSDAY: *Negative Sentences*

THE CRIMINAL WAS EXECUTED

The sentence sits in the middle of the board, drawing my eye as I walk into the room. The students are there before me, chatting or finishing off homework. I'm glad of the opportunity to confront them with this; I'm getting tired of it.

'Good morning,' I say before I've even reached the front of the class. 'Would anyone like to tell me what this is all about?'

I draw a thick black line under the sentence with the new board pen I've just picked up from the office. The students gaze at it with polite and detached interest, then Denis speaks, his tone courteous but puzzled.

'It relates to our lesson yesterday,' he says.

Of course it does. Ekrem, the message implies, was a criminal, so his death was not murder but execution. In yesterday's killing chart, we tick the *execute* box.

'I know that, Denis,' I retort. My tone, I know, is shrill. 'But who wrote it? Who thinks it's funny to keep writing these things on the board?'

I look around at their faces and notice, in passing, that there is a gap where Asil and Ahmet should be sitting. Innocence and bewilderment look back at me.

'You didn't write it?' Farid asks.

And now I understand. They think (well, all but one of

them, presumably) that I have written this up as a starting point for the forthcoming lesson. I am exasperated.

'No, I didn't write it, Farid. Does it look like my writing?'

Farid is saved from answering by a commotion at the door, and Asil and Ahmet sidle into the room, one carrying a shinily-wrapped parcel and the other a bunch of flowers.

'We are coming to say goodbye,' Ahmet explains. 'We are leaving this afternoon.'

'Leaving? Before the end of term? Has something happened at home?' I ask, and then I take in the significance of the flowers and the parcel.

'You are coming back next term, aren't you?'

They smile awkwardly and Ahmet shakes his head.

'Our government is calling us come back home, Mrs Gray. We will not return. I am very sorry.'

He thrusts the bunch of flowers towards me. I reach out for them automatically but then I stop.

'But Ahmet,' I say, 'will the police allow you to go home?'

Ahmet is too embarrassed to speak but Asil answers,

'Our government is arranging. We have immunity.'

He beams with pride as he delivers the new word. I, for once, am lost for words, so I go into familiar farewell mode. I accept their gifts, shake their hands, remind them to keep practising their English and hope they'll come back to England one day. With more smiling and shuffling they exit. *And then there were nine.*

I turn on the class.

'Did you all know they were leaving?' I demand.

They don't meet my eye. They are embarrassed and hurt. They are wondering why I'm being so aggressive to them. Why have I turned into a harpy? What happened to their nice teacher?

'Well, we'll clean this off,' I mutter as I wipe the board. 'And perhaps we'll have no more of this silliness.'

My tone would better suit a room full of toddlers, I know. I need to reassure them, to be Mrs Nice again. I take a deep breath and launch us into Spot the Error. (I give them a passage with twenty errors in it for them to identify; they work in two teams. A team gets one mark for correctly identifying an error but loses two marks for an incorrect claim). It gets both competitive and hilarious and good humour is fairly rapidly restored.

When I get back to my office, I call David Scott to see if he knows about the Turks. I've given his card to the Amiels but I'm embarrassed to find that I've memorised his number. I find his mobile is turned off so I leave a text. I'm just leaving for lunch in the SCR when my office phone rings.

'Mrs Gray?' the voice asks, crisp and prissy. 'This is Janet Chisholm here. The Principal would like to see you.'

Again? My day is sliding downhill by the moment.

'Right, Janet,' I say breezily. 'I'm just going to –'

She cuts me off.

'Right away please, Mrs Gray.'

When I get over there, I'm kept waiting for ten minutes – a deliberate ten minutes, I would say. My reception is very different from last time; there will be no coffee and sandwiches today, I feel sure. Eventually a buzzer sounds on Janet's desk and she tells me I can go in, without moving her eyes from her screen. When I get inside, I get no handshake this time, no greeting of any kind, in fact.

'Well, I hope you're pleased with yourself,' he bellows. 'This is what you wanted, I suppose.'

His face is extremely red and he seems barely under control. I resist the urge to run out of the room and I play for time, feigning confusion though I know, of course, what he's talking about.

'I'm not sure what you mean but if this is about Asil and Ahmet leaving –'

'Asil and Ahmet!' he mimics in an exaggerated falsetto. 'Asil and Ahmet! They're all leaving, the whole bloody lot, every Turk in the college.'

'Every Turk in the college?' I am genuinely amazed.

'Well, all the government-sponsored ones anyway,' he mutters. 'A few of the private ones may stay, but I wouldn't be surprised if they go too.'

He has deflated a bit but he gets a second wind.

'You know you're responsible for this, don't you?'

'Me?'

'You could so easily have prevented this. All I asked was that you had a quiet word with your policeman friend to get him to lay off a bit, but no. So in they went with their size elevens, upsetting the wives, making all kinds of insinuations about drugs and such, and this is the result. In future, the Minister of Education tells me, they'll be sending their students elsewhere to learn English, somewhere with "more sensitivity to their culture".'

'Well, I wouldn't have thought –'

'I don't care what you'd have thought,' he thunders. 'The point is, we've lost them. And it's potentially a huge market. It'll be vast when Turkey joins the EU.'

He comes across and looms over me.

'I'm expecting your resignation on my desk tomorrow morning, Mrs Gray.'

'You don't mean it!'

'On my desk!'

He is so very red in the face that a bit of my brain wonders if he's going to have a stroke, while the rest contemplates a jobless future.

'And if I don't resign?' I ask.

'Then you'll wish you had. I shall make life very difficult for you indeed.'

'Then it sounds as if I'd better talk to my union,' I say, and I turn for the door.

'You've been grossly disloyal to the college, Mrs Gray,' he calls out as I'm leaving, 'and I don't allow that, not on my ship.'

Not on my ship! I only just get out of Janet's office before I start laughing. I am a bit hysterical, of course, and I find that my legs are a bit shaky, so I head for the refectory, rather than the SCR, and order a pot of strong tea and a plate of chips.

Back in my office I call Judith Roth, my University and College Union rep. She's a New Yorker working in the Law department and she has a brisk, laconic style which I find reassuring. She advises me to start keeping a diary.

'Open a file,' she says. 'Make a note of anything – anything at all – that could be construed as bullying or harassment, with times and dates. Anything in writing, including e-mails, keep as evidence. We'll need it all if we want to argue constructive dismissal.'

Someone should have told me this during the years of my marriage. *Constructive dismissal.* Is that what my divorce was? I thought I chose to divorce Andrew, but did he, in fact, set out to make my life so impossible that in the end I resigned?

'You will need to be strong,' Judith was saying in her forceful twang. 'I should warn you, men stick it out – they're more stubborn – but most women give up in these situations. They decide it's not worth the hassle.'

'Not this woman,' I assure her with as much conviction as I can muster.

'Good girl.'

A busy afternoon of teaching puts other thoughts out of my head but as I climb the stairs to my office at five o'clock I realise that I'm dog-tired. I unlock the door, sling my briefcase across the room and find David Scott standing by the window.

'I thought,' I snarl as I kick the door closed, 'you wanted the door between these offices kept locked. I don't come wandering in there at will, even though it's my office, so I'd really appreciate it if you didn't wander in here whenever you feel like it.'

'You sent me a text,' he says, as though this justified his presence. 'I've been moving heaven and earth this afternoon to try and stop my two chief suspects from leaving the country and I've got nowhere'. He looked at his watch. 'They'll be taking off from Heathrow as we speak. How have they managed it? What did they tell you?'

'Nothing. Their government is calling them home.'

I'm emptying my briefcase and refilling it with stuff to take home.

'Our revered principal, on the other hand,' I tell him without looking at him, 'tells me that it's your fault. They've been whisked home to save them from being subjected to further police brutality and intimidation.'

'Is that right? Well that fits. I went storming in to see Superintendent Lake this afternoon, demanding to know why my suspects had been allowed to leave, and he said the Chief Super wants to see me in the morning. He's very concerned about the way I've handled the case, apparently.'

I laugh and it comes out as a rather unattractive cackle. 'Well, that's both of us with our jobs on the line then. I've been hauled over the coals for disloyalty and letting the college down. The Principal believes I could have stopped the Turkish exodus in its tracks if I'd tried.'

I stop and take a look at him.

'Poor Asil and Ahmet. Did you bully and intimidate them? Did you frighten their wives?'

'What do you think?'

I start to put my coat on, avoiding his eye.

'We've all got a mean streak in us, I suppose.'

He comes over and helps me into my coat.

'Do you suppose there's anywhere we can get a drink?' he asks.

Well, there isn't anywhere at five o'clock in the afternoon, so I invite him home and open a bottle of wine, and after a while I go off to the kitchen to make us some pasta. Annie comes in and rolls her eyes and says she'll just put a frozen pizza in the microwave and take it to her room, so David and

I eat alone. I open a second bottle and it starts to feel more comfortable between us. We stop the 'Mrs Gray'/ 'DCI Scott' business and we talk about anything but the case – holidays, books and films mainly. He's really keen on archaeology and goes to interesting sites on his holidays. He knows how to talk about them without being nerdy or boring. It's a congenial evening and I realise with a shock that he's my generation really, only six years younger than I am.

He seems in no hurry to go and I'm not sure what he has in mind, but at ten o'clock, because he has to see the Chief Superintendent in the morning, and because he's a policeman and can't drive with a bottle of wine inside him, I ring for a taxi and send him home.

16

FRIDAY: Investigation Day Nine

Chief Superintendent Hamilton's office was on the fourth floor of the County HQ, with a view of distant hills in one direction and of water meadows in the other. His desk, however, sat between these two aspects, facing the door, and Scott wondered if he ever looked out of either window at all.

He was not, at first sight, impressive: a small man, mainly bald with a ring of sandy hair. His eyes were bright and humorous, though, and Scott had been warned that you underestimated him at your peril. He gestured Scott to sit down, consulted a single sheet of paper on his desk, sat back and surveyed him in silence. When he finally spoke, his question came from left field.

'These Turks,' he said. 'Yurekli and Kurtal. Do you think they're your men?'

Scott was taken off-guard. He had come prepared with defences to all sorts of accusations, but not for this. He could feel himself flailing a bit as he answered,

'It's a very complex case, sir. I can't say at this stage. We're pursuing several lines, but that's hardly the point. As I told Superintendent Lake yesterday, I feel -'

'I can imagine how you feel, Chief Inspector. You've lost your key witnesses. No need to spell it out.' He glanced again at the sheet of paper on his desk. 'Bullying, intimidation, harassment. How much of that went on?'

'I felt they were holding out on us, sir. They had information material to the investigation and they weren't talking. I brought them into the station for questioning because I thought it would put pressure on them. And it worked. But the tapes will tell you no – '

'I've heard the tapes. And the wives? What happened to them?'

'DS Powell talked to them, sir, with a WPC. We took care that no male officers were present and DS Powell is very p.c. – very culturally aware, sir. I'm confident that she will have dealt sensitively with the situation.'

'You said this was a complex case. What makes it complex? Summarise for me.'

'It's the background and activities of the victim. He was working as an informer for the Turkish government, which won him a lot of enemies, but he was also dealing in cannabis, cocaine and probably heroin. In addition, forensics suggest there could have been a sexual motive for the killing.'

'Nice chap. And he had the protection of his government.'

The Chief Superintendent got up and walked away from the desk, his hands in his pockets.

'I'll ask you again, do you think Yurekli and Kurtal are the killers?'

Scott stood too.

'No sir. It's only a gut feeling but frankly I don't.'

'So it doesn't matter that they've gone?'

'I wouldn't say that, sir. They're a very valuable source of information about the victim.'

'Precisely. And no doubt the Turkish government knows that too.'

'I'm sorry?'

'Of course, I'm not privy to what goes on at the highest level and I've no doubt this piece of business was fixed up at the highest level – minister to minister I would say.'

'Why, sir?'

'We can all read the newspapers. It's no secret that a lot of the EU member states – this country in particular - are desperate to have Turkey join the club. As a bridge into the Islamic world, Turkey is crucial to the 'hearts and minds' approach to the Islamic threat. And the Turks themselves are equally desperate to join, for the most part – not the religious extremists, of course, but most of the rest. The only thing stopping it is Turkey's less than attractive human rights record.'

'I'm not following you, sir. How do these guys … ?'

'Think about it, Scott. It's hardly going to advance the cause, is it, to have a couple of Turks standing up in a British court and describing how the Turkish government routinely sends informers to spy and report on the private lives of Turkish students studying here?'

'So the intimidation and harassment ?'

The Chief Superintendent waved an impatient hand.

'Is a fig-leaf, yes.'

'So, what do you want me to do now, sir?'

'I assume you have some other lines to pursue?'

'Yes, sir.'

'Then I suggest you go and get on with them.'

Which was all very well, Scott thought as he took the stairs down the four flights and headed for his car, but the other lines of inquiry weren't proving particularly fruitful. Nor had they made any progress on Laurent Amiel. He was relieved, of course, that he hadn't been taken off the case, but he couldn't say he was enjoying it.

His mobile rang and he recognised the caller number.

'Gina?'

'David. There's been another development, I'm afraid. Ceren Vural has gone missing.'

'The Turkish girl? When you say *gone missing* - ?'

'She disappeared some time during the night. She went to a film with Yukiko and Christiane last night and they dropped her off at her hall of residence at about ten. When they went to pick her up to go to class at ten to nine this morning, they got no answer. Her door was locked so they got the porter to unlock it. Her bed was made, they said, everything was tidy and she was gone. They've tried calling her mobile but it's switched off. Sound familiar?'

'You sound upset.'

'I am. Laurent is flaky. He may just have taken off, and he can probably take care of himself. But Ceren is so young and she's been so protected up till now. She's never been away from home before. Even when she did her undergraduate degree she lived at home in Ankara. I personally told her parents that we'd look after her here. I feel we've let her down.'

'Leave it with me. I'll get a team on to it and I'll be over myself later. Will you be free?

'I'll be free at twelve. I'll see you then.'

As he drove to the campus, Scott acknowledged to himself that he was looking forward to seeing Gina again. Last night had been unexpected, to say the least. She had been different at home: less spiky, less superior, less amused by him. He had enjoyed himself. He liked her: he liked the house, which was messier and less self-conscious than he had expected; he liked the wine and food, which had comforted his bruised spirit; he even liked the elderly cat and the sassy daughter, who'd asked him if he carried handcuffs in his pocket.

He was waiting outside her office at twelve and noticed how tired she looked as she reached the top of the stairs. Her eyes looked strained as she smiled at him and unlocked the door.

'Have you been over to Ceren's room yet?' she asked.

'No, not yet. I've got officers in there now. I'll go over in a minute. I just want to ask you a few questions first.'

She sank into an easy chair by the window and he pulled a chair over to join her.

'I asked her, and she denied it, so now I'm asking you – do

you think there could have been anything going on between Ceren Vural and Yilmaz?'

She looked at him in astonishment.

'Ceren and Ekrem? Absolutely not! None of the girls could stand him – he was a creep.'

'But Ceren was upset the day the body was found. She'd obviously been crying when I saw her and she was on the verge of tears through most of the interview.'

'Well, maybe she was just shocked – and scared about talking to the police.'

'Maybe. Have the other girls always been as protective of her as they're being at the moment?'

'How do you mean?'

'You said they walked her to her room last night and then went to walk her the few yards to class this morning. Could they have thought she was in danger?'

'Oh God, I don't know. I don't seem to know anything at the moment. Usually, I pride myself on knowing everything that's going on with my students – a real mother hen I am – but there seem to be all sorts of undercurrents with this lot and I don't know what's going on.'

'Christiane and Yukiko seem to be together a lot. Could they be an item?'

'There you are, you see! I'd never thought of that. You have a far more colourful imagination about my students' love lives than I have. But the answer to your question is no, actually. Yukiko's not a lesbian – she fancies you for a start.'

'Don't be absurd.' He was furious to feel himself blushing.

'It's true. She gets all fluttery whenever she mentions you.'

Time to shift ground, he thought.

'What's the atmosphere like in the class at the moment? Were they surprised to see the Turks go? Do you have the sense that anyone knows more than they're telling?'

'I honestly don't know. Sometimes I think they all know what's going on. I picture a *Murder on the Orient Express*

118

scenario - they all did it and now they're having to silence Laurent and Ceren – and anybody else who's flaky. Sometimes I think they know nothing and don't really care. I told you about the grammar exercise that ended with *The man was crushed* didn't I? I couldn't work out who manipulated that, if anyone. And then there was this latest message, *The criminal was executed.* They all sit there looking at these things and they're just mildly embarrassed, as far as I can see. Embarrassed for me, I think, as though it's in bad taste.'

'I wasn't thinking *Orient Express* as much as *Seven.*'

'Someone's punishing my students, you mean? I've got Kevin Spacey in my class?'

'Well, it'd have to be two someones, in fact. I'm convinced one person alone couldn't have killed Yilmaz.'

'But who would want to punish Ceren – or Laurent? I can see that someone might decide to get rid of Ekrem because of his drug dealing – and because he was horrible - but Laurent does no harm to anyone but himself, and no-one could be more harmless than Ceren.'

He was not sure he really wanted to pursue this. What had been a vague idea just nagging away in his mind was having to be put into words, and he knew that, as he exposed it to the light of day, it was going to sound absurdly far-fetched. But he had started now so he would make the best case he could.

'That's your liberal western perspective, isn't it?' he asked. 'Suppose a couple of religious extremists - Muslims - had decided to clean things up. They kill Yilmaz because he's a dealer, they abduct – perhaps kill – Amiel because he's an addict and they take Ceren because she's behaving inappropriately for a Muslim woman. She wears jeans, doesn't cover her hair, goes to discos.'

'So do some of the other Muslim women students.'

'Yes, but this is happening to students in this particular class.'

'So, you're thinking – who?'

'Well, I was thinking Asil and Ahmet, but they'd gone home before Ceren disappeared. So, it would have to be your Iranian guys.'

'Farid and Atash? Oh David, this is absurd. They're perfectly nice guys.'

'Studying Electronics – learning how to blow us all up, you said. And they were very disapproving of *the French boys*, as they called them – Laurent and Denis – and their drug habit.'

'Of course they are. They're Iranians. They have views and beliefs that we don't share. But that doesn't make them serial killers.'

Scott stood up, and shook his head. He knew he had taken this far enough.

'Of course you're right. I think this case is just getting to me. Too many leads and too little evidence. And the feeling all the time that people know more than they're saying. Losing the Turks hasn't helped. But you're right. It's crazy. I'm going over to look at Ceren's room. Do you want to come?'

'If that's all right. We can walk across – it's not far. It'll be easier than trying to find somewhere to park.'

As they followed the path that snaked between buildings, Scott thought how odd it was that he had so resented her tagging along to look at Laurent's room, but now having her here was almost comforting. Her thoughts, however, were obviously going in a different direction. Suddenly she said, 'I'm just thinking, that message - *The criminal was executed* - it appeared on the board the day after we had a discussion about different types of killing and whether the killing of a criminal was only execution if it was done by the state. It was Farid and Atash who wanted to argue that anyone who killed a wrongdoer could be said to have executed them.'

'You mean, they could actually be claiming responsibility for Yilmaz's death in that message?'

'I find it almost impossible to believe. They really are nice guys.'

'At least the message only says *criminal* singular. There's no implication that anyone else has been killed.'

'No. Though I was thinking if you were right about the punishment idea they could be after the whole class.'

'What do you mean?'

'Well, we could all be punished for something. There's me for a start. I don't live with my husband, and I'm pretty outspoken in class about women's rights. Then Denis and Desirée live together but they're not married, Valery lives off the ill-gotten gains of drug-trafficking and prostitution, Irina has run away from her husband – and bad-mouths him at every opportunity. Which leaves just Christiane and Yukiko. Well, Christiane is quite forceful about the treatment of women in the Islamic world – and if you thought she and Yukiko were lesbians, so might others. And that cleans up the class.'

Scott stopped and looked at her.

'So, we'd better hope I'm wrong, then, hadn't we? Shall we go in?'

Hawthorn Hall was one of the original halls of residence from the college's days as a teacher training establishment. In contrast to the self-contained flats Scott had seen in Beechwood Village, here were long corridors of closed doors leading to cramped study bedrooms. The lighting was gloomy and it all looked as though it could do with a coat of paint. As they headed up the stairs, Scott noticed a communal kitchen at the end of the corridor and put his head round the door. It looked as messy and depressing as any he had known in his own student days.

Ceren Vural's room was on the second floor. The door stood open and inside two DCs, one male, one female, were carefully going through the room's contents.

'Anything of interest yet?' he asked.

It was the woman who spoke.

'Doesn't look like an abduction, sir. No sign of a struggle, all neat and tidy.'

'Anything missing?'

'We haven't found her wallet or phone. Her toothbrush is still here, though.'

She pointed to the small wash basin in one corner with a shelf full of toiletries above.

'She may have more than one toothbrush, DC Hart.'

'Yes, sir.'

A movement in the open doorway alerted Scott and he turned to see Christiane Becker and Yukiko Iwaki standing outside the door, peering hesitantly inside.

'We wondered,' Christiane explained 'if you have any news about Ceren.'

He looked at their anxious faces. They were afraid for Ceren, there was no doubt about it.

'Come in,' he said. 'You may be able to help.'

They sidled in, glancing at Gina Gray as they did so. Scott said, 'We need to know what Ceren has taken with her. Does she have a bag she uses regularly, for example, and can you see it anywhere here?'

They looked around.

'Ceren has a shoulder bag,' Yukiko said. 'A brown leather bag. I don't see it now.'

'And she carries her books in a backpack,' Christiane added.

'What colour?' Scott asked, taking out a notebook.

The two young women looked at each other.

'Blue,' they agreed. 'Dark blue.'

The backpack also was nowhere to be seen.

'What about clothes,' Scott asked. 'Coat and shoes, for example?'

Yukiko glanced along the garments hanging in the wardrobe; Christiane looked at the hooks on the back of the door. Her coat, they agreed, was missing – a long black wool coat – and her boots, but apart from that they couldn't say. Scott looked at their wan faces and wanted to comfort them.

'Thank you, girls,' he said as he ushered them out. 'That's very helpful – and hopeful really. It does look as though she planned to go. Did she ever mention anyone she knew in the UK? Friends or relatives?'

Again they checked with each other, then shook their heads. As they were leaving, Yukiko suddenly gave an exclamation.

'The bedcover,' she cried. 'What has happened to it?'

All six occupants of the little room turned their eyes to the bed, which stood neatly made up with a matching blue duvet cover and pillowslip.

'The bed has a cover,' Yukiko explained urgently. 'A blanket with patterns – checks. Like Scottish pattern.'

'Tartan?' Scott asked.

'Yes. Tartan. It covers the bed to sit on in the day.'

As she and Christiane left, Scott said, 'On second thoughts, I think we'll fingerprint this room. And we'd better get prints from those two'- he nodded at the open door – 'for elimination.'

The two young DCs exchanged glances and then looked at Scott. A missing blanket, they knew, was not such good news. A blanket was what you used to wrap an unconscious or trussed body. Scott looked at Gina Gray and saw from her face that the implications were not lost on her either.

17

SATURDAY: *Future Perfect*

We are off to a wedding. Given yesterday's events, I felt, last night, that this was the last thing I would want to do today, but this morning the sun is shining and, in spite of everything, I am looking forward to it. This is not just any old wedding, you should understand, but a grand performance in the Abbey – possibly the Marlbury Social Event of the Year. I am amazed that we have been invited, and rather touched, actually. The bride, Sophie, is the daughter of an old school friend of Andrew's. Her younger sister, Belinda, was a contemporary of Ellie's, so we saw a lot of one another when the girls were small, and they all went to Lady Margaret's College – the girls' equivalent of Marlbury Abbey School, though neither so old nor so distinguished, of course. Although you have heard me complain about the level of financial support he has given the girls, I can't fault Andrew in the matter of school fees. Well I can, of course, because I've always worked in the state system and I think it would have done fine for our girls, but Andrew finds no conflict between his radically egalitarian professional values and laying out huge sums of money to buy his daughters a head start in life.

Since Andrew and I split up, the girls and I hang on rather half-heartedly to this élite social world, and many of Andrew's friends would be happy to see us drop off the edge, especially since Freda's unscheduled arrival, but Sophie's mother – bless her – has stayed a true friend and has invited us all to the wedding. If we can take the raised eyebrows, they won't bother her. Andrew was invited too, of course, but he is in Venezuela, so we are going unchaperoned.

I have an outfit: a midnight blue silk suit, bought in the Jaeger sale last year for the annual graduation ceremony at college and for just such occasions as today. I am teaming it with a red velvet rose pinned to my bosom and a floppy-brimmed red hat. I was tempted to go for red shoes but I resisted. The shoes are navy and the bag matches. Those who are familiar with my usual sartorial style will find all this very remarkable.

I have not discussed with the girls what they are going to be wearing: I never see Ellie for long enough to discuss anything and I know that any attempt to guide Annie as to what to wear will result in her appearing in ripped jeans and safety pins. I am quite anxious about what she will dress herself in but I'm acting casual and may be fooling her. She comes down to breakfast in her pyjamas, so that gives me no clue, but she appears again twenty minutes later looking, well, lovely, really.

She is wearing a pale grey linen suit that I bought her, with a very bad grace, last summer. Marlbury College offers a three-day *Introduction to the World of Work* course every summer to post-GCSE students and I got one of Lady Margaret's snotty letters informing me that my daughter would be attending and asking that I ensure that she dressed *in a manner appropriate to a work environment*. I suggested to Annie that she should go in a boiler suit or an overall but she wouldn't play ball. It had to be a suit. We spent a fractious afternoon in the boutiques of Marlbury and eventually found the pale grey effort. She has never worn it since and I had written it off, but here she is, looking cool and elegant, her hair neatly coiled, footwear other than trainers on her feet and a challenging scowl on her face.

'Nice,' I say casually and go up to change myself.

Ellie arrives breathless as usual and looking alarmingly inappropriate in a scarlet dress with tiny spaghetti straps over the shoulders.

'Won't you be cold, darling?' I say and I listen to myself and think what a bore I am.

It's not the cold that worries me, of course, though it is a brisk March day and Annie and I are going to be chilly even in our suits. What worries me is that her outfit screams *You all think I'm a scarlet woman so I might as well look like one.*

'I've got a raincoat in the car,' she says.

Oh fine. A scarlet woman and a tramp then. We tussle for a bit over my lending her something to wear over the dress while Annie rolls her eyes and jiggles Freda half-heartedly in her buggy. None of my jackets will be any good because anything big enough to accommodate my bust will swamp her, but I find a beautiful cream pashmina shawl, hardly worn, brought back from his travels by Andrew in the days when he still brought me presents. She takes it, slings it nonchalantly over one shoulder, and we set off.

I have decreed that we walk down to the abbey: there's nowhere to park nearby and we shall get oil on our clothes if we go in Ellie's car. I push the buggy because Ellie can't manage both it and the pashmina in the stiff breeze. We turn a few heads and I must say I'm rather proud of my little entourage. We are all blond (I'm pretty dusty these days but look good enough under the red hat) and the girls have their father's height: they are leggy and willowy. Freda, I should tell you, is probably the best dressed of us all. Ellie may have got her own clothes wrong but she hasn't put a foot wrong with Freda, who is wearing a little red coat (a Christmas present from my mother), a white furry bonnet, red mittens, white tights and heart-stoppingly tiny red shoes. We look good.

The atmosphere is muted outside the abbey: people are stiff, self-conscious still in their best clothes, anxious about their hats, which threaten to fly away, and not yet loosened up by emotion and champagne. A phalanx of tail-coated ushers stands at the abbey door as I approach at the head of my posse. They part, rather reluctantly it seems to me, to let us through, and another greets us inside.

'Which side?'

'I'm sorry?'

'Which side are you?'

'Why? Is there a war on?'

I hear Ellie snort a stifled laugh behind me. The young man smiles, polite but lofty.

'Are you on the bride's side or the groom's?'

'Oh, the bride's every time, I think, don't you?'

And I sail on in. We find a pew with just a couple sitting in it. They smile politely at Freda but I can see that they think their morning is about to be ruined. I usher the girls in and I sit on the end so I can control the exits and entrances. Some people, I note, are kneeling for a little silent prayer; I allow my mind to wander.

Which side are you on? Weddings are all about union, about coupling and yet nowhere are men and women more sharply divided. Look at the clothes for a start: all that suiting for the groom and his men and nothing but bare shoulders and lacy draperies for the bride and her maids. Every wedding looks set to host the rape of the Sabine women: the diaphanous nothings cry out to be ripped off and the floating skirts and spindly heels seem specially designed to prevent flight.

Which side are you on? It is the ultimate divide – male and female. Look at what happened in the US election, in the showdown between Clinton and Obama. Race, you might think, was the great divide in American life, the fault line that threatens the stability of everything else Americans may construct, but was it the black presidential candidate who was said to divide the electorate? No, it was the woman. *She's such a divisive figure* they said of Hillary Clinton.

I have nothing against Obama, you understand. If I were American I'd have voted for him, but I did resent the way people talked about Clinton. I heard some American media type on *The Today Programme* one morning. No man, he said, could bring himself to vote for Clinton, *not because she's a woman but because she reminds him of his Third Grade teacher.* Well, let's unpack that a bit. For a start, are there any Third Grade teachers in the States who aren't women? Very few, I would imagine, so *not because she's a woman* is just a touch disingenuous isn't it? Then, why should men object to their Third Grade teacher? Most children at the age of eight or nine enjoy school and like the teacher who is opening up the world to them. Could it be that these men look back with horror to their Third Grade teachers because they look back to a time when, God forbid, a woman – other than their mothers, who naturally doted on them – had power over them? Had power and, even worse, may have failed to acknowledge the majesty of their manhood, may possibly have made the mistake of thinking they were just little boys?

I notice that a woman I know slightly is greeting me tentatively with a little wave. She looks puzzled and I realise that, in the midst of this scene of joy, my face may have inadvertently twisted itself into a rictus of rage.

It is a nice conventional service and Freda behaves very well through *Morning has broken*, The Marriage at Cana, *Speak now or forever hold your peace*, The Vows and 1 Corinthians 13 (*and the greatest of these is love*). While they are signing the register, we sing *Love divine, all loves excelling* and she gets a bit restive, so I take her outside. A little crowd has gathered, drawn by the line of limousines waiting to whisk the principals away to the reception. They look at me disapprovingly, I think. Maybe they're just disappointed because I'm not the bride, or maybe they think I'm Freda's mother and they're shocked by my antiquity.

My own mother was quite old when I was born – thirty-eight, which was old for her generation. She was a GP in a single doctor practice and it seemed to me that she worked all the time. I don't remember her showing any sign of feeling guilty about my solitary weekday teas and lonely school holidays: she certainly never overcompensated with treats and cuddles as I did with my children. It disabled me, I think, as a working mother, my own lonely childhood: I knew what it cost a child to lose its mother to work.

Her patients adored her, of course, and I was constantly told how wonderful she was. It occurs to me only now, as I'm telling you this, that she was like Andrew in this respect. Having spent my childhood in the shadow of a mother who gave generously to all and sundry but hadn't much left for me, I chose a husband who was just the same. How's that for stupidity? Interestingly, my mother took Freda's arrival without a blink. Since Ellie was studying Drama, which her grandmother considers the academic equivalent of cordon bleu cookery, she wasn't bothered about her dropping out of university and simply embraced the biological pleasure of a great-grandchild.

At the reception in a blue and gold marquee, the girls quickly disappear to join the young, taking Freda with them to be petted and admired. I paddle about in the social shallows for a bit, sipping my champagne and exchanging passing pleasantries without getting drawn into joined-up conversation. I make people here nervous, I know: many of them have known Andrew longer than they've known me, but they don't like to ask after him – or indeed to ask where he is. I suppose they imagine he hasn't come because I'm here. And then they don't know what to say about Ellie; nor do I, if it comes to that.

Eventually, I accost Tom Urquhart, headmaster of the William Roper School, where I toiled for fifteen years. He was toiling in those days too, an eager young history teacher on a mission. He stayed with it when I got out, and he got his reward. He looks horribly grey and he's sipping mineral water but he greets me with a hug and we find ourselves a couple of spindly little gilt chairs to sit on. We get through the preliminaries – work, children – and then he says, 'You've had a murder on your patch, then?'

'We have. And according to Norman Street it's all my fault.'

'Really? Tell me more!'

'I wish I could but I've already been accused of treason, so I've taken a vow of silence.'

'Is it right that the chief inspector in charge of the case is an alumnus of William Roper?'

'David Scott, yes. Do you remember him?'

'I don't think so. Do you see much of him?'

I swallow my sip of champagne with a splutter.

'What's that supposed to mean?'

'Nothing. I just meant - well, unless there's something I don't know.'

'There's a good deal you don't know, Tom, omniscient though you'd like to be thought. But there's nothing to know about DCI Scott and me.'

'I was just wondering if I could get him to come and talk to Year Twelve about a career in the police. I like to get former pupils in when I can.'

'I can give you his mobile number if you like.'

He fishes a pen and a diary out of his pocket and I start to reel off the number, until I realise that he's not writing it down but looking at me quizzically.

'I remember phone numbers,' I say defensively. 'It's just a thing I do.'

There is no stinting at this wedding: lunch, speeches and toasts all happen in abundance. So, it is late in the afternoon and beginning to get dark by the time we gather ourselves for the walk home, and it has started to rain. We make as much haste as we can but it is difficult in our wedding gear and with the wind hurling the rain in our faces, so when we reach the

High Street and see a taxi drawing up outside the County Hotel, I dash across the road to commandeer it, with the others trailing wetly in my wake. Out of the taxi emerge the Amiels, *mère et fille*, looking dry and elegant and sporting several designer carrier bags. I am aware that we, by contrast, present a sorry sight. As Mme Amiel's eyes sweep over us I am conscious not just of our wetness but that Ellie's wet dress is clinging to her, that Annie has a wine stain on her jacket and that Freda's face is smeared with chocolate. I dive into the taxi.

Back at home, it's agreed that Ellie and Freda will stay the night since Ellie won't be fit to drive for hours, so we all go and take off our damp glad rags and re-emerge, as if by consensus, in pyjamas. We close the curtains and turn on the fire in the sitting room. Ellie feeds and baths Freda and when she is settled to sleep, I make tea and a mound of cheese on toast, which we eat with our fingers, squeezed onto the big sofa, shouting out the answers to *Who Wants to be a Millionaire?*. I can't remember a happier evening we have spent together.

18

SATURDAY: Investigation Day Ten

Scott gathered up the students' statements strewn across his desk and stacked them in a pile. Not a thing. Nobody had seen anything, nothing unusual had happened, the evening of Wednesday February 27th had been entirely uneventful, except that a man had been brutally murdered in a college library.

He rubbed a hand over his unshaven face and looked at his watch. Four o'clock, and he had been here since seven. An entirely fruitless day. They were stuck, going precisely nowhere. In the night, he had convinced himself that the missing Turks held the key and railed pointlessly about their being whisked away; now he was less convinced. With Laurent and Ceren missing, he was inclining to the bigger picture: not a personal attack by two men driven wild by another's malice but a conspiracy.

There were two possible kinds of conspiracy. One was the Islamic crusade: a sort of two-man terrorist cell aiming to clean up the college. Gina Gray had pooh-poohed it, didn't believe her *nice* Iranians capable of it, but he wasn't ready to relinquish it as a theory yet. The other possible conspiracy involved the Russian Mafia and the Turkish drug trade and was potentially so far-reaching that it was hard to know where to start.

Ekrem Yilmaz and Valery Tarasov ending up in the same small UK college – that was surely no co-incidence. Yilmaz knew Valery's father. He and Anton Tarasov had both managed to dodge the bullet when Mikhail Belenki got caught and sent to jail. If Yilmaz's death was Belenki's revenge, they would never catch his killers. Without clear proof of a Russian involvement they would get no co-operation from the Russian authorities – probably wouldn't even if they had proof. But if it was associates of Belenki who had killed Yilmaz, then wasn't Valery Tarasov in danger too? Unless. Unless Tarasov was the killer – or one of the killers – saving his own skin by doing Belenki's dirty work for him. Is that what Tarasov had meant when he said, *I am safe here*?

What he could not fathom for the moment was how Laurent Amiel and Ceren Vural fitted into this. Amiel had bought his drugs from Yilmaz and had maybe picked up his connection with Tarasov. And Ceren Vural? She seemed a total innocent, but there was some connection between her and Yilmaz, whatever anyone told him to the contrary. He had talked to her the day Yilmaz's body was found and he had seen a very distressed young woman. They would have to keep digging, but he could swear they would find a connection. So, there was further work for Boxer and his team: background checks on the Vural family, more digging on the Belenki connection and anything they could get on Farid Hosseini and Atash Shirazi – anything that linked them to extremists, anything unusual at all.

He stood up. He was starving, he realised. He hadn't had a proper meal since Gina had cooked him pasta on Thursday night. Well, he wouldn't resort to bacon sarnies again; he would go to the supermarket, get a steak and a bag of salad, and some new potatoes that wouldn't take long to cook, and he would make himself a proper dinner.

The food looked good on the plate, quite professional, since the steak had come with a little pat of herb butter. As he ate, he reflected that this would be a respectable meal to cook for someone else. He remembered the way Gina had looked at

133

his trolley in the supermarket. Well, he would invite her round and show her he knew how to eat properly. She might be a vegetarian, of course - it would be like her, and that was a vegetable sauce she had put on the pasta the other night. Well, he would buy a quiche from the delicatessen then – something healthy looking. No-one could object to that. We Clean 4 U would be coming for the first time on Wednesday so the house would be respectable; he would invite her round for supper that evening and impress her with his domestic skills.

He was wondering quite why it was that he wanted to impress her when his mobile rang from somewhere upstairs. He ran up and rummaged in the pocket of yesterday's work suit.

'David Scott.'

'Hello,' said a voice he did not recognise. 'My name's Tom Urquhart. I'm the headmaster of the William Roper School. I hope you don't mind me ringing you at home at a weekend. Gina Gray has just given me your number and I thought no time like the present.'

Scott cursed silently. What did she think she was doing giving out his mobile number - unless this man had information to offer.

'Is this in connection with a current police investigation, Mr Urquhart?' he asked.

'Tom, please. No, I'm afraid not, except that I spotted your name in the local paper, with the information that you were a William Roper boy. I was wondering, you see, whether you would be willing to come into the school and talk to our Year Twelves about your experiences in the police.'

'We have a team that gives schools talks. I can pass your request on to them.'

'I really wanted the personal touch. It would be good for these young people to see someone from their school who has been as successful as you have been. A chief inspector at forty – that's quite something.'

Yes, and flattery will get you everywhere, thought Scott. Aloud, he said, 'Obviously, I am very busy at the moment, in the thick of a murder investigation,'

'I know, and I know it's an awful cheek to ask you this, but we've had a speaker cancel for the careers session on Monday afternoon. Is there any chance you could give us half an hour then?'

'I don't have anything prepared,' Scott protested.

'No problem. We find it always works better if our speakers are willing to answer questions. The students will have plenty to ask, I'm sure.'

'Then yes, provisionally,' Scott said. 'But I'm sure you understand that if there are developments in the case I may have to cancel at the last minute.'

'Understood. Many thanks. We'll see you at three-thirty on Monday, then. You know where we are, of course, don't you?'

Scott closed his phone and ate a last potato, now cold on his plate. Why had he said yes? He knew why: because he was not actually all that busy; because the harder he worked at this case the faster it seemed to run away from him; because he was mainly waiting for information, for results, for inspiration; because it would be nice to get some admiration, to play the successful detective even if that was the last thing he felt like right now.

19

SUNDAY: *Second Person Plural*

The glowing digits on my bedside radio tell me that it is 02.28 when I wake properly and listen to the sounds that have been disturbing my sleep for some time, I think. Aside from the background noise of the steady rain, I can hear someone moving around outside in the back garden - there is the swish of footsteps on the wet grass. Have they come for me? Is it my turn to disappear? They can't snatch me from the bosom of my family, can they? If I scream, will the girls rush to my aid or pull their duvets over their heads? Should I ring 999 now? Should I ring David?

While my body is experiencing all kinds of panic reactions, my mind is baulking at the melodrama of the situation. I get out of bed and grope in the dark, on shaking legs, towards the window. I look out and can see nothing. The rain is still falling and there is no glimmer of moon. I stand there for a while hoping that my eyes will adjust to the dark and then I hear a familiar sound – the outraged cry of a cat that has been trodden on. My cat, my Mog, has fallen foul of the kidnappers in the garden.

Somehow, the thought that my would-be abductors might harm my cat galvanises me into action. I put on my dressing gown and grope downstairs. In the kitchen, I find the heavy torch that hangs behind the back door and a knife out of the knife block. I have no idea whether the torch's batteries are functioning but I'm thinking of it as much as a weapon as a source of light. I unlock and open the back door as quietly as I can and then the breath is blown out of me as someone tries to knock me off my feet. I realise after a moment that it is the terrified cat and I brace myself for what is outside. With the knife in my right hand, I turn on the torch with my left and direct its surprisingly strong beam out into the darkness.

As the beam swings round, I pick out a figure - a horribly misshapen figure, bent and hunchbacked. It starts to move towards me and I realise that it is making a piteous noise. As it gets closer, I know who it is. It is Ceren. The misshapen back is simply her rucksack and she is wrapped in a blanket. She is dripping wet and as she reaches the door she throws herself into my arms and sobs noisily.

I bring her inside and stand and look at her. She is as wet as it's possible to be. Water pours down her face from her sopping hair, the blanket sheds little pools around her and more pools form from the hem of her coat. She is grey with cold and, as her sobs begin to subside, I can see her teeth chattering.

'I'm not going to ask you anything,' I say, 'until you've had a hot shower.'

We have a wet room off the kitchen, where the walk-in pantry used to be. Andrew had it put in. He liked to use his periods at home to keep fit for his real life elsewhere and he liked to be able to leap directly into a shower when he came in from cycling, running or playing tennis, without the danger of being thwarted by females doing unnecessary things in the bathroom. We hardly use it now but the shower is first rate, so I steer Ceren towards it. I get it going for her and leave her to it, with instructions to dump her wet clothes in the corner. While she is in there I turn the fire on in the sitting room, fetch pyjamas, a sweater and some thick socks from my room and get warm towels from the airing cupboard. Then, good Englishwoman that I am, I put the kettle on.

In the sitting room, cradling her mug of tea and dressed in my too-large clothes, she looks pathetically waif-like. Finally she speaks.

'I trod on your cat,' she says.

I sit on the sofa beside her and point out that the cat (who has come in to enjoy the fire) has suffered no ill effects, and then I ask, as gently as I can,

'Ceren, can you tell me what happened to you? Who did this to you?'

Tears ooze silently from her eyes and I think she is not going to answer me, but then she speaks.

'I am so afraid, Mrs Gray.'

I put my hand on her arm.

'Who are you afraid of? If you can tell me that, I can help you.'

She shakes her head violently and puts down her tea mug. She is heaving with sobs again and she has her hands over her face as she says, 'I am afraid to police. I can't to talk to police.'

'But the police are there to help you. If someone is trying to hurt you –'

'I mustn't talk to police. This is why I must to leave.'

'Leave where?'

'I am afraid, Mrs Gray. I am afraid what I can say to police. So I must to go, to leave my room and go.'

I am struggling to accommodate what she seems to be telling me.

'Ceren,' I say, 'are you telling me that no-one took you from your room?'

She draws a shaky breath and I can see the effort she is making to speak calmly.

'Asil and Ahmet have gone. Also many other Turkish students. Police cannot question them so they must question me about Ekrem. But I cannot answer. I am afraid.'

'Ceren.' I pick my words carefully. 'The police won't hurt

138

you, you know. Our police in the UK, well – they're not like the Turkish police. They just want to find out who killed Ekrem. They won't bully you. The inspector - Chief Inspector Scott – he was nice, wasn't he? He didn't bully you?'

Her eyes won't meet mine. She looks down at her lap and plucks at the stuff of the pyjamas she's wearing.

'I am afraid what I can say,' she says quietly.

We sit in silence for a while drinking our tea, and then I ask, 'So where did you go when you left your room? What were you planning to do?'

She sighs as if she is too weary to tell the tale but she is a polite young woman and I am her teacher, after all, so she answers me.

'I went to the woods, on the campus, near to Beechwood Village. I slept there. I think – thought – I can stay there one week and then is end of term and I go home, back to Turkey.'

'Why didn't you just go home right away?'

'I can't. My parents bought my ticket for one week time. I can't change. I can't to tell them what is happening to me.'

'So you planned to sleep in the wood for a week? Oh Ceren.'

'My brother, when he was young he did this. He ran away and lived three days in the wood. He was fine.'

'But not in England, in March!'

'First night was OK. Was cold and scary but OK. Then the rain came. So much rain. I was scared. I thought I would die from the rain.'

'How did you find your way here?'

'I remember we came here for tea party last term. I thought I remembered the way, but I was lost. I was walking and walking. When I got here there were no lights. I was trying to shelter in hut in garden but there are rats –'

'Mice, I think,' I say in defence of my garden shed. 'And possibly a hedgehog, but I don't think there are rats.'

'I was scared. I couldn't stay. Then I trod on your cat.'

'Don't worry about it. Cats don't understand why humans can't see in the dark.'

'And then I saw you and I thought God answered my prayer.'

She turns and looks at me, her eyes huge and trusting as a child's.

'Please, Mrs Gray, please let me to stay here with you.'

At this point there is a noise in the doorway. Annie is standing there blinking in the light. She stares narrow-eyed at Ceren, who gazes back at her.

'Annie,' I say, 'this is Ceren, one of my students. She's here because she's – in a bit of trouble.'

'Who with?'

As I struggle with an answer to this, Ceren unexpectedly says, 'With police.'

'Cool,' says Annie.

Then, as I look on open-mouthed, she advances on Ceren with her hand held out.

'I'm Marianne,' she says. 'Don't worry. We'll look after you.'

I gather up my last shreds of will-power and say firmly, 'We're not talking about this now. Go back to bed, Annie. Ceren I'm going to bring you a duvet so you can sleep down here. You'll be warmer here than in the spare room. Annie, GO TO BED.'

After I've settled Ceren to sleep on the sofa, I return to my cold bed and pass the rest of the night in complete sleeplessness. For the first time in, possibly, ten years I want to ask Andrew's advice. I want to know what my legal position is and whether I have, in fact, already broken the law. I could ring him on his mobile in Venezuela and I conclude vaguely that, being some hours behind us, it may still be evening there. I won't do it though: I can't bear to give him the opportunity to tell me what to do. I can't bear having to respect his professional opinion, I can't bear seeming to need him, I can't bear giving him the chance to be nice to me.

At seven I can stay in bed no longer so I go down to the kitchen to make myself some breakfast. I make a big pot of tea and, since lack of sleep has made me ravenous, I cook scrambled eggs and eat them on a thick slice of buttered toast. While I'm eating, I make a list of the arguments that have accumulated in my mind against letting Ceren stay in my house any longer. Actually, I make two lists, one for Ceren and one for Annie, because I'm going to talk to them separately. I'm not going to let them gang up on me: the combination of Ceren's tears and Annie's ferocity will be more than I can deal with. One list, scrawled on my shopping list pad, reads:

Ceren
Parents will be told she is missing
*NB their **distress***
Ceren must contact them.
Then what?
Think again about police – why so afraid?
Must talk to them

The list for Annie reads:
Annie
*Distress to Ceren's parents (take **seriously**)*
Ceren witness in murder case.
*I am committing **crimes***
    a) wasting police time
    h) conspiring to pervert course of justice.

NB
I SHALL LOSE MY JOB AND GO TO PRISON

I look at the two sheets side by side. They look compelling to me, but then I'm a mother and a responsible citizen. I am also, I have to admit (and you will notice that this appears on neither list) interested in having some sort of relationship with a policeman. Specifically, with Detective Chief Inspector David Scott, who is leading this murder investigation.

I'm not just worried about losing my job and going to prison. Oh, who am I kidding? Of course I'm worried, I'm frantically worried. There is something else, though. I think Ceren knows something about Ekrem's murder. In my sleepless hours, I've been replaying my conversation with her last night. Her tears and her problems with modal verbs made what she said unclear, but when she said, 'Police want to question me about Ekrem, but I cannot to answer. I am afraid. I am afraid what I can say', isn't the obvious implication that she knows something and she's afraid the police will get it out of her?

Clearly, she didn't kill him herself; the police are sure that it took two strong men to do it. But she knows something about why or how he was killed and she is afraid. Is she afraid of the murderer, perhaps – afraid of being punished for talking? So what should I do? Persuade her to talk to the police and possibly put her life in danger? Protect her and help a murderer to go free?

My agonisings are interrupted by Ellie, carrying a hungry Freda. By the time I have made her a bowl of Ready Brek, cooked some more scrambled eggs for Ellie, who has looked longingly at the remnants of mine, and finally packed the two of them off home, I feel sure we've made enough noise to wake Ceren, even if Annie is still sleeping the determined sleep of the righteous. I put some clothes on and go into the sitting room.

Ceren is awake, I feel sure, but would like me to think she isn't. I sit down by her feet and say gently,

'Did you manage to sleep?'

She nods. She is still pale and her face looks thin, surrounded by a mass of dark hair, usually tied back in a neat pony tail but now wildly curly after its night in the rain.

'Would you like a cup of tea?'

She shakes her head and whispers, 'No, thank you.'

'Ceren,' I say, 'we need to talk about your parents.'

I see the panic in her face but I have to go on with this.

'Tomorrow, someone from the college will have to ring them and tell them that you're missing. That someone should be me, really, but if I don't do it then someone from the International Office will. I'm sure you know how worried they'll be.'

By way of an answer she slides down further under the duvet and turns her face into the pillow. I push on.

'I know how worried I would be if one of my daughters went missing in a foreign country – and I know what I'd do. I'd be on the first flight I could get. I'd go straight there to find out what was going on.'

She looks helplessly at me and, mercilessly, I carry on.

'And, quite honestly Ceren, if you know something about Ekrem's death – about who murdered him – then you should tell the police. It's your duty. You don't need to be afraid; the police will protect you.'

She says nothing but a veiled look comes into her eyes and I feel I've lost her.

'Think about it,' I say. 'Think about your parents. I'm going upstairs to talk to Annie now. Then I'll ask her to find you some clothes. Yours aren't dry yet.'

I dash upstairs and go into Annie's room before I have a chance to lose my nerve. She is semi-dressed and sitting on the bed getting her clarinet out of its case. This is a surprising turn of events since the clarinet has not been heard in the house for several months. It is carried to and fro to school occasionally and I assume that Andrew is still paying for lessons, but not a note has sounded within these walls. I comment to this effect.

'It's for Ceren,' Annie says. 'She plays. We had a chat last night and she told me.'

'When last night?'

'After you'd gone to bed.'

'I told you to go to bed. Why do you never do as I ask you?'

She says nothing but continues to fiddle with the clarinet.

'Annie, we need to talk and you need to be sensible. There could be a lot of repercussions if we let Ceren stay here. For a start, what am I to tell her parents? She's one of my tutees and she's officially missing. It's my job to let them know.'

'Well, pretend,' she says, before trying a note.

'What do you mean?'

She looks at me.

'Tell whoever you have to tell that you're going to ring her parents and just don't,' she says, with the pitying air of the quick-witted for the slow.

I am appalled.

'I can't do that! It'd be dishonest. I'd be lying to my colleagues. I could lose my job.'

'Oh, your job,' she says dismissively, and I flare into a rage.

'Yes, my job!' I shout. 'The job that pays for all this – stuff, for a start.'

I sweep my hand around the clothes, the heap of shoes, the computer, the shelves of CDs, the MP3 player and all the rest of her accumulated *stuff*.

'We wouldn't get far without my job.'

'There's always Pa,' she says.

'Unfortunately, that's just what there isn't, as you well know. There is very occasionally Pa, as a matter of fact.'

I'm getting diverted. She's always able to do that. She wants to follow in her father's footsteps and she's argumentative and manipulative enough to make a very good lawyer. She's been practising her courtroom techniques on me for years. I have another argument, however, beyond the moral one.

'Anyway,' I say, 'if Ceren stays 'missing' the police will contact her parents – they'll want information from them. If I haven't even told them she's missing, they're going to get a very nasty shock, and I'll be in serious trouble.'

'This is all about you, isn't it?'

'No it's not all about me; it's about you too. This isn't a game, Annie. Ceren probably knows something about the murder that happened at the college and she doesn't want to tell the police about it. The police are looking for her. If I hide her here and don't tell the police where she is then I'm pretty sure I'm committing a crime: *wasting police time* at the very least, and almost certainly *conspiracy to pervert the course of justice*. I could go to prison, and then what would become of you? Actually, they could charge you too.'

'Fine. Ceren needs sanctuary and it's our moral duty to give it to her. If the police want to charge me then they can. I'm prepared for that.'

'No, you're not. It's all very fine, the grand gesture, but just think about it. You might not go to prison but you'd have a criminal record. No decent university will take you and bang go your chances of becoming a lawyer.'

'So you're just going to turn her out, are you? Or are you going to let your friend the policeman know where she is?'

'Neither. You know I wouldn't do that. I think I can persuade her to go back to college and put herself under police protection, if you don't interfere. So just keep quiet, Annie. I don't want any of your histrionic poses. I want to get her to be sensible.'

'Oh, sensible!'

I swear her lip curls with the weight of disdain she gives to the word.

It's my fault, of course. I should never have called her Marianne. It won't have escaped the notice of those of you of a literary disposition that I seem to have channelled *Sense and Sensibility* in naming my daughters Eleanor and Marianne. A foolish idea, you might think, since Austen endows her Elinor (different spelling, of course) with all the desirable qualities (intelligence, moderation, self-control, unselfishness) while giving Marianne irrationality, excesses of emotion and a penchant for the wilder shores of romantic poetry. In my own defence, I didn't plan it: I named my firstborn Eleanor because I liked it and because I've always been impressed by Eleanor of Aquitaine, one of the most thoroughly bloody-minded women in English history. Then, when a second daughter came along, Marianne seemed the only name to pair up with Eleanor. Ellie lived up to her name quite spookily for years: she was sensible, quiet, hard-working at school, Deputy Head Girl. Then she produced Freda and threw it all over. So, I'm hoping my Marianne will follow her in thwarting her name's expectations (she has, after all, made it her business to thwart me in everything else in the past sixteen and a half years).

Like Milne's little bears, as one gets worse, perhaps the other will get better. I live in hope, never more than now, and I leave the girls together while I cycle off to do the weekend's shopping because, whatever gets decided, we still have to eat.

20

MONDAY: Investigation Day Twelve

'So why did you tell me Yilmaz was a drug dealer?'

Farid Hosseini's face was impassive, the eyes blank, as he answered, 'Because you asked for information about him.'

'You didn't tell me right away, though, did you?' Scott objected. 'Why did you change your mind?'

'I have no experience of UK police. I didn't know if I can trust. I talked to our teacher, Mrs Gray. She said I can trust you.'

Scott, together with Paula Powell, was questioning Hosseini in an interview room at the station. He had shown no emotion on being taken in, neither surprise or resentment. Now he sat, apparently relaxed, facing them.

'How did you know about the drug-dealing?'

'I heard the French boys talking. They don't know I understand French. I worked two years in Algérie. My company sent me.'

'In Algeria?'

'Yes.'

Paula Powell leaned forward across the table.

'Have you ever taken drugs, Farid?'

'No.'

'Why not?'

For the first time, Farid Hosseini looked surprised.

'Why ask me that? It is a crime. Why I should do it?'

'It's not just a crime, is it, Farid?' Paula Powell asked. 'It's a sin for you, isn't it? Isn't it forbidden in the Koran?'

'The Koran tells us we must put nothing into our bodies that changes us. Nothing to make us lose control of ourself. So we take no drugs, no cigarettes, no alcohol.'

Scott took up the questioning.

'Tell me, drug dealers are sentenced to death in Iran, aren't they?'

'Sometimes.'

'Do you think that's right?'

'It is our law.'

'And what about our laws in the UK? Do you think they're not tough enough?'

'I have no opinion.'

'Surely you must have. Don't our laws seem lenient compared with your laws in Iran?'

'I have no opinion.'

Scott glanced at Powell and she asked, 'Did it upset you to see a fellow Muslim dealing in drugs, Farid? Was it worse because he was a Muslim?'

'It is for him. For his soul. I am not his judge.'

'Do you think he has been punished now?'

'That is for Allah.'

Scott allowed a pause and then asked, 'What do you think has happened to Laurent Amiel?'

'How should I know? This is your job, I think.'

'But you must have an opinion. You've studied with him for six months. You must know him quite well.'

Hosseini leaned across the table and glared into Scott's face, his eyes dark and fierce.

'I have no interest. These rich boys with all their privilege, they throw their lives away and I don't care. I must sit in class with them but I don't need to interest in them. I study Electronics. For that I am here. The university says I must also study English, so I study. I sit with these people and I learn with them but I don't need to know them. I have no interest.'

Frustrated by this interview, Scott decided to let Atash Shirazi cool his heels for a bit before talking to him. He thought he might be the easier nut to crack. He rang the English Language office and asked when Gina would be free. He was told that she had just come out of a class so he rang her mobile but got no answer. He went to the canteen, where he found Paula Powell drinking coffee and eating a doughnut. He joined her for coffee, resisting the doughnut though comfort food was appealing in his present mood, and they went up together to interview Shirazi.

As they entered the interview room, Shirazi gave a nervous start but then turned a broad smile on them.

'Good morning,' he said. 'Very good coffee.'

He indicated the plastic cup on the table in front of him.

'I don't think so,' Scott said, 'but I'll tell the duty sergeant you enjoyed it.'

He sat down and looked at Shirazi.

'So what else do you like about living in the UK, apart from the coffee?'

'I like to study. I like to learn English.'

'Nothing else? The weather, for example?'

Shirazi laughed a little too heartily.

'I was here only in winter. Perhaps summer weather I shall like.'

'I wouldn't bank on it. What about British culture? Our way of life?'

The Iranian smiled again.

'Ah, multi-culture,' he said. 'Our English teachers like multi-culture very much. We discuss a lot. *How is it in your country? Oh how interesting! In our country is different! How different culture!*

He acted out his parody with heavy irony, then shrugged.

'They like. It's fine.'

'But you like your own culture best, do you?' Powell asked.

149

'Of course. Like everyone. Why not?'

'Do you think,' she asked, 'that living here might be bad for Islamic students? Do they forget how they should behave?'

'I try hard to be good Muslim. I am not forgetting. Why are you asking this?'

'I wondered how you felt about Ekrem dealing drugs. You did know he was selling drugs, didn't you?'

There was a moment's hesitation before he agreed that he knew something about it. Paula Powell went on,

'And Ceren. Ceren doesn't cover her head, does she? And she wears western clothes. What do you feel about that?'

'She is Turkish. There is different. There is *secular society*. Before women cannot wear headscarf in university in Turkey. But now is changed. Law is changed and students can wear. Prime Minister's wife now wears headscarf in Turkey. Is good, I think.'

'Does it make you uncomfortable to see Ceren with her head not covered, when you know she's a Muslim? Is it difficult for you to sit in class with her?'

Shirazi looked at her for a long time.

'It's OK,' he said. 'It's fine.'

Further questions elicited nothing more and with no evidence against either man, there was no option but to let them go. Scott went back to his office, tried Gina's mobile again and found it was switched off. He tried her office number but found his call was diverted to the English Language office. It was twelve-thirty and he was due at The William Roper School at three-thirty. He was debating what to do next when he got a call from reception: Mme Amiel had called earlier, while he had been interviewing. She wanted to see him and would be coming in that afternoon. That decided him: he would go to the college and see if he could take Gina to lunch. Maybe, he told himself, she had thought further about the Iranians and might have an angle they could use.

He got no response when he knocked on her office door, but he had the odd sense that she was in there, hiding from him. He was tempted to go in via the inner office, to which he still had access, but it felt too much like being a stalker. Instead, he went over to the Common Room to see if she was having lunch there. Failing to find her there either, he went over to the library, still closed and barred with scene-of-crime tape. He walked round to the porter in the foyer and got him to unlock the staff door. He went through into the librarian's office and then beyond into the library itself.

He walked up and down the rows of stacks, drawing the stale air of the place into his lungs. He looked into cupboards that opened off the library: a stationery cupboard, another with a trolley in it and boxes of books with post-it notes stuck to them, 'awaiting repair', 'to be accessioned'. There were certainly enough places for three men to hide on an evening when the library assistant was in a hurry to go off duty.

He walked on until he stood before the winding mechanism that controlled the stacks which had killed Yilmaz. He tried to imagine the scene as he had pictured it. He was no believer in ghosts but he felt himself infected by something of the victim's panic.

He paced Yukiko's walk down to the main doors and then back to the library office and he stood in the office looking around him. It was no wonder the body in the library had been a murder mystery cliché. It was irresistible, order and silence shattered by violence and confusion.

He walked down to the emergency exit, opened it and stood outside, smoking, looking across at the English Language building just as he had on the morning the body was found. Perhaps, he thought, he could conjure Gina out from her office to stand there shivering without her coat as she had done then. And what had he achieved since then, twelve days in? Pathetically little. A half-baked theory, no evidence, his prime suspects whisked away from him and two more students missing. Looked at that way, it was amazing he hadn't already been taken off the case.

He ground out his cigarette and went back inside, closing the emergency door carefully behind him. As he turned to walk back along the rows of books, he realised that he was in the Archaeology section. Of course. In his experience, books on archaeology were always consigned to the outer reaches of libraries: they were large and not much read. His eye was caught by a title: *The Destruction of Cultural Heritage in Iraq.* It was a fairly new book and he wanted to read it: he'd not been as angry as many people at the invasion of Iraq, though he had thought it was stupid, but the wanton destruction of sites and artefacts had driven him wild. He pulled the book off the shelf and heard something clatter to the ground. Something that had been pushed in beside the book on the shelf. A knife, an ordinary, small kitchen knife with a black plastic handle. He took out his handkerchief and used it to pick the knife up. Though incongruous in this setting, it would have been a harmless enough object, the blade no more than seven centimetres long, had it not been for the fact that both handle and blade were encrusted with a brownish substance that he recognised without doubt as dried blood.

He stood looking at it as it lay on his handkerchief, nestling in his palm, and willed himself not to hope for too much from this. Before he even started speculating he needed to know if the blood was Yilmaz's. He took out his mobile and called the station. The first of his team to be found was Boxer. He gave him a terse account of his find and told him to get over right away with evidence bags.

'And Steve,' he said, 'let forensics know we're going to want a DNA comparison and fingerprints, top priority. Let Dr McAndrew know we're going to need the knife matched up to Yilmaz's stab wounds, and tell the SOCOs I want them back here to finish their fucking job.'

While he waited for Boxer he couldn't help speculating,

whatever he told himself about not running too far ahead. If this was the knife that was used, then the killers dumped it here before going out of the emergency exit – nothing else made sense. But the emergency exit was closed when Clive Davies did his rounds at ten-thirty, so someone had to have closed it from inside. Maybe one of the killers went out that way and the other closed the door and went out through the office. Easier for one to slip past the porter unnoticed than two, they may have thought.

He thought about cancelling his talk at the school now he had this new development to think about, but it was going to be all waiting for the next twenty-four hours – waiting for the forensic results, waiting for Lynne McAndrew's assessment of the knife as a weapon. He might just as well go.

The school was unrecognisable as the place where he had spent seven years. As he approached the imposing front entrance, Scott read on the glossy sign that The William Roper School was now a city academy, *pursuing excellence*, funded by private money. A corporate logo was etched into the double glass doors and a card swipe controlled the entrance. He rang the bell beside it, gave his name and was admitted. A woman behind a reception desk summoned *today's runner* and a girl of twelve or so appeared to lead him to the year twelve common room.

The logo (a twisted 'W' and 'R' in red and black, surmounted by an academic-looking scroll) was everywhere. The uniform had been designed to match too: the girl was wearing a knee-length black skirt and a public school-type red and black striped blazer. He asked a few questions, more out of politeness than anything, as she led him along a warren of corridors and she answered them dutifully, attaching 'sir' to the end of each reply. Well-drilled, he thought.

The common room was nothing like the cosy shambles he remembered from his sixth form days. Upholstered chairs were grouped in a wide circle, a wall of windows with a view out to the abbey gleamed on one side, while on the other, as he was shown, a door opened onto an enclosed, glass-sided bridge leading to the Senior Library. About thirty students had gathered to hear his pearls of wisdom. They were not in school uniform – a post-sixteen privilege they had not lost in the school's makeover, though he would bet there was a no jeans rule, since no-one was wearing them. As Tom Urquhart had promised, they had plenty of questions. He joked that it was odd to be on the receiving end of questions for a change and at first he found himself being grudging in his answers, as unwilling as any police interviewee to divulge more than he needed to.

Q. What made you go into the police?
A. I've always liked problem-solving.

Q. Did you go to university?
A. Yes, I went to Nottingham University.

Q. What subject did you study?
A. Archaeology and Geography

Q. What 'A' levels did you do?
A. Geography, English and Classical Civilisation

And so on. But he warmed up after a while, became more discursive, told a few carefully anonymised true-life stories of life in the force, and the forty-five minutes were soon slipping away. He was quite surprised to hear Tom Urquhart say, 'We've just time for two more questions, I think.'

'What's the worst thing about being in the police?'

The question came from a boy who had not spoken before. Scott considered it. In his darkest gloom over the weekend he would have said, *It takes away your life, eats you up and spits you out*. Now, he said, 'It can be frustrating. When the public won't help. When we believe people know something but won't tell us, because they're afraid or they don't trust us. When we're pretty sure who the criminals are but we can't get the proof. That can really get you down.'

'What makes you stay, then?' a girl asked.

He smiled.

'Well, the pay's not bad. And sometimes, just sometimes, you get a lucky break and it all falls out for you, and then there's nothing like it.'

As he drove back towards the station, he realised he was passing More Street. He wondered if Gina would be back from work yet and, without quite intending to, he turned off and stopped outside her door. He wouldn't tell her about the knife yet, he thought as walked up the path, but his interviews with the Iranians were a plausible enough reason for calling. He rang the bell, which appeared not to work, and then banged the knocker. He could hear movements inside and eventually the door was opened, not by Gina but by the daughter he had met the other evening.

'Oh, hello, Detective Chief Inspector,' she said, and gave him a cool, appraising look. 'Have you come to arrest my mother?'

21

MONDAY: *Present Tense*

I am treading a fine line, skating on thin ice, standing on a volcano, sitting on powder keg, playing with fire. Alternatively, I have tempted Providence, put my head in the lion's mouth and taken my life in my hands. I am certainly out of my depth and sailing too close to the wind. I rehearse these metaphors as I pedal into college on Monday morning. I could make a language exercise out of them: *now let's see if we can arrange these idioms in order of seriousness.*

Things did not go as well as I hoped yesterday: Ceren has not been persuaded to return to college and I would not – cannot – throw her out. She has promised me, however, that she will ring her parents today, and I have no option but to trust her. What she will say to them I have no idea. Annie still looks dangerously willing to go to the stake for her cause, and to take me with her.

As soon as I get onto the campus, before I've dropped my bag or taken my coat off, I go into the International Office. Better to get this over as soon as possible. I don't actually go into the office, but put my head round the door, as though this will make what I'm about to say deniable.

'Ceren Vural,' I say breezily to Monica, the adsministrator, who has just walked in and also still has her coat on. 'Don't worry about contacting her parents – I've got it in hand.'

This is approximately true; I have, after all, told Ceren to ring them. This, however, is not what Monica thinks it means, nor what I intend her to think it means. Though my utterance is superficially true, its perlocution – that Monica should believe that I have spoken or will be speaking to the Vurals – is a lie. For forty-five years I have regarded myself as a truthful person, perhaps pathologically so. I don't even go in for white lies in the interests of sparing feelings (my daughters, I know, felt I was unnecessarily frank, especially in my assessment of their performances in school plays and concerts), but now I am lying, and when Monica says, 'Oh, thanks, Gina. How did they take it?'

I am forced to confront my lie and, panicking, I take to my heels.

'Sorry, Monica,' I call as I turn tail. 'Nine o'clock class. I'll catch up with you later.'

As I push my bike over to the English Language building and trail up the stairs to my office, I rehearse my cross-examination in court when I stand charged with conspiring to pervert the course of justice. I used to do this when the children were small. I would leave them in the charge of a first-time babysitter and go out to the theatre, or drop them at the house of a friend who had a small pool in her back garden and go and do the shopping. Then, as I sat in the theatre or trawled the supermarket aisles, I would imagine myself in the coroner's court. *And how much did you know about this fifteen-year- old you had engaged to care for your children, Mrs Gray? Had you ascertained to your satisfaction that she would be able to cope in an emergency? In retrospect, would you say you had behaved like a responsible mother? Or, And you had no qualms, Mrs Gray, about leaving a five-year-old – a five-year-old who could swim only with the assistance of inflatable arm bands – in the charge of a woman with three other children to take care of?*

Today I hear the prosecution counsel:

You knew, did you not, Mrs Gray, that Ceren Vural had

information that could be helpful to the police in tracking down a murderer?

And I hear my own shamefaced mumble:

I thought she might have.

And yet you kept her secreted in your house? You hid her from the police, not only depriving them of vital information but causing them to waste valuable resources looking for a young woman who was safe and well and living in your spare bedroom? How can you possibly justify that?

I didn't feel that I could throw her out when she was unwilling to go.

Why? Was she homeless? Did she have nowhere else to go?

Well, not really. She –

Did she not have a room waiting for her on the campus, not to mention parents who would have been glad to welcome her home?

She didn't want to go back to her room, or to her parents.

She didn't want to? And that was enough, was it, to justify your criminal behaviour?

My daughter felt very strongly that she should be allowed to stay.

Would you tell the court the age of your daughter?

She's sixteen.

And you are prepared, are you, to blame a sixteen-year-old – a child – for your own irresponsible actions? What kind of mother are you, Mrs Gray?

I stand in my office gazing out of the window. How did I get myself into this? And how am I going to get myself out? I have to stop sleep-walking. I must take control. My phone rings and Gillian in the department office tells me that Mme Amiel wants to see me. This is more than I can manage this morning.

'I'm teaching. Tell her I'm teaching all morning. And I have a meeting at lunch time. And busy this afternoon. If she leaves a mobile number, I'll ring her.'

This lying business becomes quite easy with practice, I

find. I feel guilty, but only slightly. My empathy with Mme Amiel's distress is moderated by the memory of all those designer carrier bags.

I teach the Two-year Master's class at ten o'clock and find that now there are only six of them – the sad remnants of the original unlucky thirteen. No Ekrem, of course, no Laurent or Ceren, no Asil and Ahmet and now no Farid or Atash, since they are being interrogated at the police station. I feel terrible about this, of course, because if I had told David Scott that Ceren was all right, he would have seen that his theory of the two-man punishment squad really didn't stack up.

So here they sit, the six survivors, Irina and Valery, Desirée and Denis, Yukiko and Christiane. What shall I do with them? It seems impossible to have a proper class. Since I have some homework to return to them, I decide on impromptu tutorials. I give them an exercise on phrasal verbs to get on with (*stand up, stand down, stand for, stand out, stand in, stand to, stand by, stand up for, stand in for* and so on) and I go over their work with them.

It is odd to sit so close, poring over their work. I seem to feel the tension in each of them, vibrating quietly beside me, as they, no doubt, can feel mine. And none of them looks quite well. It's a bad time of year, of course – we all have an end-of-winter pallor – but young faces shouldn't look like this, so weary and hollow-eyed. What is happening to us all?

As I head for the SCR for coffee, my mobile rings and I see that it's David Scott calling. I can't talk to him. If I talk to him, I shall have to lie to him – by omission at the very least. I switch my phone off. Now I'm running from him as well as from the Amiels and there is no hiding place. Normally, when I don't want to be tracked down in my office, I go over to the library but that's obviously not an option at the moment. I lurk in the SCR, anxiously eying both entrances the whole while, then take a circuitous route back to my office to pick up my books for my next class. I enter fully prepared to find

David lying in wait, but he is not, so I collect my things and head off.

At the end of the morning, I decide that the only safe thing is to leave the campus, so I walk into town and buy myself a toasted cheese and tomato sandwich in the café on the top floor of Waterstones. No-one, I'm pretty sure, will think of looking for me here. It is ridiculous, of course, to be reduced to skulking like this but I promise myself that it's only temporary. I refuse to spend another day like this. When I get home tonight, the situation with Ceren must be resolved.

I remember, though, that I shan't be going straight home after work: I am summoned to a Parents' Evening at Lady Margaret's College to discuss Annie's progress into the Upper Sixth (Lady Margaret's has no truck with new-fangled nonsense and years twelve and thirteen remain the Lower and Upper Sixth as far as they are concerned). Decisions have to be made about which subjects she will take only to AS level and which she will carry on to A level. She is doing Latin, History, Economics, Drama and Art. She likes Drama and Art best but they won't get her a place to study Law, which is what she and her father have decided she wants to do.

When Andrew first proposed sending the girls to Lady Margaret's College, I protested that I would never feel comfortable there: I would resent the tone of the place, which seems to ask whether you are good enough for it rather than what it can do for you, and I would despise the teachers, who had found a soft option, who couldn't hack it in the front line. (I was still in the front line myself in those days. I've since found my own soft option but at least I did my time. I have paid my dues). Andrew said I was being ridiculous (when was I ever anything else?) but it was true and remains true. As soon as I enter the school's hallowed portals I have an urge to behave badly, and when teachers complain that my daughter is *disruptive*, I want to grab them by the ears and tell them what disruptive is really like. I know, you see, what this evening will be like; the script is already written. Usually I am able to ride their complaints about Annie with a judicious mixture of modified agreement and cheerful optimism, but today I'm really not feeling strong enough.

After an afternoon of pretty mediocre teaching, five-thirty finds me cycling up the drive to Lady Margaret's amid the four by fours, the Rovers and the occasional Bentleys. I am swearing quietly under my breath. I start, of course, at a disadvantage on these occasions because we are supposed to come in pairs. Tables are placed at intervals round the vaulted hall, with a teacher sitting behind each. Facing her (or occasionally him) are two chairs to accommodate a brace of parents. I am anomalous. I'm not the only lone parent here, of course, but I'm unusual enough to feel conspicuous.

I start with the Latin teacher. Mrs Emily Duncan (MA Oxon, as the white card in front of her identifies her) is younger than I expected from Annie's account of her, and not bad-looking, though lamentably badly-dressed in a green and orange patterned jumper with a black and white check skirt. She is reasonably up-beat to start with. Annie has *quite a flair for unseen translation*, she tells me, but she is *terribly careless in prose composition* and she will really have to *buckle down to learning the set books* if she's going to get a good AS grade. I promise that I will make sure she does, though I suspect that we both know that I can't deliver on this, and when I discuss the possibility of her going on to 'A' level, she is clearly rattled.

'But I understood from Marianne that she wasn't planning to carry on. And I really do think that's wise.'

'Her father wants her to carry on,' I say, 'because she wants to be a lawyer.'

She actually looks at the empty chair next to me, as though Andrew might possibly be the invisible man. Then she smiles at me and says, 'Oh, I think AS will be quite enough for that. After all, all sorts of people do law degrees these days, don't they – I mean from quite disadvantaged schools?'

'But this,' I retort, 'is an outrageously advantaged school, isn't it? And one of its advantages is that our daughter can take A level Latin.'

Why am I doing Andrew's dirty work for him? Do I care whether she does Latin or not? Is arguing just a habit with me?

'Marianne seems quite sure that she wants to drop it,' she persists.

'And her father is quite sure he wants her to carry on, so they're just going to have to fight it out,' I say.

'Who do you think will win,' she asks nervously.

'It's hard to say,' I tell her. 'They're pretty evenly matched. But I think my money's still on him.'

Miss Eileen Porter (BA London), Annie's History teacher, is a different proposition altogether. She is fiftyish, plump and pallid, with flat colourless hair and an ingratiating smile that is belied by her beady little eyes. She is dressed this evening in layers of brown and sits behind her table like an oversized brown hen. I know her of old as she taught Ellie too. She usually prefaces her remarks about Annie with the observation that *of course, she's not like her sister*, but since Ellie's fall from grace I think we can assume that she'll drop that as an opening gambit this evening. She tells me instead that she finds Annie *challenging* and *opinionated*.

'Oh good,' I say. 'That's good, isn't it? Having their own opinions, challenging received truths, that's what we want from our young people, isn't it?'

A slight pink flush suffuses her moon face.

'Not altogether. As a teacher yourself, Mrs Gray, I'm sure you'll agree that opinions need to be backed up with knowledge and that a certain amount of deference to superior knowledge and experience is desirable.'

I laugh.

'Ah, deference,' I say. 'I must admit that's not one of her strong points. We have always encouraged our girls to speak their minds at home, I'm afraid.'

'Frankly,' she says, growing ever pinker, 'I find Marianne very attention-seeking. My lessons are constantly interrupted by her observations and questions. There is a great deal of factual material to be covered in this syllabus and I cannot afford to be stopped every five minutes by –'

I am conscious of a movement at my side. I turn to see Andrew slipping into the seat beside me and I must say I admire the cool way I simply say, 'Oh, hello.' as though he wasn't the last person I expected to see. He has a Venezuelan tan and is wearing an Italian-looking jacket. He is a good-looking man and I've always liked being seen with him even if I couldn't stand living with him.

'Miss Porter was just telling me,' I say, 'that our daughter is opinionated, challenging and not over-deferential. I made the mistake of thinking those were the qualities we wanted to encourage in the young, but apparently I am mistaken.'

Andrew doesn't miss a beat. He gives the wretched woman his sharkiest smile and says, 'With all due respect, Miss Porter, I wonder if you're in danger of perpetuating an outmoded female stereotype here. Does this school really want to go on producing young women who undervalue themselves, who fear confrontation and who want only to conform?'

She makes a feeble effort at self-defence.

'Mr Gray, I must protest! I never said anything about –'

But her poor little wings are broken and Andrew drives on relentlessly.

'More than twenty-five years ago, we boys at the Abbey School were being encouraged to hone our wits and our arguments, to have the confidence of our own opinions. I appreciate that you have taken refuge in a girls' school in order to avoid the challenge of teaching boys, but don't you think this school has a duty to offer these young women an education that will fit them to participate as equals with men in a modern world? If not, then I don't know what you think you're doing.'

I am gaping at him, torn between admiration and outrage. These are *my* arguments, many of them in my very words. I have been binding on about this for years and Andrew always batted away my opinions as though they were so much irritating trivia. Of course, he's just a lawyer; he'll use any argument that comes to hand to win a point. I have no idea whether he believes any of it or not.

I turn to make some ameliorating remark to Miss Porter, but she has risen and is hurrying out of the hall. I am almost sure she is crying. I am ashamed. I have allowed my ex-husband, a man who gets paid to bully people, to destroy this poor little woman and I have provided him with the ammunition to do it. All right, I admit I've got no time for her and women like her, but I still shouldn't have let it happen, especially as I know what Annie can be like when she gets the bit between her teeth. She is probably being a complete nightmare in History lessons.

We stand up and I shrug a sort of apology at the parents sitting waiting for their interviews with Miss Porter before grabbing Andrew's arm and tugging him out into the corridor.

'What the hell did you think you were doing?' I hiss.

He looks injured.

'I thought you wanted me to weigh in,' he says. 'You invited me to.'

'I just wanted a bit of support. I wanted you to stick up for Annie.'

He looks at me.

'You know your problem, Gina,' he says. 'You content yourself with biting people's ankles. You're never ready to go for the jugular.'

Oh, so *that's* my problem, is it?

'What are you doing here, anyway?' I ask. 'I thought you were in Venezuela.'

'I just got back. I'm practically straight off the plane.'

'How did you know this was happening?'

'Annie told me.'

'Why?'

'She thought I'd like to be involved. I do pay the fees.'

'And neither of you thought to tell me you were coming?'

'I wasn't sure till the last minute whether I'd be able to make it.'

I see what Annie is doing. She wants Andrew to meet the teachers. She knows he wants her to drop Drama and carry on with Latin. She wants him to see for himself how much her Latin teacher doesn't want to teach her any more, and she wants him to meet her adored Drama teacher, the only bright spot, it would seem, in the sunless landscape of Annie's school life.

I send Andrew along to the refectory where, I know, the PTA will have provided a substantial tea for parents coming straight from work (by parents they will mean fathers: the assumption in the quaint world of Lady Margaret is that mothers still spend their days gossiping, gardening and golfing). He protests that he has been eating aeroplane food all day, but I send him anyway. I need to talk to the Economics teacher, a nervous young man who, I suspect, is being baited unmercifully by Annie and her friends and should be protected from Andrew at all costs.

I find Mr Aidan Trevelyan (BA Exeter) without a queue and I slip into the seat in front of him, causing him to give a nervous little start. I decide to approach this interview differently. I shall be disarming.

'I'm Marianne Gray's mother,' I say, 'and before you say anything, I should tell you that I know she can be a nightmare. I've lived with her for sixteen years, so I should know.'

I give a jolly sort of laugh. He peers at me with pale eyes beneath fluttering eyelids.

'To be frank,' he says, 'I find them all a nightmare. Marianne isn't the worst.'

'Really?' I say, disconcerted.

'No. At least she's well-informed. And she seems quite interested. Unlike some of the others. They seem to think it's some sort of game.'

I consider him. He's only middle thirties but has a greyish aura. *He thought he'd found a safe haven coming here,* I think, *but he's found himself in a nest of harpies.*

'She certainly seems to be enjoying the course,' I say.

This is overstating the case, but you will remember that this is my day for being creative with the actualité. What Annie has in fact said is that Mr Trevelyan is a wimp and a dickhead but the course *isn't bad* and she *doesn't mind* carrying on with it.

'Yes she seems to enjoy it,' he says. Then, 'They have so much energy those girls. It makes me tired just being in a room with them.'

I am terrified that he is going to have his nervous breakdown right here in front of me.

'She definitely wants to carry on to A level,' I tell him bracingly.

'Oh good,' he says with the faintest flicker of surprise.

'How,' I ask tentatively, 'do you think she will do on the AS papers?'

'Quite well, I think,' he says sadly. 'She writes very well, and that's half the battle.'

Is it my imagination or does he flinch slightly as he says *battle*?

'That's good news,' I say as I stand up, and then, because it would be inappropriate to give this sad little man a hug, I put out my hand and say, 'Thank you so much for all you're doing for Marianne.'

I sound ridiculous to myself but he takes my hand and gives it a limp shake.

'I do my best,' he says.

As soon as Andrew reappears, I steer him in the direction of Mrs Emily Duncan (MA Oxon) to discuss Annie's Latin plans. I stake a place in the queue for Head of Drama, Ms Kirsten Donald (BA Cantab, MA Warwick) and I watch the encounter between Andrew and Emily Duncan from a distance. I see from Andrew's body language that he is in gallant mode. He's leaning towards her, listening intently, nodding and smiling. He might as well be seducing the woman for God's sake.

By the time he has finished with her, I have reached the head of the queue for Ms Donald. I'm not surprised this queue is so long: Kirsten Donald is completely gorgeous. A natural redhead with clear green eyes and creamy milkmaid skin, she looks no more than twenty-five. I wouldn't be surprised if there were fathers in this queue just standing here for the pleasure of looking at her.

When we announce who we are, she leans across the table and seizes our hands.

'I am so pleased to meet you,' she says. 'I'm sure you know it already, but I have to say it: you have a very remarkable daughter.'

I am prepared for most things on these occasions, but not this. I stare, speechless, and she sweeps on. Marianne, she tells us, is *a star*. She is *not just talented*, but *creative, original, thoughtful, disciplined, a natural leader* and *hugely supportive of others*. We gaze at her in wonder. How has she achieved this miracle transformation in our child? What kind of witch is she?

Andrew rallies a bit.

'Unfortunately,' he says, 'she won't be able to continue with Drama beyond AS level. She'll need three academic subjects for the university course she wants to do.'

'She wants to be a lawyer, doesn't she, and she's doing History and Economics A levels?' Her voice is lovely, her accent soft, seductive Scottish. 'I think she'll find that Drama is a perfectly acceptable third A level for a law degree. And very useful. What is a courtroom, after all, but a place of theatre?'

She turns the green eyes full on to Andrew.

'You're a lawyer yourself, aren't you, Mr Gray? Would you not agree that a sense of theatre is important in your job? Are you not a bit of an actor yourself? Would that not be where Marianne gets her talent from?'

And Andrew, for once, is utterly nonplussed. He grins foolishly but he is speechless, silenced. The cat, it appears, has got his tongue. I sit and savour this unprecedented state of affairs. The woman, I tell myself, really is a witch. Then he does the only possible thing and removes us from her magic circle. He clears his throat, thanks Ms Donald for her time, says that we shall have to discuss the question further and now it is he who bundles me out of the hall.

Outside he recovers a bit and suggests that he comes back with me to talk about all this. He probably hopes I'll give him supper too. He can't come back to my house, though, because I'm harbouring a wanted woman in my house and I've vowed not to let Andrew into that imbroglio.

'I'm knackered, Andrew,' I say (perfectly truthfully). 'It's been a hell of a day. How about a pub lunch tomorrow? Check your diary and give me a call.'

Then he climbs into his shiny monster of a car and I mount my bike and pedal off home.

The house is silent when I return; it feels deserted. I find Annie in her room, though, lying on her bed, listening to music. She doesn't ask how the evening went and I'm not volunteering anything till I'm asked. She doesn't turn the music off either, so I shout over the top of it,

'Where's Ceren?'

For answer, she hands me an envelope (one of my own envelopes, I recognise) addressed to 'Mrs Gray'. I open the letter, which reads as follows:

Dear Mrs Gray,

I am safe and I stay with my friends. Please tell the police they not worry for me. Please not to telephone my parents.

Thank you that you are kind teacher.
Ceren Vural

I know what this is: this is my get-out-of-jail card. How carefully she has written it; no-one would guess that she has been living in my house. My first response is pure relief, I must admit, before I start to worry about where she has gone. Has she really gone to friends? If so, who? Will they look after her? Does whatever she knows put her in danger?

'What did she say when she left?' I ask Annie.

'She was gone when I got back. She left a note for me too.'

'Do you mind if I see it? You can see mine.'

We exchange letters and I read:

Dear Marian,

Thank you so much you are so kind to me. I enjoyed talking and music with you. I must leave now because I make trouble to your mother and you.

Don't worry to me. I am fine. I hope I see you again.
Ceren

'She knew you didn't want her,' Annie shouts, still without turning her music off. 'We let her down. She came to us for help and because you're so thick with the police all of a sudden, we let her down.'

I go downstairs and put two pizzas in the oven, and in the twelve minutes I am instructed to leave them in there, I down a glass of red wine. We eat in silence. Annie has nothing to say to me and I know better than to raise topics of conversation only to have my words frozen in mid-air by her icy contempt. I swallow another glass or two of wine and get up, still in silence, to clear our plates. As she is leaving the room, Annie says, 'Your policeman friend called, by the way.'

'When? What did he want?'

'He wanted to see you, I imagine. He certainly didn't come to see me.'

'What did he say?'

'All sorts of things. We had quite a chat.'

'You didn't let him in?'

'Of course I did. I thought it would look suspicious otherwise.'

'But Ceren – '

'Ceren had gone, hadn't she? There was one thing though. She'd left that scarf thing she wears behind. It was on the sofa. I noticed it as I took him into the sitting room, so I spread it out over the back of the sofa like a throw. Quick thinking, I thought.'

Panic, on top of the wine, is making me dizzy. I sit down.

'Oh God, Annie! Did he say anything about it?''

'No. It was fine. Then I made him a cup of tea and we talked.'

'What about, for Heaven's sake?'

'You, mainly. He wanted to know all about you. And about Pa and all of that. He told me all the boys fancied you when you were his teacher. And he was very keen to tell me that he's only six years younger than you.'

'What did you tell him?'

'I said that being a mother and a grandmother had made you old before your time, that you weren't interested in men and that you and Pa were still like *that*.'

She brandishes her linked index and middle fingers at me before she sweeps out of the room.

22

Tuesday: Investigation Day Thirteen

'The blood on the knife is Yilmaz's,' Scott was telling the team, 'but we've had no luck yet with the fingerprints. There are two sets on the handle but no match with the database. So –'

Simon Kerr interrupted.

'Are we going to take prints from the students, then?'

'We can't, Simon. There's no hard evidence against any of them. We've no justification for treating them as suspects. They just happened to be doing the same course as Yilmaz. They're our suspects because two others in the class have gone missing and because of those messages that have appeared on the classroom board, which we assume were written by one of the students. Some of you are sceptical about those, I know, and you may be right. They could be something and nothing. The Director of English is convinced that they're significant, but I'm not sure.'

Scott saw Kerr's eyebrows go up as he and Boxer exchanged a quick look before Boxer asked, 'So what happens now?'

'We keep digging. The SOCOs are back at the crime scene. I've told them I want them crawling over every inch of the place this time.'

'How the hell did they manage to miss a bloodstained knife last time round?' Paula Powell asked.

Scott raised his arms in a despairing shrug.

'Said they didn't realise they were expected to examine every book in the place. They concentrated on the area round where the body was found, the office, entrances etc. It just happened that the knife was hidden next to a book I was interested in. Luck. The only bit of luck we've had in this case.'

His phone rang and he saw that it was Gina, finally returning his calls, he assumed. Well, not now. He cut off the call and continued, 'We do have something from forensics. Fibres found near Yilmaz's body are Indian cotton, pink, green and white, and the hairs found nearby aren't Yilmaz's. They're dark and the DNA is female. We've no idea whether they're significant. They could have been dropped there any time. The cleaners go in on alternate mornings, so they last cleaned on the Wednesday morning, the day of the murder, but they admit that they only sweep between the rolling stacks where they're standing open. They don't move them apart.'

He looked around at their faces, blank with discouragement.

'Any progress on the Mikhail Belenki connection, Steve?' he asked.

Boxer shook his head.

'Nothing yet. The Russian police won't play ball any way. Official line is there's no Russian Mafia. All an invention of the West, apparently. We may get something from the Turks, though. I'm waiting on that.'

'And Amiel? Any credit card or phone activity?'

'Nothing. And he doesn't seem to have bought a new phone – not that we can trace.'

'OK, Thanks. Keep at it. And let's hope the SOCOs come up with more. Oh, and though we can't fingerprint the students, we have got something - a pen from one of the classrooms – a boardwriter they use for the whiteboard. Apparently the students as well as the lecturers write on the board. They're looking for a match with the knife handle. We should have those results by tomorrow.'

As he left the room, his phone beeped the text message signal and he read:

Have heard from Ceren.
Safe and sound.
Ring me 4 details. Gina

Turning back to the room he had just left, he put his head round the door.

'Stop press,' he called, brandishing his phone. 'Ceren Vural has made contact with the college. Safe and sound apparently. So we may only have one missing student, which is something. As soon as I get more details I'll let you know.'

If he had lingered a moment longer before leaving the room, he would have seen Boxer and Kerr exchange another significant look.

When he called Gina back, she was just about to go off to teach.

'Ceren sent me a letter,' she said.

'So you haven't spoken to her?'

'No.'

'Any postmark?'

'It was hand-delivered.'

'I'll need to see it. When can I come and get it from you?'

'I'm teaching all morning and then meeting – someone - for lunch. You don't need to see it. I'll read it to you. *Dear Mrs Gray, I am safe and I stay with my friends. Please tell the police they not worry for me. Please not to telephone my parents. Thank you that you are kind teacher. Ceren Vural.* I've read it with errors and all so you can hear it's genuine. And it's definitely her writing. So, panic over.'

'When can I pick it up from you?'

'Why do you need to?'

'For God's sake, Gina. The girl was reported missing. That note may have been written under duress – haven't you thought of that? We need our handwriting experts to look at it. Is it dated?'

'No, but – '

'So, we don't know when it was written, we don't know where she is, we don't know why she disappeared and we don't know who is holding her. That note is vital evidence and I need to see it. You can either leave it in the department office for us to collect or bring it in to the station yourself this afternoon.'

'You're being very masterful all of a sudden. You find that goes down well, do you, with women of a certain age?'

'I'm just doing my job, and I don't know why you think it's a joke. So what's it to be? If you bring the letter in, we can do your fingerprints at the same time.'

'*My* fingerprints! Why?'

'Come on, Gina, you're not usually slow. We need to know how many people handled the letter – whether others were involved in writing it – so we'll want to know how many sets of prints there are and it'll help if we can eliminate yours. We've got Ceren's own from stuff in her room. Have you shown it to anyone?'

'No. I told the International Office and the English staff, and I rang you.'

'So no-one else has handled it as far as you know?'

'No. Oh, well, Annie might have picked it up.'

'Annie? Do you mean it was delivered to you at home?'

'Well, yes. What did you think?'

'I just assumed it was sent to you at work. Does Ceren know your home address?'

'She's been to the house – David, what is all the interrogation for?'

'And the other students? Have they been to the house too?'

'Yes. I had a tea party. Before Christmas. Yes.'

'Doesn't it worry you that whoever may have abducted Ceren knows where you live, and has been to your house to deliver that letter?'

'No-one's abducted Ceren, David. She's staying with friends. She says so.'

'Why? Why would she disappear of her own accord and then send you such a deliberately vague message about where she is? Why would she want to run away?'

'I don't know. She's twenty-one. Boyfriend trouble? I don't know.'

'Does she have a boyfriend?'

'I DON'T KNOW.'

'I thought you prided yourself on knowing all about your students' private lives.'

'Well I obviously don't know everything.'

'And that's an admission I didn't ever expect to hear. You don't know everything. In that case, perhaps you'll let me do my job and bring me that bloody letter. At your earliest convenience, of course.'

'Certainly, Chief Inspector. Shall we say two o'clock?'

Scott spent the rest of the morning dealing with the heaped contents of his in-tray, ate a sandwich at his desk, then stood at his window looking out at the station forecourt, sipping a mug of coffee, waiting for Gina. At two fifteen, as he was beginning to get angry – with her and with himself – a remarkable car stopped in the forecourt. An MG Roadster in a distinctive blue-green. He was no car buff but he guessed it dated from the 1960's. And he guessed, just a few seconds before she emerged, that Gina would get out of it. He watched her as she slid out, waved a casual farewell and strode towards the station doors. Then he looked back at the car and caught sight of the driver as he turned it – a glimpse of thick grey-blond hair and a winter tan. Movie star looks. Who was he? The ex-husband she was still so pally with, according to the daughter? Or someone else he didn't know about?

He went down to the foyer to meet her and brought her up to his office.

'Good lunch?' he asked.

'Stimulating,' she said curtly, which told him nothing.

Up in his office, she handed him the letter without a word; he glanced through it and sealed it in an evidence bag. He pulled up two chairs and sat down beside her.

'You understand why we need your fingerprints, don't you? And we'll need Annie's too.'

'I'm sure she'll be thrilled. When do you want her?'

'As soon as she gets home from school would be good.'

'It'll be easier for her to come straight from school. I'll send her a text.'

'Fine.'

There was a silence. She was refusing to look at him. Was she still annoyed about having to hand over the letter?

'The thing is,' he said, 'we've found a knife in the library.'

Now she did look at him.

'What do you mean?'

'We've found a knife with Yilmaz's blood on it hidden in the library. Yilmaz had knife cuts on his arm and face. We've always thought that one man kept him in the stacks at knife point while the other rolled them together. We appear to have found the knife.'

'And there are fingerprints?'

'There are. And if they match prints on this letter then we'll know Ceren's in danger.'

'Are you going to fingerprint the students?'

'No. We can only fingerprint people who are suspects, or for elimination purposes, as in your case. We do have that pen you gave us, though. It's got a lot of prints on, as you warned me, some of them, presumably, from this group of students. It's possible we'll get a match and then we would be justified in fingerprinting them all.'

'I've got something else for you, actually,' she said. 'Another board message.'

He groaned.

'Please, not another. My team think I'm off my head to take them seriously at all.'

'Oh well, if you don't want to know – '

'No, no. you'd better tell me.'

'I can show you.'

She produced her phone and fiddled with it.

'Look.'

INSTEAD TO BE GOOD MUSLIM
HE SOLD THE DRUGS. HE WAS KILLED
WHY NOT?

'And what nationality would this be?' he asked. 'As if I couldn't guess.'

'Your guess would be right. It's Iranian. They're classic errors. The *why not* question tag and the infinitive instead of the gerund – *to be* rather than *of being*.'

'But they know they're under suspicion. They're hardly likely to advertise themselves like this, are they?'

'No. Which makes me think –' She hesitated.

'Think what?'

'That someone's playing games with us – with me, rather. Someone's been playing games all along, I'm afraid.'

'How?'

'Well, look at the messages there have been. I made a list of them, here. Number one: *If I would kill him I would be happier* – a classic German error that *would* in the 'if' clause. Then we had *If the man wasn't being a drug addict he wasn't disappearing*. Classic again. Turkish this time – misuse of the progressive in *wasn't being* and *wasn't disappearing*. Then we had *The criminal was executed*. No errors this time, but it directed us towards the Iranians and could only have been written by someone who had been at the discussion in class the previous day. And now this – implicating the Iranians again. Whoever wrote these knew that I would see the errors and spot the nationality. The question is, is this just a rather macabre game or is the phantom writer the killer?'

'If you're right, then we should look at which nationalities haven't been implicated. Logic would point to one of them as the guilty party, unless they're being very subtle.'

'No Russian, Japanese or French errors as yet,' Gina said.

'And if we're looking for pairs of killers, they provide some convenient options. Valery Tarasov and Irina Boklova? Irina's a big woman. Armed with a knife, she could probably have kept Yilmaz between those stacks. We're still working on the way Yilmaz was tied up with Anton Tarasov. He may have been involved in his death. Valery could well have had a motive – as could Irina, if Yilmaz was threatening to tell her ex-hisband where she was. Then there's the French pair –'

Gina interrupted with a hoot of laughter.

'You're not suggesting Desirée was involved! What? And get blood all over her clothes? I don't see her as Lady Macbeth.'

'I meant the pair of French speakers – Amiel and De Longueville. Both were getting drugs from Yilmaz, both could have been being blackmailed. It's possible Amiel was panicky afterwards and Longueville decided he was a danger. So he's got him locked up somewhere, or he's given him the money to disappear, or he's killed him too.'

'I don't think Denis is a killer.'

'You don't think any of them are killers, but somebody is.' Seized by a mounting rage, he went on, 'Somebody is, and we don't know who, and I can spin these theories and they're all quite plausible but there isn't a shred of evidence for any of it, and it's nearly two weeks since the murder and we've got fucking nowhere.'

She looked at him.

'I bet you feel better for getting that off your chest,' she said. 'I don't expect you can shout at your subordinates like that. Anyway, you've got a weapon and some fingerprints now, so who knows what may happen? Talking of which, perhaps I'd better go and do the deed.'

When the fingerprinting was done, he walked her to the front doors.

'You haven't got your bike, have you?' he said. 'I noticed you got a lift. Your lunch date, I assume?'

'Oh yes, the precious MG. I did Andrew a service divorcing him really. It meant he could go and live somewhere with a garage.'

'A bit drastic. You could just have moved house.'

He was treated to a mocking smile.

'We could. How sensible you are.'

'How dull, you mean?'

'Not necessarily. I'm going to get a cab from the rank outside the town hall. I need to be back in college for three o'clock.'

'I'll walk round with you. There's one more thing I want to ask you.'

'Oh yes?'

'When I called at your house yesterday evening –'

'Yes, I'm sorry I wasn't in.'

'No, my fault. I should have phoned first. But when I called, Annie asked me if I'd come to arrest you. Why did she ask that?'

She was rummaging in her bag.

'That reminds me,' she said, 'I must text Annie about the fingerprinting. Sorry, what were you asking? Oh yes, why did she say that? Well because that's what policemen do, don't they? They arrest people. It's typical Annie – a mixture of melodrama and mockery.'

She was busy texting. Like a teenager, Scott thought, walking, texting and talking all at the same time. She and Annie were remarkably alike, he realised, and he visualised Annie sitting talking to him yesterday with her poise and her cool amused look. And in his picture, Annie had something behind her head, something that had been on the edge of his thoughts since that morning.

'I noticed,' he said conversationally, 'that you had a rather nice ethnic-looking thing on your sofa that I don't remember seeing before. Is it new?'

'What am I now? Your design consultant?' she snapped, her eyes still on her phone, thumb still texting. 'Are you gay, David? Only gay men notice soft furnishings. And I don't know what you're talking about. I don't think I've been into my sitting room since Sunday – yesterday was the day from Hell. It's probably some thing Annie's bought at a Traidcraft sale at school. She goes for third world products. They make her feel noble.'

Without saying goodbye, she slid into a taxi and slammed the door.

23

TUESDAY: *Concessive Clauses*

Annie is still glowering at me in the morning but I don't care. I have slept well – the sleep of the just, or at least of the woman who is not about to be arrested. I am cheerful as I breeze into College, light-hearted as I pop my head round the door of the International Office and inform Monica, with perfect truthfulness, that Ceren has made contact. By the time I pick up the phone to ring David I am positively euphoric, and when he doesn't answer I send him a cheery little text assuring him that all is well.

Sadly, this is as good as the day gets. By five past ten I've had a snappy conversation with David about Ceren and found a really horrible message on my classroom board – nasty both in its content and its linguistic incompetence – so I'm in a pretty evil mood by lunch time, when Andrew sweeps through the college gates in that ridiculous vehicle of his and takes me off for lunch.

We go to his *local*, a dark, malodorous little place of which real ale is the major feature. The food is traditional in a spotted-dick-and-custard kind of way and you'll not be surprised to hear that I am one of only two women spending their lunch hour here. Andrew orders veal and ham pie and a pint of something called Old Peculier (*sic*), while I go for potted shrimps and a glass of elderflower pressé. I've been having issues with Malcolm in my department about his being under the influence in the afternoons and I have to set a good example.

When we are settled with our drinks, I present Andrew with a brief resumé of last night's meeting.

'So that's that,' I say, 'and I haven't got long, so let's keep discussion to a minimum.'

'What did you say to Annie about the meeting?'

'Nothing.'

'What do you mean, nothing?'

'We didn't discuss it.'

'Why not?'

'She didn't ask. You know what she's like. There was no point in raising it if she didn't want to know. Anyway, I know what she'd have said.'

'Which is?'

'That she'll give up Art, which we all know she's not much good at; that she'll carry on with Economics and with History, though – or possibly because – Miss Porter would like to be rid of her; that she wants to drop Latin because it's mega-boring; and that if she's made to give up Drama she'll leave school.'

'That's just being histrionic. She doesn't mean it. I can soon talk some sense into her.'

'Of course. You can talk anybody into anything. That's what you're for, but in this case –'

At this point our food arrives and I eat a buttery shrimp or two before trying a more emollient approach.

'The thing is,' I say, 'for once I agree with Annie.'

'Because, as always, you want to disagree with me.'

'Oh, for God's sake! Can I point out that this is about Annie, not about us?'

'And can I point out that in your determination to thwart me you're ruining Annie's chances of getting a place at Oxford?'

'Andrew, she's not going to Oxford. Apart from anything else, she's not clever enough. Look at her GCSE grades.'

'They weren't that bad, and you remember Hugo Stott – read Law with me at Oriel? He's a Fellow now. Our paths cross from time to time. I'm sure I could have a word with him and –'

'ANDREW!' I shout, and heads turn in our direction. Throttling my exasperation, I hiss, 'It doesn't work like that any more – hasn't for years. She has to compete in the open market, with people who have twelve A*s at GCSE and predictions of four As at A level. Anyway, she doesn't want to go to Oxford.'

'Why not?'

'Probably because we were there. She wants to go to York.'

'Why York?'

'Because it's got a lake, probably. I don't know. Given her record so far, she'll be lucky to be offered a place. I'm pinning my hopes on Kirsten Donald, the Drama teacher. She's rather wonderful.'

Andrew puts his knife and fork down with a huff of irritation.

'Well,' I retort, reckless now about being too loud, 'she'll be a wonderful person to have on my side and I could certainly do with one of those because, frankly, bringing up Annie single-handed isn't getting any easier and although you've decided to take an interest this late in the day, I doubt it'll last. You're obviously at a bit of a loose end at the moment but it only needs another interesting case to come along and we shall disappear right off your mental map again.'

He pushes his plate away from him and gives me a long look.

'You know, Gina,' he says, 'you're the only person I know who always thinks the worst of me. I wonder why that is.'

I laugh.

'I can think of several reasons,' I say, 'all of them unkind. But I take it that's an oblique way of giving up the argument? I'll tell Annie Drama it is, shall I?'

'As long as it's clear that she's not doing Drama at university, It was bad enough when Ellie –'

'She won't do Drama. She wants to be rich and she wants to feel important. You can count on her becoming a lawyer.'

I gather up my bag and coat.

'Can you drop me at the Police Station?' I ask. 'I have to go and get my fingerprints taken.'

This is irresistible to the lawyer in Andrew, of course, and he wants to know all about it. He is suspicious about *for elimination purposes* and says I have to be sure that they destroy my prints once the case is over. I begin to worry that he's going to insist on coming in with me and kicking up a fuss, but he drops me and drives off. I don't tell him that Annie has to be fingerprinted too; that would certainly freak him out.

David is mildly apologetic about the fingerprinting business and, possibly as a peace offering, he gives me a titbit of information about the case. He has a little rant about his frustrations, which makes him seem young again and puts me in danger of feeling maternal, which isn't how I really feel about him at all. We do the fingerprinting and it is just like they do it on the telly: I have to press my fingers on an ink pad and then a policewoman presses my hand down and rolls it to and fro to get complete prints. It feels peculiarly unreal.

Then he walks me to a cab and this is where the trouble starts. As we're walking the mere hundred yards, David asks, oh so casually, about the nice ethnic thing he saw on my sofa yesterday evening. Now, when I'm rattled I resort to verbal aggression – mindless insults if necessary. Annie is just the same. When I took her to her first day at infant school (a trendy, uniform-free institution) two older boys, waiting to go into school, laughed at the clothes she was wearing. Without a blink, she clapped a hand over her nose and said, 'Cor, you stink!' and they melted away. So this is me: when David asks about the ethnic thing, I accuse him of being gay. *Accuse* is the operative word. I sound like the worst sort of homophobe, and I like gay men usually – probably more than I like straight ones. I think I deflected his suspicions but I am ashamed of the way I did it.

The Two-year Masters class is back up to eight students with the return of Atash and Farid, but they are looking pretty glum so I do a little performance about the fingerprinting, displaying my still-inky fingers to entertain them, and then I do something really irresponsible: I tell them what David has just told me – that they've found a knife in the library. I don't know what possesses me. David didn't actually tell me that it was confidential but I know that it was for my ears only. Really, I'm just showing off, and I'm ashamed all over again.

When I finish their class at four, I pack up and go home. I want to be there when Annie gets back from the Police Station; I feel a bit guilty about sending her on her own. As I come down the road towards the house, I see the MG standing outside and Annie talking to her father through the window.

'What's going on?' I ask as I approach.

'I rang Pa,' says Annie, 'when I got your text.'

'I can't imagine what you were thinking, Gina,' says Andrew, all self-importance, 'expecting her to go to the Police Station alone.'

'I'd have been fine, Pa,' Annie contradicts him, 'but I thought as I had a lawyer on hand -'

'You thought you'd like to be picked up from school and carried off in the fairy coach,' I cut in, with a wave at the MG. 'And I've no doubt Pa didn't mind having it admired by the girls either.'

'You're so cynical, Ma,' reproaches Annie. 'I'm sure you're a bad influence on me.

'As you are on me.'

'I was just asking Pa if he'd like to stay for supper.'

I look at Andrew and he at me. He declines.

'Thanks, but I've got a lot of work to get on with. One way and another, I've not managed to get much done today.'

He doesn't actually say that, between us, we've wasted his day, but I read the subtext.

As Annie and I walk up the garden path, I ask, 'Did Pa talk to you about A levels?'

'Yes. He said it's all right about Drama.'

'Your Ms Donald was pretty persuasive.'

'She's ace,' she says, glowing with a rare pleasure. 'But Pa said it was you who really persuaded him.'

Then, as I'm fumbling for my door key, she adds, 'So I have to say on this occasion you've been pretty ace too.'

I am so astonished at this unlooked-for accolade that I drop my key. Annie says, 'Oh for God's sake', picks it up, opens the door and bundles me inside.

24

WEDNESDAY: Investigation Day Fourteen

'There's a Miss Iwaki to see you, sir,' the desk sergeant told him when he got into work at eight-thirty.

He found her sitting in Reception, formally dressed in a pinstriped grey suit and white shirt. As he ushered her up to his office he remembered her explaining the need to change before going to dance at the SU: *Those were library clothes. They weren't dancing clothes, you see.* Presumably today's outfit was *visiting the Police Station clothes*.

He showed her to a chair, offered coffee, which she declined, and asked how he could help. He had absolutely no idea what might have brought her here. Gina had joked about her fancying him; he hoped this wasn't some flirtatious little game. He wasn't in the mood. He regarded her neutrally – not aggressively, he hoped, but without any effort to be friendly or reassuring. She tucked her hair behind her ears in a little nervous gesture and then said,

'I am sorry for disturbing you, but I heard you found a knife in the library?'

'Who told you that?'

He heard the rough edge of surprise and anger in his voice and saw her flinch slightly.

'Mrs Gray told us, yesterday. I'm sorry if –'

'Told who exactly?'

'Told our class.'

'I see.'

Damn the woman for blabbing, and damn his own stupidity in blabbing to her. With an effort at sounding calm and reasonable, he asked, 'And why did you want to see me?'

She dropped her head for a moment but then raised it and looked him straight in the eye.

'I think the knife is mine, maybe.'

'Yours?'

It was impossible to hide his astonishment.

'What on earth do you mean?'

She answered calmly. She had prepared this little speech, he thought.

'As you know, I was on duty in the library the evening Ekrem passed away. I was there from five-thirty so I had no time for dinner. I took some food with me – some salad and an apple. I took a knife from my flat to cut up the apple. I don't like to bite it like English people.'

'So what happened?'

'I'm not quite sure. I ate my food and put the salad container in my bag. I meant to wash my knife before I put it away, but I don't remember if I did – I got busy then, issuing books. The next day when I unpacked my bag I found no knife. I realised I left it in the library, but of course it was impossible to go back now. Then I bought a new knife and I forgot about it.'

'So where did you leave it?'

'I don't remember. I ate in the Library office, so maybe on the table there.'

'What was the knife like?'

'Just small. Like cutting vegetables knife. Maybe this long.'

With her fingers she indicated a length of about twelve centimetres.

'What was the handle like?'

'Black. Just plastic – not wood.'

He sat looking at her for a moment and then got up and

walked across to the window to think. Could this be true? Could the murder of Yilmaz have been so spontaneous, such a piece of improvisation that the killers came unarmed and just happened on a fruit knife left behind by a ditzy young woman preoccupied with getting off to meet her friends for a girls' night out? He had thought it an odd weapon, that little knife. Hardly the weapon of a professional killer. But if her story was true, the finding of the knife really got them no closer to the killers all. He turned back to her.

'I'll need to get you to look at the knife when the forensic experts have finished with it. And we'll need to take your fingerprints, for comparison with those on the knife.'

'Actually,' she said, 'you took my fingerprints already. Because I was in Ceren's room.'

He was thinking about her story. It was plausible enough and why would she tell him the knife was hers if it wasn't? Still, he didn't have to take it at face value. There were a couple of things he could check. He phoned for a WPC to come and sit with her for a short while, then he went down to the Incident Room and called for the forensic report on the contents of the library waste paper bin on the morning of February 28th. He also rang and harassed Forensics for details of what, beside blood, had been found on the knife. He was snappy with everyone, he knew, impatient and curt. He saw glances exchanged among the team, silent comments on his black mood.

The report on the contents of the bin was lengthy and complex, largely because they had included, among other things, the Deputy Librarian's breakfast. There was no mention, though, of what Scott was looking for - an apple core. When Forensics called him back, however, he was informed of minute particles of vegetable matter round the base of the knife handle, including a trace of malic acid - apple.

Returning to his office and dismissing the WPC, he said to Yukiko,

'When you'd eaten your apple, you threw the core in the bin, presumably?'

She laughed.

'I wonder why you interest in my apple core! Is this a weapon too?'

Getting no answering smile from him, however, she continued,

'No, actually. It would smell bad in the morning. I put it in my salad box to take home.'

So that was it. He had no doubt that she would identify the knife as hers or that one of the sets of prints on the handle would be hers. There was just a chance that the other prints would lead them to a killer but he couldn't see how. The randomness of the killers picking up a knife left lying about confused his picture of the crime. Everything else had been so professional, he felt: the unseen entry and exit of the library, the absence of forensic clues, the ferocious efficiency of the killing itself. It was true it didn't smack of a Mafia-style punishment killing – no bullet between the eyes - but the KGB had used some imaginative elimination methods in the past – a poisoned umbrella tip and a radioactive supper among them – so he supposed the Russian connection was still top of his list of possibilities.

'Well, thank you for coming in,' he said to Yukiko. 'That's certainly helpful. I'll see you down to Reception.'

As they took the lift down, he said, 'I suppose Mrs Gray told you she'd had a letter from Ceren?'

'No.'

She was genuinely startled, he could see.

'I thought she would have told you,' he said. 'She seems so keen to share information with you all. Ceren's letter said that she was staying with friends. But you haven't seen her?'

'No, I'm afraid not.'

There was a pause and she seemed to feel that something more should be said.

'But it is good news Mrs Gray has a letter,' she said. 'This makes us very happy. And makes her parents happy, I think.'

As he walked back up to his office (part of a newly-conceived plan for keeping fit) he thought about this conversation. Why had Gina not told the class that she'd heard from Ceren? She knew how anxious Yukiko and Christiane were about her. There was no doubt that Yukiko really had been surprised to hear it. And there was something else. Yukiko had said it would make Ceren's parents happy. When Gina had spoken to him on the phone yesterday, he'd asked her if she'd shown the letter to anyone. *No*, she'd said, and he was almost sure that she'd said, *I told the International Office and the English staff and then I rang you*. What about Ceren's parents? Weren't they a priority? Well, maybe the International Office called them. Still, it was odd.

25

THURSDAY: *Imperfect Tense*

I know as soon as I walk into the Department building that something disastrous has happened; the air vibrates with drama. From the bottom of the stairs I can hear my office phone ringing insistently and Gillian runs out of the Department office, pink with agitation.

'Gina, something terrible. There's been – there's been *another death.*'

The last two words are delivered in an urgent whisper. Then she drags me into the office to give me the details. When I stagger, reeling, into my office, my phone is still ringing. It is Monica from the International Office confirming what I've just been told: Valery is dead. I can hardly believe it even as I write the words. He is simply dead, shot in his room in the early hours of this morning.

I am reaching for my phone to call David when it leaps into life in my hand. When I pick up the receiver, the Principal's voice explodes in my ear.

'Oh, so you're in at last are you?' he spits. 'Well, perhaps you can tell me what the hell's going on over there in your department.'

I open my mouth automatically to answer but find I have nothing to say. I sit mute and helpless as he rages on.

'Not so ready with your clever answers now, are you? Two students missing and two murdered in the space of two weeks.

A bit remiss in the pastoral care area, wouldn't you say? Or is it your admissions policy needs looking at? Do you do any checks on the backgrounds of these people you're bringing over here? Well it wasn't the Turks this time, was it? It looks like their government did right to get them safely home. Who knows what might –'

Unable to bear the sound of his voice any longer, I lay the receiver down on the table and walk over to the window. I'm not sure how long I stand there but when I pick the phone up again it is dead. Then something shocking happens: I start to cry. I am not a woman who cries; I never have been. My mother loathed what she called *dripping*. I don't remember her crying even when my father died. I did. I was thirteen. It may be the last time in my life that I cried properly. Now, I almost don't recognise what is happening to me: I feel the rising convulsions in my chest and wonder if I'm about to vomit. Then the sobs come, great, blubbering, undignified, snotty sobs, and at the same time my head is full of violent rage. This is better; this is familiar; this I can deal with. I rampage around the room, swearing, sobbing, hiccupping, kicking the furniture, hurling things about.

I don't think it lasts long. I stop; I take a few deep breaths; from my desk drawer I get out the box of Kleenex kept for weeping students; I blow my nose. Then I pick stuff up off the floor (I never throw books in my rages, incidentally; the taboo on messing with books must be deeply embedded in my psyche). After that, I get a new ring-binder folder out of a cupboard and write a label for it: PRINCIPAL HARRASSMENT. Then I sit at my computer and I type out, as far as I can recollect it, what the Principal said to me on the phone. I date and time it and I supply brief context – *The murder of a student, Valery Tarasov, had just been reported.* I print it out, punch holes in it and insert it into my new folder. I make a cup of strong coffee.

As I'm drinking my coffee, I try to work out what triggered

the snotty blubbering. Not grief for Valery: I never made any connection with him, really. I tried to establish a rapport at the start of the year with my usual repertoire of little jokes and comments but he blanked me out, as he did everyone, it seemed to me, except Irina. So, if not Valery then was it the unexpected diatribe from our revered Principal so early in the morning? Surely not. I have never in my life let a bully reduce me to tears, let alone a man I despise as much as I do Norman Street. Shock? Well, I've had shocks before without going drippy.

I conclude in the end that I wept in pure frustration, that though I bitterly resent the Principal's making me responsible for what is happening to my students, I do actually feel responsible myself. I feel I should be able to protect them, I feel I should be able to sort this out, and I can't. How often I've said, hyperbolically, that something was *a complete nightmare* when it actually wasn't at all; the situation didn't resemble a nightmare in any way. This really is like a nightmare, though, where the everyday becomes sinister and familiar faces turn monstrous and threatening. In the past two weeks, I have seriously considered the possibility that almost any one of my nice, polite, friendly, civilised students could be a vicious murderer. And I shouldn't have to be doing this; that's what is sending me into a rage. It's the job of the police. It's David Scott's job, and he sat here in this very office two days ago, wailing about the fact that he was getting nowhere and expecting sympathy from me. No wonder I'm in a rage.

I am due to teach in ten minutes, so I go to the loo and with the help of a lot of cold water and a bit of makeup I manage to get my face looking normal enough not to scare my class of Business Studies students. I pick up my books and go downstairs to spend an hour practising the vocabulary of business negotiation.

Back in my office, I ring David for an update on Valery's murder, but he is brusque and uncommunicative.

'I'd rather not discuss it,' he says. 'We can't afford any more leaks.'

'Have there been leaks?' I ask, but I know what he means: the knife.

'What did you think you were doing telling the students that we'd found the knife? You must have known it was confidential.'

I should apologise, I know, but I'm angry with him so instead I shout.

'How was I to know it was confidential?' I demand. 'You didn't say. Anyway, I did you a favour, didn't I? I flushed Yukiko out. How long would it have taken you to work out by yourselves that it was Yukiko's supper knife? Forever, if the general rate of progress of your investigation's anything to go by.'

'How did you know it was Yukiko's knife?'

'She told me. Yesterday. After class. Was she not supposed to? Was that confidential too? I do think you should make it clear when things are supposed to be confidential. We're all a bit confused.'

'Well, what confuses me,' he says, and I can tell he's working hard at keeping his temper, 'is that you're so free with some information but you didn't tell the other students about your letter from Ceren. Why was that?'

Now the answer to this is that when Ceren said in her letter that she was staying with friends, I assumed she meant Christiane and Yukiko and I didn't want to raise the subject because they might have revealed where she was and I'd have been in the position of withholding information from the police all over again. If nobody actually tells me where she is, then I don't know. Since this answer isn't an option, I go for shouting again.

'Because you made me feel bad about that letter,' I snap. 'I was so relieved to get it and thought the panic was over and then you came up with all that stuff about it being written under duress and delivered by her kidnappers and me being in danger and God knows what else. I didn't want to get their hopes up if she wasn't actually safe.'

'OK,' he says, and cuts me off.

When I go in to teach the Two-Year Masters' class at twelve, it is clear that there won't be any teaching going on today. In place of the eerie normality that followed Ekrem's death, there is disarray. The women are huddled at one end of the table, heads together, round a weeping Irina. At the other end of the table, Farid and Atash are looking awkward and discomfited; Denis is pacing the corridor outside. It is astonishing to see Irina weep – as astonishing as my own tears earlier this morning. She is no more practised at it than I am, snuffling noisily and wiping her face clumsily with the flat of her hand. Yukiko is offering a handkerchief and Desirée tissues, but they are waved away in the vigour of her grief.

I talk to Farid and Atash, give them the comprehension exercise I've prepared for this session and suggest that they find an empty seminar room and work on it there, taking Denis with them if he wants to go. Then I sit down to talk with the women.

Gradually they give me the details David denied me. Valery, I'm told, lived in the same hall as Ceren, though on the men's corridor one floor down. At about three thirty that morning, students in the neighbouring rooms had been woken by the sounds of gunshots and running feet. By the time they had roused themselves and got out into the corridor, they caught sight only of a man disappearing down the stairs at the far end. Seeing Valery's door open and the light on, they went in and saw him lying bleeding on the floor. One of them called security and another called an ambulance. The night porter arrived and phoned the police. When the ambulance came, Valery was declared dead. All the students in Hawthorn Hall had been made to stay in their rooms until they had been searched. Another Russian student had called Irina with the news.

The tale is told piecemeal, each of them contributing their

bit. Irina quietens as the story unfolds and, as it finishes, she turns to me.

'Police ask me to identify Valery,' she says, as if in explanation for her tears. 'He was not boyfriend, but he was friend. He was good for me. I don't understand this. I never thought this would happen. He always said he was safe here. *I am safe,* he said. *This is UK isn't it?'*

It has been a very long morning and I would love a drink, but no alcohol is served in the SCR (though, ironically, it is served freely in the Student Union). I content myself with more coffee and my usual cheese and coleslaw sandwich. The rest of the English Language staff gather in my corner and I tell them what I have learnt. We are subdued, apprehensive and weary. We just want this to stop.

I return to my office, log on to my e-mails and find a message from the Principal's secretary.

Please complete the attached forms asap and return to me, it instructs me curtly, but when I open the attachments I can see that they're not going to get completed in a hurry. First I am asked to estimate student numbers for the next academic year. Since it is only March and overseas student applications generally come in much later than those coming through UCAS, this is impossible and Norman Street knows it.

Second, is a form requesting me to define my department's admissions policy. I am required to give *clear criteria, both academic and other* for the acceptance or rejection of applicants. Has Janet been made to knock up this form this morning specially for me? Have all directors of studies been sent one? I think not. Street knows the answer to this one too: we accept anyone who's got enough money to pay the exorbitant overseas students fees and enough English and academic competence to get through the course. And he wouldn't want it any other way. I can imagine his reaction if we started turning away students with the money in their hot little hands because we didn't think they were very nice.

Finally, and most threateningly, comes a clutch of forms for me to complete, showing 1) exactly how many hours each of my staff spent a) in teaching, b) on admin over the past two terms, and 2) how those hours might be reduced to save time and money in the event of student numbers being lower than expected next year. *Please bear in mind,* it adds in bold, *that the Director of Studies may be required to teach a full teaching schedule in addition to administrative duties.*

I phone Judith Roth, the UCU rep.

'I've begun keeping a record,' I say. 'I think it's started.'

'Well, if you will go shooting your students,' she says, 'what can you expect?'

26

THURSDAY: Investigation Day Fifteen

When the phone rang, he incorporated it into his troubled dream. He was in a library, which was on fire. He knew it was his job to clear people out, but no-one was paying any attention and he couldn't make himself heard however loudly he shouted. They milled about, laughing and chatting, among the constantly moving stacks, ignoring the strident alarm which rang and rang and rang.

When he surfaced and grabbed the receiver, he heard Mark Tyler's voice.

'I'm at the College, sir,' he said. 'There's been another death.'

He arrived at Hawthorn Hall at the same time as Lynne McAndrew and they surveyed the body together. Valery Tarasov lay on the floor near the bed, dressed in pyjamas, with one bullet wound in his head and another in his chest. As Scott straightened up from leaning over the body, he saw two holes in the wall beyond, where bullets had missed their target. Not a really professional job, then, he thought: not a crack shot and possibly wasn't wearing gloves.

'Any idea about the gun?' he asked Lynne McAndrew.

'At first glance, I'd say a 9mm semi-automatic, but I'll need to do the autopsy to be sure.'

'Can you make that a priority, Lynne? Time's going to be crucial with this. We're probably already too late with the road blocks. This guy will do a runner. '

Leaving her to get into her scrubs, he went back into the corridor. Tarasov's room was at the end of the corridor farthest from the stairs. It was a long way to run after firing a gun; no wonder the guy had done it when even night owl students were likely to be sound asleep. A couple of students were hovering in the doors of their rooms, their pale faces betraying both shock and excitement. Scott spoke to them.

'Have you given your names to DS Tyler? Good. Then I'd like you to wait in your rooms, please. Someone will be along to interview you shortly. And I'm afraid you won't be able to leave the building until we've searched your rooms.'

They would learn, he thought, that violent death was not that exciting for those caught up in it; it was mainly inconvenient. He went downstairs to where Tyler was talking to the SOCOs.

'... and for God's sake don't fuck it up,' Scott heard him say before he turned at the sound of his approach.

'Thank you, DS Tyler,' he said. 'You took the words right out of my mouth.'

Then, as always, it was a waiting game. Statements were taken from Tarasov's neighbours, who had raised the alarm but they had seen nothing but the back of a running man wearing a black padded anorak; fingerprints were taken from them and from the ambulance personnel who had answered the 999 call; Lynne McAndrew confirmed that the weapon was a Smith and Wesson 9mm semi-automatic, so common it didn't suggest any particular type of killer. It was someone in the criminal world, though – someone who knew where to buy a gun. Road blocks netted no-one but a couple of drivers over the limit, who had thought they were safe at that hour of the morning.

At eleven o'clock Scott's phone rang and he answered it eagerly, hoping for news, but it was Gina, on the scavenge for information, and he was in no mood to give it to her. She was at her most unreasonable too, and for once he felt he couldn't be bothered with her.

In the late morning, Tyler called him with news about fingerprints and he went down to the Incident Room.

'The SOCOs got clear thumbprints,' Tyler told him, 'and partial index and middle finger prints on the inside and outside handles of the door to Tarasov's room. We've ruled out his neighbours and the paramedics, so it looks like these might belong to our man. We're checking the database now.'

'And I'll bet you good money you won't find a match,' said Scott gloomily. 'If he's a Turk or a Russian, the chances are he's got no record here. He'll be out of the country in twenty-four hours and without a name or a description there's nothing we can do to stop him.'

'They've checked the prints against the knife handle, by the way. No match, I'm afraid.'

'That'd be too neat, wouldn't it?' Scott said sourly.

'Isn't it worth alerting ports and airports, though? If we're sure about the Turkish/Russian connection, we could put an alert out for Turkish and Russian men travelling alone – and we've at least got the black anorak for description. They can take them out and rattle them a bit - take their bags apart.'

'And we can risk being accused of harassment or racism. I'm tempted though.'

Boxer, who had been locked in communion with his computer screen and hardly seemed to be aware of these new developments, suddenly swung his chair round with a triumphant cry of 'Yesss!'

'I've got it,' he shouted 'I've finally got it. Yilmaz's police record in Turkey. And it makes some reading. Come and look.'

As Tyler and Scott came over to join him, he said,

'It's been like pulling teeth getting it. He's obviously got protection from the Turkish Secret Service and their police didn't want to play ball with us. But I finally got hold of the guy who was prosecuting officer in the 2003 case, when Yilmaz and Belenki got off on drugs charges. He's obviously pretty pissed off that they got protected by people higher up the food chain and the judge ordered some of the evidence inadmissible when, according to him, it was sound as a bell. It's taken a while because he doesn't speak English and I had to use an interpreter. Then, when he sent the stuff, I had to get it translated. Anyway, here it is, and worth waiting for.'

Scott and Tyler stood either side of him, watching the screen, as he scrolled up to the start.

'It starts in 1994,' Boxer narrated. 'He's twenty-one and he's picked up for pimping and supplying drugs. When you get into the detail, you find he was actually trafficking women from Eastern Europe: promising them jobs, getting them hooked on heroin, putting them to work in brothels in Ankara.'

'Was he convicted?' Scott asked.

'That time, yes. Sentenced to six years but mysteriously released after two. Compassionate grounds.'

'Any detail on that?'

'Not really. A very vague medical report which says *his health is not strong enough to withstand a prison regime.*'

'Lynne McAndrew found no signs of previous ill-health,' Scott commented.

'I don't suppose she did,' Boxer said. 'Look where we find him next. 1998, he's a student at the University of Ankara and giving evidence against some fellow students involved in Kurdish separatist activities. They were each sentenced to nine years in jail.'

'So we think he was released from jail early and sent to university on condition he worked undercover for the Secret Service? I wonder why they picked him from all the other traffickers and dealers they have in their jails.'

'I can tell you that,' Boxer said. 'He graduated from high school.'

'And you don't find many Turkish high school graduates who choose organised crime as their preferred career?'

'Exactly. He can pass as a student, and it becomes his speciality. After Ankara, he moves to Istanbul, where he crops up as a trial witness a couple more times – in 2000 and 2001. Both times his occupation is *student*. But he's getting on a bit now. He's thirty. He can't pass as a student much longer, so they make him a lecturer. I don't know if he ever got a degree, but now he's a lecturer – in Turkish History. He's sent to Samsun, on the Black Sea coast and that's where he is in 2003, when he's prosecuted for drug-dealing, along with Mikhail Belenki. Belenki was bringing the Afghan opium in and Yilmaz was passing it on to labs in Turkey to be turned into heroin, ready for the European market. The police got a tip-off and rounded up the whole ring. My contact said it was the best bust of his career. No wonder he was pissed off when Belenki and Yilmaz walked.'

'And we can assume plenty of others were pissed off too, though they're all sweating it out in jail,' Scott said.

'They'll have friends on the outside ready to take their revenge for them,' cut in Tyler. 'And they're ready to take out Tarasov too, for what his father's done.'

'What happens to Yilmaz after the trial, Steve?' Scott asked. 'Anything to suggest a connection with Anton Tarasov?'

'Nothing. He seems to have gone to ground. No prosecutions, no witness statements. I can try and find out where he went, though. I'll bet Anton Tarasov was in with Belenki at his end of the drug route. There was a falling out and Tarasov informed on Belenki. Our friend Yilmaz will be in there somewhere.'

'You know what, sir,' Tyler said. 'I wonder what we're doing here. Yilmaz was a piece of shit and no-one's sorry he's dead. Yet we're pouring resources into finding his killers when we could be out looking for our own villains. Don't you ever wonder what's the point?'

27

FRIDAY: *Present Progressive*

Term has ended. With everything else that has been going on,
this has somehow sneaked up on me. Officially it doesn't end
till today, but we've accepted that no-one turns up to classes
on the last Friday, so there is no teaching today. Annie's term
finished yesterday too, and she is off to York today for an
Open Weekend for prospective students. At the end of it, she's
to meet Andrew at Leeds-Bradford airport and fly with him to
The Hague, where he has work to do. This attempt at father-
daughter bonding so late in the day is a bit of a puzzle, but I
assume he wants to impress Annie with the exciting life of the
legal eagle just in case she's tempted to backslide. Ellie has
offered to drive her to York (which terrifies me), giving herself
an excuse for going over to Manchester for the weekend. I
hardly need to tell you who will be holding the baby.

Although term has ended, it not actually very convenient
to be in charge of Freda today as I'm taking the train out to the
seaside – to Dungate where, bizarrely, there is a Greek
Orthodox church. One of my students is having her son
baptized there and has invited me to attend. Out of politeness,
affection and curiosity, I have accepted. Afrodite, my student,
is a captain in the Greek army; the army is paying for her to
take a Master's degree in Business Administration and she is
here with a toddler, a baby and a husband, who is also taking
an MBA. She is intelligent, humorous and determined, a

thoroughly modern young woman, but she wants her baby baptized before she flies home with him for the vacation because she fears that if the plane crashed and he died, his unbaptized soul wouldn't get to heaven.

Afrodite has assured me that it will be fine for Freda to come to the baptism, so I set out for the station with the buggy and a bag of nappies, wipes, bottles, rusks, assorted toys and a change of clothes (for Freda, that is, though it's possible that I shall need a change myself before the end of the day). Freda is wearing the outfit she wore to the wedding but she is also enclosed in a fleece-lined bag as it is bitterly cold. I am not wearing my silk suit but a sensible full-length coat and knee-length boots. I also have a scarf which I can drape over my head if need be. I meant to research the protocol for a Greek Orthodox church but there hasn't been the time.

As I stand on the platform waiting for the once-an-hour train, I watch passengers getting off a delayed train from London. Journalists, many of them, I'll be bound. The media scrum started yesterday, as soon as the news of a second murder was out. Interest in Ekrem's death has been muted – partly, I think, because of the way the news leaked out: an unexplained death, first of all, possibly accidental, and then later the murder inquiry. Perhaps his age makes him less interesting too: he doesn't fit the conventional student stereotype – doesn't press the right buttons. Valery's death is a different matter: a young man, a Russian, shot in his bed in a college hall of residence, has all the makings of tabloid drama. Most of the papers have already got hold of the story of Anton Tarasov's murder, I see from a scan of the front pages at the station news stall, and the Daily Mail's headline speaks for all: RUSSIAN MAFIA MENACE HITS UK. A good day to be off campus, I would say.

I spot Yukiko coming down the platform, evidently bent on the same errand as me, as she carries an immaculate parcel – a present for baby Serafin, I guess. (My own gift, an awkwardly-wrapped teddy bear, is lying, hopelessly squashed I fear, among the nappies). I wave.

'Going to a baptism?' I call as she approaches. 'How do you know Afrodite?'

'We both go to Italian class,' she says. 'Wednesday lunch time.'

'Italian class!'

I'm amazed. On top of an MBA and two tiny children, Afrodite goes to Italian classes?

'Why does she think Italian will be useful?' I ask.

'Not useful.' She smiles reproachfully. 'She thinks it's nice language. So do I. Excuse me, I must just -'

She gets her phone out of her bag and texts a message with that lightning thumb action I so much admire.

On the train, we chat amiably and avoid, without difficulty, the subject of murder. We start with babies. I look at Yukiko's parcel, with its neatly printed gift tag, and she tells me it's a book of Japanese folk-tales written in English. She asks me what Freda's baptism was like and I make a bit of a production out of describing the Naming Ceremony Ellie concocted in our back garden, involving home-made poems read by Freda's secular godparents, followed by cake, ice-cream and beer. I also describe Ellie's christening in Marlbury Abbey, though I don't tell Yukiko how forcefully I was press-ganged into it by Andrew and his parents, nor how bitterly I resented it. Neither do I tell her that by the time Annie came along, Andrew seemed to have lost interest in the idea and how, perversely, I resented that too, on Annie's behalf.

We move on from this to the eclecticism of Japanese religious practice: Shinto shrines for loving Nature, churches for weddings and Buddhism for funerals are the preferred options. Yukiko says it wasn't till she came to the UK that she realised how odd this pick-and–mix attitude seemed to people who are stuck with the religion they were born into or pick one and stick with it.

This is an endlessly stopping train and we never get up much speed, but eventually we step out into the blustery chill of an eastern sea coast and emerge from the little station to look for the Church of St Photino. Afrodite has drawn me a little sketch of its position and it appears to be right on the sea wall, so we set our faces towards the sea in the teeth of the gale. The force of the wind sets Freda howling and I lean over the buggy to make comic faces at her, which has little effect but amuses Yukiko anyway.

Down on the front, we struggle along the sea wall until we see the church. It is actually the end of a little terrace of cottages and was obviously just a cottage itself until it had a sort of Greek pediment and a couple of pillars bolted onto the front of it to give it a more ecclesiastical appearance. It reminds me of an extraordinary little chapel constructed by Italian prisoners on Orkney during the war. In essence, it's just a Nissen hut, but it has had a cement façade put on the front so that it looks just like a tiny Italian church, and inside every inch of wall and ceiling has been painted with frescos and patterns. It takes your breath away. We don't know if the Church of St Photino will take our breaths away, however, as the door is firmly locked.

We are early and the Greeks will be late. We pace up and down and then, to keep Freda from wailing, we take it in turns to run up and down with the buggy, crying *wheee* with exaggerated enthusiasm. I am hugely relieved to see, eventually, a tall, black-clad figure striding along the wall towards us: the priest. He is, rather puzzlingly, carrying a broom and I wonder if this features in the ceremony – driving out the Devil, perhaps?

We stand back while he unlocks the door and the function of the broom becomes clear: he starts to sweep out the dead leaves that have made their way under the door and accumulated in the lobby. It's obvious that the little church doesn't get much use. We hear the Greeks approaching before we see them, like a particularly vigorous flock of gathering birds, and after a hubbub of geetings and embracings we all go inside. I am prepared for dank chill, but it 's quite warm. The practical priest has seen to this too.

We sit at the back, which is Yukiko's inclination and suits me as I can make a quick dive outside if Freda becomes vocal. From where we sit we can see what's going on in the little lobby, and I'm appalled: they are removing all the baby's clothes. Surely this isn't going to be total immersion? That sort of thing is all very well under a Mediterranean sun, but could easily kill a baby off in Dungate.

'Did you know it was total immersion?' I whisper to Yukiko.

She nods.

'I googled,' she explains.

The baby is now being brought in, wrapped in a large white sheet. His mother and several other women unwrap him and start to rub oil all over him – a precaution against the cold I'm glad to see.

'It's extra-virgin olive oil,' Yukiko whispers.

I think she's making a joke, so I grin, but she whispers, 'No, really.'

This makes me quite uncomfortable. It's all right for Greeks, who no doubt use olive oil for everything, but I can't get out of my head the image of a fat little baby rubbed all over with olive oil, sprinkled with salt and pepper and a bit of oregano, and popped in the oven. I close my eyes and snuggle Freda a bit to clear the picture away, and when I open them again, the baby is going into the font and the priest is speaking.

I don't understand a word, of course, and I decide that this is good for me. Hooked on language as I am, so pathologically alert to small nuances of feeling and tiny distinctions of meaning, it is therapeutic for me to sit without comprehension, simply taking in the pictures. So I see the baby taken out of the font, swaddled in a white towel that has been warming on a radiator and carried over to a side table, where he is dressed from head to toe in new white garments, each carefully extricated from tissue paper wrappings. Things are said - blessings and pledges, no doubt – but I really enjoy watching this tender little robing ceremony. Then it's all over and we're outside and the kissing and weeping, embracing and laughing are redoubled.

As we stand around, waiting to move on to the home of a friend of Afrodite's, who lives in the town and is hosting the party, I stand on the sea wall and look down onto the beach. A little way along, a group of four lads in hooded anoraks are crouched on the pebbles, smoking. As Freda shouts a greeting at some seagulls, one of the lads looks up towards us and I see his face. It is Laurent.

'Laurent!' I shout, waving furiously.

He makes no acknowledgement, but I see him turn back, say something to his companions and pull his hood further over his face.

I shout again but get no response, so I shove the handles of Freda's buggy at Yukiko and run along the wall to a place where there are steps down to the beach. Awkwardly, in my long coat and high-heeled boots, I clamber down the steps and stagger across the pebbles. I have no breath for shouting again, but they must hear me coming and I'm afraid they'll get up and run away. I certainly won't be able to catch them if they do, but I see, as I get closer, that they have a sort of camp here: sleeping bags, blankets, rucksacks, even what looks like a primitive barbecue with a pile of driftwood beside it. They won't want to risk leaving all that behind.

Laurent's friends have edged away from him slightly by the time I get to him, but they look at me belligerently enough. I haven't thought what I'm going to say to him and I'm pretty out of breath, so I just stand in front of him and say, 'Well?'

'Well?' he echoes back, with a shrug.

'I suppose you realise the police are looking for you?' I demand.

'Pouff.'

He makes this little sound of dismissal, then looks round at his companions, who grin back. He is the naughty boy in class, egged on by his mates.

'You might at least have let your mother know that you were all right,' I say. 'Did you know she's over here looking for you?'

'Ah, my mother!'

The way he says *mozz-air* burnishes the contempt that is inserted into the word, but I am not to be deflected.

'Yes,' I say, 'and your sister. They're really worried about you.'

'My sister!' he says to the others. 'You'd like my sister!' and they snigger on cue.

'I'll let them know you're all right then, shall I?' I say.

When he says nothing, I turn away. This is fruitless and I need to retreat with some dignity. I want to take a photo of him to show to his mother and to David, but I need to take him by surprise. Walking away slowly, with my back to the group, I get my phone out and switch it to camera, then turn and call,

'Oh, Laurent, by the way –'and as he turns to look at me I snap him.

There is an angry roar and a couple of his mates jump up. I see I've been foolhardy: they can so easily take the phone off me and may injure me in the process. I realise, though, as I turn to hurry away from them, that some of the baptism party have come down onto the beach to see what's going on, several large Greek men among them. The lads spit a bit of abuse at me and sit down. I rejoin the party.

'A runaway student,' I explain. 'It's amazing what some students will do to get out of English classes.' And we depart for *mezethes* and *baklava*.

It is mid-afternoon by the time Yukiko, Freda and I board the train back to Marlbury. The rolling stock used on this line is competing for a medal in the oldest-still-in-use category: the heating isn't working on our train and we can hardly see out of the windows for the encrusted grime. Freda is exhausted by all the socialising and falls asleep on my lap. In spite of my coat and boots, I'm cold and I'm glad of the extra warmth of her little body in its fleecy bag. I look at Yukiko, sitting opposite me, and think she must be freezing in her smart little coat.

We are both glad of a break from talking, I think, and Yukiko has the Japanese gift for being comfortable with silence, so we each sit with our own thoughts. I peer out of the filthy window at the flat fields and allow my mind to empty. Lulled by Freda's steady breathing and the clattering rhythm of the train, I fall into a half-dozing state myself. Images flash onto the screen of my consciousness, seen once but not examined, now retrieved from the recycle bin of my memory. The gift tag on Yukiko's present, Yukiko's new coat, Yukiko's knife; Christiane playing her viola; those conditional sentences on the day of Ekrem's death and Ceren's empty chair; Ceren's tears the next day, which had so puzzled David Scott. *The day before*, I tell myself. Why had nobody thought to ask what had happened *the day before*?

It is an epiphany of sorts and I'm afraid I may have spoken the words out loud. I look across at Yukiko, who senses me looking and turns away from the window to meet my gaze.

'You look frozen,' I say. 'What's happened to that nice tweed coat you were wearing all winter?'

My voice sounds all wrong – husky and tense – and my attempted casualness pathetically fake. She looks back at me, unblinking.

'I wore it all winter,' she says calmly. 'It's boring, isn't it?'

'I hope you gave it to a charity shop. Someone would be glad of it, I'm sure.'

Stop it, Gina. Leave it. You're not fooling anyone.

Yukiko just smiles and turns back to the window, as do I, but I am seething with an excitement that threatens to bubble up in me like a geyser. I know how it was done and I know why it was done. I do my best to keep my face blank, but the next time I look at Yukiko she is regarding me with an expression I can't read and don't like. I've never gone along with the cliché about *inscrutable orientals.* Young Japanese women, at any rate, seem to me to be highly expressive, moving along on ripples of amusement, embarrassment, horror or delight, but I can't read Yukiko now, perhaps because she is trying to read me. She is watching me fixedly and though she looks away when I catch her eye, I feel her gaze come back to me.

I meanwhile am thinking furiously. If I'm right – and I'm sure I am – about Ekrem's death, a look at the library rota will confirm it. I have to get into the library office, just for a moment, but the whole library is still locked up. I concoct in my mind a story for the porter on duty in the Social Sciences building: a book, crucial to one of my courses and ordered by me for the library, received by the library before the murder and now lying, waiting for me, in the office. It is, I will tell him, vital for me to have it over the vacation to plan a course for next term. Just five minutes in the office, I will plead, and I shall be able to find it.

You may be asking yourselves why I don't ring David. He is, after all, in charge of the murder inquiry and he wouldn't have to fabricate stories about essential books; he could just walk in and demand the library rota, no questions asked. So why am I planning to bumble around in this amateurish way when the cream of the county's CID is available? The thing is, I love a puzzle; I like solving things; I like being clever. So, I want to solve this mystery, and I think I may have done – at least part of it – and I want to know if I'm right, but if I am right, I'm not going to like the answer and I'm not going to know what to do with it. If I get David involved, then he'll have no choice about what to do. He's operational man and he'll follow standard procedure. Me, I'm just an amateur and I have choices. I can do what I like, though I have the feeling I'm not going to like anything about this scenario very much.

When we arrive in Marlbury it is beginning to get dark and Yukiko says she will take a cab to the college. I tell her I have something to pick up from my office and we share the cab. On the campus, the driver drops Yukiko at Beechwood and Freda and me on the main campus. As I push the buggy towards the glass front of the Social Sciences foyer, however, I can see that I may be thwarted. There is a reception going on. The foyer, with its atrium-like design, is a favourite venue for drinks before public lectures, pre-conference receptions, small celebrations and leaving parties.

On a mission now, I am undaunted. I plunge in with my buggy, windswept and slightly crazy, and manoeuvre through the genteel champagne drinkers, running over a few feet, spraying apologies hither and yon, to get to the porter's desk. Only there's no-one there. The booth is dark and closed. It is after five o'clock and term has finished. He has gone off for a break and won't return until this shindig has finished. With a furtive glance around, I try the door to the library office; it is locked, of course. If I were on my own, I would hang around until the porter returned, but I am encumbered with a weary and grizzling Freda. There's nothing for it but to swallow my fizzing impatience and come back tomorrow. I push Freda home through the unfriendly gloom.

28

SATURDAY: Investigation Day Seventeen

With the murder of Valery Tarasov, the inquiry had become the centre of a media scrum. As if from holes underground they appeared, running, jostling, snapping, shouting. The Principal had forbidden staff or students to talk to the media, but he was pissing in the wind, Scott knew. Anyone who could claim any sort of connection with Tarasov could be guaranteed to have their words recorded as golden truths by a hungry reporter; it was irresistible.

He had been forced to do a press conference himself, which he hated at the best of times. This was worse because there was so little to say: he knew very little as yet and what he did know he was not prepared to give away. He had resorted to clichés. Was there a connection between this murder and the death of Ekrem Yilmaz? It was too early to say. Was there a connection with the death of Anton Tarasov? It was one of a number lines of inquiry being pursued. Was there a link with organised crime? It was too early to say. Did he believe that other students were in danger? Students remaining on campus for the vacation should stay calm but remain vigilant. Apprehending the killer or killers was a priority and all possible efforts were being made. Here he broke into a small peroration: resources would be expanded, all police leave had been cancelled, no stone would be left unturned.

Scott, chewing his breakfast toast, reflected on his

performance of the previous afternoon and winced at the prospect of Gina's sardonic take on his barrage of banalities. *No stone left unturned* he could hear her say with her mocking lilt. *Oh really, David.* As if brought to life by this thought, his mobile rang, bringing the voice of Gina herself.

'I thought you'd be up,' she greeted him. 'Why aren't you out turning stones?'

'You read it?'

'I saw it. You were on the telly. You looked very dashing but you should have let me write your script.'

'It doesn't work like that, unfortunately. But thank you for the dashing bit.'

'Don't mention it. Now, I've got something to tell you.'

Her voice, he now realised, was vibrating with excitement.

'Yes?' he asked cautiously.

'I went out to Dungate yesterday, for a baptism. The details are irrelevant but who do you think I saw on the beach?'

'Who?'

'Guess!'

'Gina, I haven't got time for –'

'Laurent!'

Her tone was so triumphant that his first response was irritation. *I found him*, she seemed to be saying, *when you couldn't!*

'Where was he?' he asked, deliberately flattening surprise from his voice.

'I told you – on the beach. With a group of mates – other druggies, I assume. They seemed to be sort of camped there – sleeping bags and so on.'

'Did you speak to him?'

'Of course. He wasn't at all pleased to see me though, after I ruined a perfectly good pair of boots walking over the pebbles.'

There was something feverish in her tone, he thought, something more than excitement at spotting Laurent.

'Whereabouts on the beach?' he asked.

'Near the Greek Orthodox church. I've got a photo of him if you want it.'

'I'll take your word for it. Will you let his mother know? Meanwhile, I'll send a couple of officers to pick him up.'

'I should think they'll have moved on from there if they've got any sense.'

'We'll find him,' he said grimly.

'But he hasn't actually committed a crime, has he? He just disappeared. We're all entitled to do that if we want to. He didn't deceive anyone – he just walked out.'

'He wasted my time!' Scott thundered. 'And he'll have drugs on him, won't he? So I'd like to talk to him about that. Or are you going to tell me that's not a crime either?'

'Well, possession is –'

'Just leave it, Gina,' Scott said. 'Just leave it.'

'Fine. I may have something else to tell you later. Shall I ring you or would you rather I left that too?'

'It's going to be a hectic day. I'll call you.'

This conversation had held him up. Leaving his breakfast things on the table, he went straight to his car and headed for the station. As he crawled round the ring road, his phone rang again and he heard Tyler's voice.

'Where are you, sir? We've got a development.'

'Good or bad?'

'Good. The best.'

Two overexcited calls before eight o'clock. Some way to start the day.

'Tell me.'

'We've got him. We've just got him.'

'Got him? Amiel, you mean?'

'Amiel?' Tyler sounded confused. 'No. The killer. We've got the killer.'

'What are you talking about, Mark? We don't even know who he is.'

'We do now. Caught with the gun on him. And wait till you hear who it is.'

'I'm five minutes away, Mark. Keep it till I get there.'

Entering the Incident Room was like arriving late at a party. His team sat sprawled in chairs, propped on tables, talking and laughing, the air fizzing with relief. The mugs of coffee might just as well have been flutes of champagne. A small cheer went up as he came in.

'I seem to have missed all the fun,' he said. 'I was delayed by a phone call. I might as well tell you my news, then you can tell me yours. Laurent Amiel's been found. Not kidnapped, just living rough in sunny Dungate.'

Another cheer rose, more raucous this time.

'OK. We'll deal with him later. Now, tell me, Mark. You've picked up our man, with his gun?'

'Not us, sir. Traffic.'

'Traffic? But the road blocks have –'

'Not here. Near Heathrow.'

'Heathrow? OK, I won't ask any more questions. Just tell me the story, Mark. The floor's yours.'

Bowing to ironic applause from the team, Tyler started.

'At four fifteen this morning, Traffic picked up a driver going the wrong way down the A4 near Heathrow Airport. He was a foreigner and seems, temporarily, to have forgotten to drive on the left.'

He waited for the cheers and laughter to die down before continuing.

'When they got him out of his car to breathalyse him, he tried to do a runner, so they took him into custody and gave his car a good going over. Among other things, they found a map of the Marlbury College campus and a Smith and Wesson 9mm semi-automatic. On his phone, they found photos of a man they recognised because his face had been all over the front pages – Valery Tarasov.'

'And this man is?'

217

'A Turk, travelling on a Russian passport. Goes by the name of Direnç Yilmaz.'

Amid whoops and whistles from the team, Scott said, 'Irina Boklova's husband?'

'The very same.'

Scott could see Irina's composed face, the contemptuous twist of her small, lipsticked mouth, and he heard her words: *my husband is simply loser, actually.*

'Where is he now?'

'On his way here,' Simon Kerr broke in, eager for some of the glory, unable to allow Tyler the limelight any longer. 'We sent a squad to pick him up and bring in the car. Should be here any time now.'

When Scott and Tyler walked into Interview Room One two hours later, they found Direnç Yilmaz flanked by two young women: a Turkish interpreter in a headscarf, who introduced herself as Leyla Mirza, and Emma Bright, the solicitor. When Scott looked at Yilmaz himself, he knew immediately where he had seen him before: outside a seminar room, squinting in through the glass door panel at the class inside, on the day when Scott too had been waiting outside – waiting to interview Valery Tarasov. How long ago was that? A week or more. This guy had been stalking Tarasov for some time then. He surveyed him. There was a passing similarity to his cousin Ekrem – not to the battered body he had seen in the library, but to the passport photo. Direnç was younger and his face showed only a hint of the heavy jowliness that would come. It was a self-indulgent face, though this morning, pale and unshaven, it looked simply weak and scared. *Sad man* Scott heard Irina saying.

Having greeted the interpreter and the solicitor and introduced Tyler, Scott turned on the interview tape and addressed Yilmaz.

'I see you have an interpreter, Mr Yilmaz,' he said. 'Do you speak any English at all?'

Yilmaz turned to the interpreter and they exchanged a few words in Turkish before she said.

'He doesn't speak any English.'

'Then we'll proceed through you, Miss Mirza. You've done this before, I assume?'

'Yes.'

'Fine. Mr Yilmaz, you were stopped by the police this morning for a traffic offence and a gun was found in your car – a gun for which you appear to have no licence. Can you explain what it was doing there?'

After the necessary delay, the answer came through the ventriloquism of Leyla Mirza.

'I don't know anything about a gun.'

'It has your fingerprints on it.'

'I don't know anything.'

Tyler joined in.

'When the police stopped you this morning, you tried to run away. Why did you do that if you're an innocent man?'

'I was in a hurry. I had to get to the airport for my flight back to Moscow.'

'And how were you going to get to the airport without your car, Yilmaz? Run?' Tyler laughed.

Yilmaz muttered something to Leyla Mirza.

'He has nothing to say,' she said.

Scott took a new tack.

'What are you doing in the UK, Mr Yilmaz?'

'I am a tourist.'

'And you've been in the UK for nearly three weeks?'

'Yes.'

'Where have you visited?'

'Many places.'

'Including Marlbury?'

'Maybe.'

'Definitely. I've seen you there myself, on the campus of Marlbury College. The campus you had a map of in your car.'

'OK, I was there. That's not a crime, is it?'

It was odd to hear Leyla Mirza's quiet tone leeching the aggression out of his answer. It made it difficult – difficult to maintain momentum, difficult to feed off the aggression.

'That depends on what you were doing there,' Scott said. 'Why did you choose Marlbury? There are plenty more obvious tourist spots to visit.'

'I have friends there.'

'Friends like your ex-wife and your cousin?' asked Tyler as a DC entered with a written message for Scott.

'I'm not interested in my cousin Ekrem. I came for my wife. I wanted her back. I did her no harm. She can't just get tired of me and throw me away. I won't allow it. I came to take her back.'

Again the blandness of the interpreter's tone was disconcerting, disorienting.

'So what were you going to do?' Scott asked as he finished reading the message and folded it. 'Take her back to Russia at gunpoint?'

'No. I didn't want to hurt her. I wanted to persuade her. I thought she would listen to me.'

'But she didn't?'

'I never spoke to her. There was always Tarasov with her. As soon as I saw them I knew it was no good. I watched them always laughing and joking together in the class. I knew he was her lover.'

'So you shot him?'

Yilmaz ran his hands through his hair before he replied in a low voice. Leyla Mirza seemed to ask for confirmation before she said, calmly as ever, 'Yes, I shot him.'

'And now perhaps you'd like to tell us who put you up to it,' Scott said.

Leyla Mirza hesitated.

'Put you up to it?' she queried.

'Persuaded him to do it,' Tyler explained.

'Or paid him,' Scott added.

She nodded and relayed the question.

'No-one,' came the answer. 'I did it myself. He was my wife's lover. I shot him. That's all.'

'According to our information,' Scott told him, 'he wasn't her lover actually. If you'd spoken to her, she'd probably have told you that. Did she even know you were here, by the way? Did you just spy on her?'

'She never saw me. I made sure. I didn't want to give her the chance to shame me.'

'Well, let's leave that aside. We know you shot him. This –' He indicated the slip of paper he had received '– is a report from our ballistics expert. The bullets that killed Tarasov were fired from the gun with your fingerprints on it, found in your car.'

He paused for Leyla Mirza to translate before adding, 'So, you see, we don't really need your confession. What we need is for you to tell us who paid you to do it.'

'No-one paid. I have pride, I did it myself.'

'Yilmaz, according to your ex-wife, you have no money, and according to you, you speak no English. Do you really expect us to believe that you were able to fly to the UK, stay for three weeks, hire a car, buy a gun and kill two people with no help from anyone else?'

Scott saw the surprise start into Yilmaz's face as the question was translated.

'Why do you say two people?'

'I assume that, eventually, you'll admit that you killed your cousin Ekrem as well. What happened? Was he sniffing around Irina too?'

'I had nothing to do with killing Ekrem. Nothing at all. I killed Tarasov. I did it alone. I have nothing more to say.'

'What about the money?' Tyler asked. 'Tell us where the money came from for this little trip.'

'I have money. You should not believe my wife. I am a business man. I have money.'

'What sort of business?'

'Buying and selling.'

'And the name of your company, Yilmaz?' asked Tyler, getting a pen and notebook out. 'It's registered in Russia, I assume? How many employees do you have? What's your annual turnover?'

Yilmaz's reply to Leyla Mirza seemed longer than her translation.

'It's not like that. It's an informal company. I work by myself.'

'But you earn enough money to go flying off on a holiday in the UK? I wonder who's looking after this business of yours while you're away,' Tyler commented.

Yilmaz made no reply.

'Let me suggest a situation to you.' Scott leaned back in his chair. 'Let me paint a picture for you.'

Yilmaz, in his turn, slumped back in his seat.

'Five years ago, you were working in a tourist resort on the Black Sea – buying and selling to the tourists. You meet a young Russian doctor who's on holiday there and you can't believe your luck. You persuade her to marry you, to take you back to Russia, get you Russian citizenship, support you on her earnings until you make the fortune that you're bound to make in the brave new Russia.'

He paused to let Leyla Mirza catch up and wondered if that was a look of reproach on her calm face. He continued, 'But it doesn't work out that well, does it? You find that fortunes aren't as easy to make as all that and your wife finds that she's made a terrible mistake. You're a loser, you're a drag on her. What you haven't reckoned with is how easy divorce is for women in Russia - compared with Turkey anyway. Before you know it, she's dumped you.'

Again, he waited. Again the interpreter's gaze shamed him.

'Now, you're on your own. You try hard to bully your wife

into changing her mind, but it's no good. You actually drive her out of the country. Without your Russian wife you're an outsider, and you have no money. You try a bit of this and a bit of that and soon you're on the wrong side of the law and you're making enemies in the criminal world. This is when you need protection and here the friends of Mikhail Belenki come in.'

He pronounced the name with care, distinctly, and had the satisfaction of seeing the flash of recognition that crossed Yilmaz's face.

'They offer you help. They'll protect you – maybe even pay you – if you'll do a little job for them. They want Ekrem Yilmaz and Valery Tarasov killed. Maybe just for revenge because they landed Belenki in prison, maybe because they know too much about Belenki's business and can't be trusted. Conveniently, they're both studying in the same college in the UK, and even more conveniently for you, your ex-wife is there too.'

Pausing once more for Yilmaz to take this in, he went on, 'So this is the deal. They'll book your flights, hire the car, provide the gun, give you all the money you need, and you just have to do the deed. And maybe you'll be able to bring your wife back too. Well, that didn't work out, but you nearly got away with the rest, didn't you? If you'd remembered to drive on the left, you would have got clean away.'

Yilmaz slumped forward for a moment, resting his head on his arms, then sat up to give his reply.

'I didn't kill Ekrem. I know nothing about that.'

'Which means that I'm right about the rest?'

'I told you I killed Tarasov. I did it alone. Your story is nonsense.'

'Yilmaz,' said Scott, 'you're going to be convicted of his murder and you're going to get a long prison sentence. If you co-operate with us, we can make things easier for you. You could serve part of your sentence in Russia, for example, or in Turkey.'

Yilmaz broke into rapid and urgent talk with Leyla Mirza and she turned and spoke not to Scott but to Emma Bright, who had been uncharacteristically silent so far.

'He does not want to go back to Russia,' she told her, 'or to Turkey. He is afraid.'

The solicitor looked, in turn, at Scott.

'Of course he is,' he exclaimed. 'He's been and screwed up and he'll get punished by the Belenki gang, who'll believe he's fingered them whether he has or not. His only hope is a good long stretch in a nice, safe British jail. Perhaps we should do the deal the other way round: we'll promise to keep him in Britain if he'll spill the beans.'

Emma Bright gave him a questioning look.

'If you're serious,' she said, 'I shall need to discuss options with my client. I'd like to request a break to talk to him.'

'Fine. If you wouldn't mind staying, Miss Mirza?'

As Scott and Tyler were leaving the room, Yilmaz spoke, looking directly at Scott, and Leyla Mirza translated.

'If I killed Ekrem, why didn't I shoot him too?'

'And that,' Scott said to Tyler when they were outside the door, 'is a very good question indeed.'

29

SATURDAY: *Third Person Plural*

I am woken at six by Freda's dawn chorus, and for once I don't mind. I've been sleeping only in snatches and I'm planning to be at the Social Science block on the dot of nine, when the porter comes on duty. There are, however, three hours to kill. I feed Freda and myself, then dress us both with care, aiming to be as appealing as possible to the holder of the key to the library door. After that, I have a go at the Guardian's Saturday quiz and do the quick crossword. It is now seventhirty. I could start the cryptic crossword or the sudoku but my concentration is all to pieces, so I decide to phone David instead. With a second murder on his plate, I assume he won't be having a leisurely Saturday morning, and I'm right.

He answers right away and I can tell he's stressed. I shouldn't tease him about his press conference yesterday, but I do, which probably doesn't improve his mood. Even so, I must say he's pretty ungracious when I tell him about finding Laurent. I've done his job for him, for God's sake, and I don't get a word of thanks. He gets all punitive about Laurent and wants to bring him in and bang him up. I'm pretty pissed off with Laurent myself but I begin to feel quite sorry for him. Precipitately, I hint that I may be on to something else, but he's not interested – freezes me off. Well fine. He'll just have to come begging later, won't he?

At eight-thirty I'm strapping Freda into her buggy, tying

Piglet to the straps and setting off through a grey drizzle. Very few people are around on this unappealing morning, but a couple of times, as I'm manoeuvring over crossings, I catch sight of a couple of youngsters in hooded anoraks behind me and I wonder if these are friends of Laurent's and if, by any chance, I'm being followed.

I arrive too early at Social Sciences, and Freda and I do a circuit of the building to keep warm. The tapes have been taken away from the front of the library, but a notice on the door declares it to be closed until further notice. When we get back to the foyer, though, Clive Davies is just arriving. Hallelujah! If I could have wished for anyone, it would have been Clive. I have put time and effort into my relationship with Clive over the years - not with any ulterior motive but because he's a nice guy and he likes to talk. It's often he who unlocks the English Language building first thing, and in our morning exchanges, I have heard about his holidays, admired photos of his grandchildren and even sympathised over the state of his garden (rain, drought, slugs, greenfly, whitefly, blackfly), though my interest in and knowledge of gardening is zero. Now, just possibly, I shall get my reward.

'Clive!' I cry. 'I'm so glad it's you.'

This is, sadly, the only true thing I'm going to say to him this morning. I accompany it with what I hope is a dazzling smile and it's possible that I put my head on one side in a winsome sort of way. Yes, I'm almost sure that I do. Then I introduce Freda who, trouper that she is, gives him a wide, gummy smile that far outshines anything I can produce.

'And what can I do for you, Gina?' he asks cheerfully.

'You can save my life, Clive,' I cry, 'but I'm afraid you're going to tell me it's more than your job's worth.'

Clive addresses Freda.

'Ooh, she's trouble, isn't she, your Gran?'

Freda gurgles her agreement.

'I'll tell you what it is, Clive,' I say. 'Weeks ago I asked the library to get me a book that I need for a course I'm teaching next term. It came in, I know, because they sent me an e-mail about it, but I didn't have time to pick it up before – all this happened.'

I gesture vaguely towards the library door.

'Now,' I bash on, 'I'm desperate for it. I can't write my lectures for next term without it.'

'Well that is bad news,' he says, deadpan, and I'm not sure how I'm doing.

'So I wondered,' I say, gazing up at him from beneath my specially-mascaraed lashes and wishing I were twenty years younger, 'if you could possibly let me into the library office for five minutes, just to pick it up. I know where it'll be and I promise not to touch anything else. I'd be eternally grateful.'

I pause and wait. He looks at me unsmiling. Then he says, 'You said it was more than my job's worth, and you're right. If anyone found out, I'd be shot.'

But his hand is moving towards a pair of keys hanging on the board at the back of his booth and I know I'm there.

'Come on,' he says and, amazingly, we're walking towards the library door.

I go first, along the little corridor and into the office. Clive follows, pushing Freda. He's not going to leave me alone in here, I can see, so I'm going to have to be quick. The door through from the office into the library is closed and I shut my mind to what may lie beyond it still. There is an odd smell, partly general staleness, partly, I think, blood, but I need to concentrate. I get my glasses on and scan the walls while Clive is still managing the buggy, and I spot the rota over by the far door. Under the pretext of looking through a pile of books nearby I manage a long enough survey of the rota to find the date I want: *Tuesday 26th February*, there it is, and the name beneath it. Yes, yes, yes, yes, yes! Afraid that I may betray myself, I grab a book at random (when I get it out later it will turn out to be a survey of midwifery services in the UK) and slip it into my bag.

'Got it!' I cry to Clive Davies, and we turn to leave.

I thank him profusely and depart the building in a rush. As I back out through the swing doors, pulling the buggy after me, I see what I'm sure is the hooded pair who seemed to be following me earlier, disappearing round the corner of the building. I'm tempted to go after them and challenge them but I've got too much else to think about.

I head to my office as a place to do my thinking. Up to now, I've just wanted to be clever, to solve the puzzle. Now I know the truth and I don't know what to do with it. It's so extraordinary, so painful, so burdensome that I don't even know what to think about it. I reach the English Language building and lug Freda and her buggy up the stairs. In my office, I sit her down on the floor with a paperweight to play with and sit down at my desk to think. Only moments later, there is a knock at my door and, unthinkingly, I call, 'Come in.'

My stomach plunges as two hooded figures enter the room and then plunges again with dizzy recognition as they throw off their hoods. Those two. Of course. I should have known.

'Good morning Mrs Gray,' says Christiane as she walks across the room and picks up Freda. 'Hello Freda.' She pronounces the name the German way, with a guttural 'r'.

Irina, meanwhile, stands with her back to the door, silent. Stupid, stupid, stupid. How stupid I've been. They've been ahead of me all the time and now, here I am on a Saturday morning in the vacation, trapped in my office where no-one will hear me scream, with my baby granddaughter and a pair of murderers.

'Did you follow me all the way from my house?' I ask, and my voice emerges surprisingly steady.

'We did. You were up very early,' Christiane replies, perching on the windowsill and dandling Freda on her knee. 'Yukiko told us you had guessed something and we weren't sure what you would do. Yukiko will be here in a minute, by the way. We've had no visit from the police, so we guessed you hadn't told the Chief Inspector yet. We don't know why you went into the library, though. We can't work that out.'

'I went to look at the library rota. I wanted to know who was on duty on the night before the murder. When I saw who it was, I understood everything – well almost everything. There are still a few questions I'd like to ask.'

'You should start with telling us what you know.' Irina speaks for the first time. 'Then you can ask your questions.'

'OK,' I say, 'let's start with this.'

There is a small whiteboard behind my desk, which I use for reminders, 'To Do' lists, phone numbers et cetera. I wipe it clean, pick up a board pen and write:

If he had not raped our friend, we would not have killed him.

'Yes,' Christiane says, 'you do know. So what are we going to do about it?'

What will they do to stop me from spreading my knowledge around? They've killed once – perhaps twice. What will they do to me? To Freda? What might Christiane do to her? Would she threaten to throw her out of the window? Would she do it? I want to run, to snatch Freda from Christiane's arms and run somewhere where I can attract help, but Irina's bulk is guarding the door. Involuntarily, my eyes go to the door to my inner office. If I sauntered over in that direction to make us a cup of coffee, could I get in there and lock the door? Well, I'm not going anywhere without Freda, am I?

There is a disturbance outside the door and Irina steps aside. Yukiko appears, followed by Ceren.

'Well, this is quite a party,' I say. 'Do sit down, everyone.'

Ceren sits in the room's only armchair and Yukiko perches on the arm. Christiane and Irina stay where they are.

'What have you said?' Yukiko asks Christiane, who gestures wordlessly at my message on the board.

'Ah so, I see,' Yukiko says, looking at me.

'But there are things I don't know,' I say, 'so do you mind answering a few questions?'

What do I have in mind? A sort of reverse *Arabian Nights*? Keep them talking because all the time they're talking they can't be thinking about how to shut me up? Well, in the absence of a better idea, it's worth a try.

'First off,' I say, 'what were all those messages on the board about?'

They exchange glances but before anyone answers there is a knock on the door behind Irina. She opens it a chink, then throws it wide to reveal the unexpected figure of Desirée. For the first time that morning I am truly surprised.

'Desirée!' I say in astonishment, 'I didn't think you'd –'

'You didn't think I'd care?' Desirée interrupts me. 'Or you didn't think I'd want to spoil my clothes? You always misjudged me, I think, Mrs Gray. Because I am a good Frenchwoman and must be soignée at all times, you think I have nothing in my head, that I care only to keep my man. I gave you a sentence, Mrs Gray, the day we killed Ekrem Yilmaz. *If I were a man, I would be happier*, I said. You thought I was not serious, but I was. It is truly no pleasure to be a young woman, you know, even in France or the UK, where we are *liberated*! What is it like for the millions of women like her?'

She waves her scarlet-tipped fingers in Ceren's direction.

'It sounds as though we've got plenty to talk about,' I say. 'Do have a seat, Desirée, and Irina, you really don't need to guard the door any more.'

Desirée sits in the chair facing me across my desk, crossing her elegant legs, and Irina takes the only other chair in the room, in the corner near the window. This is better. I feel like the teacher again. I begin to feel in charge.

'Tell me how it happened,' I say, 'from the beginning. Tell me the story.'

There is a silence. No-one looks at anyone else and I'm

230

afraid they're going to refuse, but then I see Yukiko bend down and whisper something to Ceren, who begins to speak.

'So,' she says, gesturing at my whiteboard, 'the story starts with me.'

She is not looking at me, or at anyone else. She is fingering the edge of her scarf, teasing a thread from the fraying edge.

'I was on duty in the library on Tuesday evening. At the end of the evening I let the students out and locked the door. Then I was walking back to the office when he grabbed me.'

'Ekrem?'

'Yes. He was hiding between the shelves. He grabbed me and dragged me back there. I tried to scream but he said – he said if I scream he will kill me. He will tie me up there and push the shelves together to crush me. So I didn't scream. I pushed my scarf in my mouth to stop screaming and he – did what he wanted.'

There is a long silence in which only Freda makes any noise at all, sitting on Christiane's lap, playing with strands of her long, sandy-blond hair. When Ceren speaks again she has her eyes closed, though her fingers are still working away compulsively at the edge of her scarf.

'After, he asked me if I like it. He said we can do again many times. It is our secret. He said if I tell anyone, he will shame me to my parents. He will tell everyone I am bad girl, not moral. He said he has protection. He works for Turkish government. No-one will believe me.'

Yukiko puts out a hand to her, and she takes it between her own before she goes on.

'I was fainting, I think, so he was nearly carrying me out. He gave the keys to the porter and he told him I was sick and he was looking after me. Then he took me outside and left me there.'

She releases Yukiko's hand and opens her eyes.

'I don't know how long I was there. In the end I went to Irina. She has room in same hall as me and she is doctor.'

As if handing on the baton, she sits back in her chair and closes her eyes again. Irina clears her throat.

'I examined her,' she says. 'She was not too bad. I have seen much worse, in hospital in St Petersburg, many women. Russian men are animals when they're drunk. Ekrem Yilmaz was animal too, but Ceren was OK. No need for hospital. But she was in shock. She was crying and crying. I gave her painkillers and sedative but still she was crying. So I called Christiane, and she and Yukiko came over.'

'I wanted she should go to the police,' Christiane chips in. 'I thought it was the only thing to protect her from that man and to protect other women, but she could not. After she fell asleep, we three went on talking. Yukiko understood better than us why she cannot go to the police. It is too much shame. In her culture, being raped is always the woman's fault. Her parents would disown her and she would lose everything – her family, her chance to marry – everything. So what else could she do? What could we do?'

'The idea to crush him with the stacks was just a joke at first,' Yukiko says. 'Ceren told us how he threatened her and we said it was a pity we couldn't do the same to him. We talked how we might trap him there and Irina and Christiane said they were strong enough to turn the handle. Irina does weight training in the gym.'

'And you have a strong right arm from playing your viola,' I comment to Christiane.

'I have. People don't realise how much force is needed. My right shoulder is bigger than my left. But we didn't plan anything then. We talked most of the night but in the morning we had no plan. One thing I did useful, though. I went to a pharmacy for a 'morning after' pill.'

Irina spoke from her corner.

'So at least she won't be pregnant.' Then, in a tone gentler than I have ever heard from her, she adds, 'When she is stronger she will need to have HIV test, and for other sexual disease.'

From her chair, where she is huddled with Yukiko's arm around her, Ceren gives a sob. Yukiko takes her hand and says,

'On Wednesday afternoon, before your class, Mrs Gray, Ekrem spoke to me. He thought he was so clever. He asked was I going to be on duty in the library tonight and he said he would see me there. I knew what he meant. Maybe he thought Ceren had told no-one what happened to her. Of course, I didn't have to go to the library. I could call sick, or change duty with a man, or have someone with me, but I saw how we could trap him. I saw we could really do it.'

'So,' says Christiane, 'after your class we stayed behind in the classroom and made our plan.'

Now it's my turn.

'Let me see if I can pick up the story now,' I say. 'Yukiko went to do her duty and the rest of you went to the SU for Women's Night. At ten o'clock, Yukiko cleared the library of everyone but Ekrem, who, she knew, was lying in wait for her. She called Christiane to say she was ready – and I blush to think how I laughed at Chief Inspector Scott when he questioned why you were all calling one another that evening. Yukiko let Christiane and Irina in through the emergency door, then she held Ekrem at knife-point while they turned the stack mechanism for all they were worth. The police thought it had to have been a man, but two strong young women working together could easily do it.'

I stop for a moment to imagine the scene.

'You couldn't know that, though, could you? Supposing you hadn't been able to move it fast enough? Supposing he'd got out? Had you thought about that?'

Irina speaks.

'We didn't plan to kill. We wanted to scare him, to humiliate him. We thought we could make sure he never tried the same thing again. We knew he could tell no-one. He would be too ashamed – to admit what he did and to admit that some girls

233

could catch him like that and do this. But then the wheel turned so easily and he said such ugly things, so we just kept turning and turning – until he stopped.'

I look at Christiane's calm face, like that of a flaxen German Madonna as she sits with Freda on her knee, and I picture that frenzied turning and Yukiko dancing before Ekrem with her little knife. Like maenads, I think, like Bacchae.

'Then Yukiko let you out of the emergency exit, closed it and went out through the office, delivering the keys to the porter as usual. The whole thing hadn't taken ten minutes. Then she joined the rest of you over in the SU, where Ceren and Desirée were ready to swear Christiane and Irina had been with them all along.'

'We were there,' Desirée says suddenly.

'I'm sorry?'

'Ceren and I, we were there. Yukiko couldn't manage alone to keep him in there. We were there too. You look amazed, Mrs Gray. You still don't comprehend. Two of my friends have been raped in Paris. You believe here that French men are such great lovers, but it's a myth. They think no woman can resist them, of course, and they think *non* is not meaning *non*. They think it's a joke but it's not a joke to us, not to my friend who is sick now.'

'But Ceren,' I say, 'how could you –'

'I needed,' she whispers without looking at me. 'I needed being there.'

There is another long silence before I turn back to Yukiko.

'Tell me about the knife, Yukiko. You'd planned it all so carefully, how did you come to leave it behind?'

'Ah!' She gives a little shout of anger. 'This is my mistake. I didn't plan to take a knife, but then I was afraid. I would be in the library alone with Ekrem before the others came. Suppose he caught me before? So I took the knife from our kitchen. I did use it for my apple, actually, but then I put it in my coat pocket when I went to lock the main door. Then when we

234

were keeping him in between the stacks, he was fighting hard and I remembered I had the knife, so I used it. I stabbed him. Many times.'

'And the blood got on your coat and you had to throw it away.'

'You noticed about my coat. The police man would not notice.'

'But why did you leave the knife in the library?'

'I didn't plan it. I had gloves to wear when I went to let the others out of the door, for fingerprints, but I had to put down the knife to do it. I pushed it among the books so no blood showing. I meant to take it again when I left, but when the others were gone I was alone – just with his body – and it was horrible, so I just ran out. When I realised, I hoped no-one would find it.'

'Why did you tell the police it was yours?'

'It had my fingerprints, and the police had too – from Ceren's room. I thought they will check, so it is better to tell, to seem innocent.'

She smiles at me, perched neatly as ever on the arm of the chair.

'I simply can't imagine it,' I say, 'you stabbing a man with a knife and watching him get crushed to death.'

She stands up and comes towards me.

'For ten years,' she tells me, fixing me with her eyes, 'as Junior High School student, as High School student, as College student, I travelled every day on metro in Osaka. Always in rush hour, always standing up, because we are young and must give up seats to our elders. So these old businessmen are always sitting down, always with their hands up our skirts, stroking up. Up. Even inside our panties. And we can say nothing. Not a word. Christiane and Irina, they say *why didn't you shout, swear at them, stamp on their foot?* But we cannot. We are not taught like that. It would be more shame for us than for them. And so we put up. But we have anger in us like flower bud and one day it must blossom. So for me that day it blossomed.'

'You wrote the messages on the board, Yukiko. Only you could write so neatly. What was that about?'

Christiane answers.

'That was my error. The day after we – after the death, Ceren was afraid to come to class, but we knew she should come or she would be in suspicion, so we took her to the classroom earlier, before the class, and we took away Ekrem's chair. The conditional sentences were still on the board and we showed them to her. Suddenly, I saw how we could make a new sentence from them and I erased everything except *If I would kill you I would be happier.* To make it say what we wanted, I changed *you* to *him* of course. It was just to amuse us and I meant to erase it, but I forgot. When we came back later for the class, you had erased it and as I sat in class I realised there was an error. It's the error I always make because of how German is. I put *would* in the 'if' clause.'

'And you knew I would notice the error and connect it with you?'

'Yes. So the only thing I could think was to write another message with a different error to confuse you.'

'A Turkish error. Didn't you feel bad about implicating Asil and Ahmet?'

'They were innocent. We couldn't do them any harm. We have faith in UK justice.'

She smiles, conscious of the irony.

'And the same goes for implicating the Iranians, I suppose?' I ask.

'Yes. We worried that the police were too interested in Denis, so we needed to distract them. The Turks had gone home, so it had to be Iranians.'

'Does Denis know what you did?' I ask Desirée.

'Yes. I couldn't lie to him, but it was difficult when the police got interested in his little bit of cannabis.'

'Just one more question. What about the disappearing sentence? How did you manage that?'

'We talked about that afterwards,' says Desirée. 'We didn't plan it, of course. We couldn't. But maybe we all had death in our minds.'

'I added *was crushed*,' Irina says. 'Maybe I could use another word for how the man died when he fell, but *crushed* came in my head. Then, when we destroyed, Ceren changed subject of sentence. It was *my father, the man on the trapeze,* but she took out *my father* so *the man* was subject, and Christiane -'

'Took out *on the trapeze*,' says Christiane. So the final sentence had to be *The man fell* or *the man was crushed*, but Irina took out *fell*.'

'And I never noticed that all the crucial changes were made by you four. I'm mortified.'

'It was just a game,' says Christiane. 'We were a bit hysterical, I think. We didn't sleep much those days.'

She gets up, brings Freda across to me and hands her over.

'So now you know everything, what are you going to do? Will you tell the police?'

'Will you let me?'

'How can we stop you? Oh, do you think we're going to say, *Now you know too much. We can't let you live?*'

There's a ripple of laughter and I say,

'We haven't talked about Valery. What happened to him? Did he know too much?'

Irina erupts from her chair in the corner, with a great sweeping gesture of her arm, so she looks like an operatic Valkyrie.

'We don't understand about Valery,' she cries. 'He was nothing to do with this. I loved Valery. We did nothing to him.'

'How would we get a gun?' Desirée asks softly from her place just across my desk. 'We are not professional killers, you know.'

'But you admit you killed Ekrem. If I tell DCI Scott and he questions you, will you confess?'

'Oh no,' Yukiko answers. 'We shall deny. Because you have no evidence, have you? I threw away my winter coat is all. A weird thing to do, but not crime.'

'I know one thing I didn't know before,' I challenge her. 'I know that Ceren was carried out of the library in a half-fainting state the night before the murder and the porter will confirm that. I also know, as you don't, that Ekrem's semen was found on the library floor. I think the police could use that as a starting point.'

Christiane, who is still standing near me, opens her eyes wide as she looks at me and says,

'Would you do that to Ceren?'

Would I do that to Ceren? I look at her as she sits huddled in her chair, her knees drawn up to her chin. She would be so easy to break, and she knew it. Why else had she been so desperate to run away?

'Where have you been, Ceren? Where did you go when you left my house?'

'I went to Afrodite,' she whispers. 'Yukiko took me to Afrodite.'

She sees my surprise and gives the faintest of smiles.

'You think we can't get along together because I am Turkish and she is Greek? Well, Yukiko told me Afrodite has a loving heart and I found it's true. '

Of course she did, and she'd have been at baby Serafin's baptism, thinking she was safe out there in Dungate, if Yukiko hadn't sent her a text, warning her that I was on my way.

'Tell me something,' I say, looking round at them. 'How is what you did different from the actions of a lynch mob?'

'We knew he was guilty,' Desirée says. 'He was absolutely guilty.'

'But you don't believe in capital punishment, do you, Desirée? Not even for murder. Nor does Christiane. I've heard you argue against it. So how do you justify killing a man for rape?'

'We really didn't intend to kill him, Mrs Gray,' says Christiane. 'We wanted to hurt him and to scare him so much that he wouldn't be a danger to any other women. Of course we would have preferred that he went to jail, but we couldn't achieve that, so we did what we could and we went too far.'

'Why? Why did you go too far? You could easily have stopped.'

'Because we were angry, but more because we were frightened. If we let him out, what would we do with him? He was shouting and threatening. We could only keep turning. It's like killing a snake. You find the biggest stone and you smash it over the head and then you do it again and again because you are afraid.'

I take a deep breath.

'You'll have to leave this with me,' I say. 'I need to think.'

I stand up and go to put Freda in her buggy.

'There is one thing I can tell you,' I say as I look round at their pale young faces. 'Ceren doesn't need to worry about an HIV test, or STDs. DCI Scott told me Ekrem was perfectly healthy. They did a blood test at the autopsy. He wasn't HIV positive.'

Ceren gives an extraordinary howl and I see Yukiko almost lift her out of her chair. Then they are hugging and laughing and weeping and the others are there too, all of them hugging and weeping and talking in a babel of languages.

Am I going to tell what I know? Am I going to let David Scott know that Ceren is the weak point, that he can unpick his mystery by unravelling her first? Am I going to let Ekrem Yilmaz, drug-dealer, spy and sexual predator, cast his blight on these five lives? Am I going to let these five murderers walk free?

As I watch them, they remind me of sixth-formers getting their A level results. Only it's no kind of success they're

239

celebrating; it's just a reprieve. No glimpse for Ceren of a sunlit future, just the merest lightening of a lowering sky. I think about the quality of mercy. I have no right to be doling out mercy, I know, but it is twice blessed and we all have most need of blessing, so on the whole, I think, I'd rather go with mercy than anything else.

When they've gone, I cart Freda and the buggy downstairs again and smoke a cigarette as I stand in the morning drizzle and look across at the library's emergency door. Then, it being Saturday, we set off for Sainsbury's and the weekly shop.

30

MONDAY: Investigation Day Nineteen

'So both the missing students have turned up safe and well?'

'Yes, sir.'

'And where had they been?'

'We found Amiel living rough with a group of others, on the beach near Dungate. We brought them in and charged them with possession of heroin. Amiel's mother has paid bail for all of them. As we thought, Yilmaz was his supplier and when he died, Amiel went where the new supply was.'

'How did you find him?'

Scott hesitated.

'A tip-off from a member of the public,' he said.

He was sitting once again in the Chief Superintendent's airy office at County HQ. He had plenty of positive news but was struggling to convey his lurking sense that the arrest of Direnç Yilmaz didn't tie up the whole business.

'That's what we like,' said the Chief Superintendent cheerily. 'Outcome of good community policing, wouldn't you say?'

'Yes, sir.'

'And the Turkish girl?'

'Ceren Vural. She'd been staying with friends, as her note to her tutor said. We had a call from her tutor. Ceren had been into the college to see her.'

'Any idea why she went AWOL?'

'No. She was clearly upset by Yilmaz's death, though she claimed she hardly knew him. I was always puzzled by that. It's one of the things that makes me wonder still whether we've –'

'Whether you've got a double murderer in custody? I really don't see what's bothering you, Scott. You say you've got a confession to the Tarasov murder from this chap you've got, and plenty of forensic and ballistic evidence to back it up. You say Tarasov and Ekrem Yilmaz were definitely involved in Tarasov senior's trafficking business and there's a grudge with a Russian mafia boss. You're not seriously trying to tell me that both of them getting murdered within two weeks of one another is a coincidence, are you?'

'Direnç Yilmaz insists that his motive was personal – he wanted his former wife back and he thought Tarasov was her lover.'

'But you don't believe that, do you?'

'No, I don't think I do,' Scott answered slowly. 'Yilmaz isn't over-bright, he doesn't speak any English and he doesn't seem to have a job. I don't see how he could have found the money to get over here or known how to get hold of the gun without criminal connections. And I can see why he'd claim it was personal – he'd be terrified of retribution from the Belenki gang if he implicated them.'

'Well, there you are then. You've addressed your own doubts, haven't you?'

'Not altogether, sir. There are some loose ends. There's the matter of the semen – Ekrem Yilmaz's semen, found on the library floor near where he died, but left there twenty-four hours or so before he died.'

'From all you've said, he was a pretty unsavoury character. I don't think it takes too much imagination to think what he might have been doing in the privacy of those stacks, does it?'

'I suppose not, sir. But then there's the question of the

second man. There had to be two killers involved in Yilmaz's death – one to hold him at knife-point, the other to turn the wheel.'

'Surely that's obvious.' The Chief Superintendent looked at him in surprise. 'He got Tarasov to help him. Tarasov agreed, hoping to save his own skin, and then he got what was coming to him.'

'But why kill Ekrem Yilmaz that way, sir? That's what really bugs me. He'd gone to all the trouble of getting hold of a gun. Why didn't he shoot both of them? Why that complicated and risky business with the stacks?'

'Come on, Scott, use your imagination. He thinks he can make these deaths look like accidents. No police investigation. Much less hassle. He has a gun because his paymasters provide one, but he's keeping that for protection only. The first job goes fine, but he's not, as you say, over-bright and he hasn't recognised that no-one's going to believe it's an accident. Then Tarasov gets edgy and it's difficult to get him into a situation where another 'accident' can be staged – hence the time lag between the two deaths. In the end he decides to cut his losses, shoot him and do a runner.'

Scott studied his face. Could a competent police officer of any rank possibly believe such an unconvincing farrago? Could he believe that even a complete idiot would think that he could make a credible accident out of a man's apparently crushing himself between library stacks at dead of night, and acquiring self-inflicted knife wounds at the same time? Of course the Chief Super didn't believe it. He simply wanted this case cleared up and a killer in the hand suited him very well.

As if to confirm his view, the Chief Superintendent spoke again.

'You say he's scared of being sent back to Russia, don't you. Offer him protection here and he'll tell you whatever you want to know, believe me.'

'Yes, sir,' Scott said rising. 'Thank you.'

Outside, he thought about the other loose end – a literal one, he reflected wryly – which he had not mentioned. Those threads they found near the body. Pink, white and green cotton. He knew what they made him think of: that throw affair he had seen on Gina's sofa, the one she had been so snappy about when he had asked about it. It had to be a red herring; he really didn't think she was one of the murderers, did he? Still he wondered if he could drop in on her and get another look. Whatever rapport there had been between them seemed to have come unravelled recently, but it might be worth a try.

31

MONDAY: *Finite Clause*

I wake to the strange stillness of an empty house. It is a sensation so unfamiliar that I feel for a moment as though I've been deprived of hearing, like that temporary deafness you get after a loud explosion. I don't think I've woken in an empty house for twenty years, but here I am now, on my own.

Ellie came by to reclaim Freda late yesterday evening and Annie is meeting Andrew at Leeds-Bradford airport at this very moment to fly with him to The Hague. I have no-one to tend to, no-one to argue with, nothing to get up for at all. Since it's vacation and I haven't even any students to teach, I could stay in bed and listen to *The Today Programme*, but instead I get up, go and rout the cat out from wherever she's lurking in the garden and give her breakfast. Then I put on some old trousers and a sweater and do a burst of tidying round the house, which is looking more rumpled than usual after Freda's weekend sojourn. After that, I get on my bike and cycle into college.

My intention, as I put it to myself, is to *tie up some loose ends*. I've tied up a few over the weekend, actually. I rang and told David I'd seen Ceren – I thought he deserved that, at least – and found him cock-a-hoop. Irina's ex-husband killed Valery, apparently, on the orders of some Russian Godfather. Poor Valery. And David and his merry men think he killed Ekrem as well. So, as far as they're concerned, the case is closed, which I ought to be pleased about, though I can't help feeling a bit disappointed that they can be so crass.

My loose ends this morning consist mainly of the pile of punitive forms sent to me by the Principal some days ago. As a stalling manoeuvre, however, when I get into my office, I log on to my e-mails, not checked since Thursday, and there, amid the spam and trivia, I find a message from Janet, the Principal's secretary, with the subject heading, *Recruitment*.

I can't handle this now, I really can't. What with the dark secret I'm keeping buttoned up in my head, and the realisation that, before long, I shall be waking up to an empty house every morning, and the fact that I haven't yet dealt with the Principal's last piece of harassment, I just don't feel up to it. I feel feeble and pathetic, in fact, and I want to throw in the towel. I could get weepy if I were that kind of woman, but instead I smoke a cigarette, make a cup of coffee and call Judith Roth.

'I've had another e-mail from the Principal,' I tell her.

'What does it say?'

'I don't know. I haven't opened it.'

'Gina!' Her tone is bracing. 'He's got you rattled. You can't let him get you rattled. I expected better of you. Now open the damned e-mail and call me back.'

I want to snivel that she doesn't understand, that I've got all these other things going on in my life, but I still have some self-respect and I don't. I return to my computer and after a bit of preliminary skirmishing – deleting spam, dispatching acknowledgments – I open Janet's message. This is what I read:

Dear Gina,

The Principal has asked me to let you know that we can expect between eighty and a hundred students next year from the Fudan University of Shanghai. They will be taking a variety of courses, but all will include an English Language component. He wanted to inform you immediately so that you can start planning for such a large number, including taking on extra staff as necessary.

I should add that the letter which the Principal has received from the Deputy President of Fudan University makes a particular point of the presentations you made to Faculty Heads when you were in Shanghai with other representatives from the College last year.

The Principal hopes you will have a restful Easter break.

Yours,

Janet

There is a slight delay while the full impact of this message sinks in, then I'm on my feet, punching the air like an athlete who has won Olympic gold and dancing round the room bellowing, 'Up yours, Norman Street!'.

I am just picking up the phone to call Judith Roth when there is a knock at my door. Irina comes in first, followed by the other four. They stand in a row in front of me, smiling, each carrying a wrapped parcel. They look different: they have all dressed up. For my benefit? And here I am in my baggy old cleaning trousers. Christiane looks older in a black trouser suit and white shirt; Irina is muted in a sage-green dress; Desirée is immaculate as ever but her face looks worn beneath the make-up; Yukiko looks older too, in a severe pinstripe jacket. And Ceren? Ceren looks startlingly Islamic, her scarf not loosely draped round her shoulders but wound tightly round her head.

Yukiko speaks

'We have come to say goodbye,' she says, her voice high and formal. 'We are all leaving tomorrow.'

'And not coming back?' I ask.

'And not coming back.'

'What will you all do?' I look round at them. 'Irina?'

'I have no ex-husband to bother me now. I can go back to Russia. I can be doctor again.'

'Christiane?'

247

'My sister has just had a baby. I shall go and help her and then I shall start a Law course in Hamburg in the autumn.'

'Desirée. What about Denis? Is he leaving too?'

'No, he will stay. We are separating. Denis has been loyal and I can trust him, but he feels differently about me now. I am not the woman he thought I was.'

'So what will you do?'

'I wrote a piece for a French magazine about the experience of being a student in England, and they published it. I am going to try to be journalist.'

'Ceren?'

'I shall go back to my parents now. Perhaps later I will take Master's degree in Ankara. We shall see.'

'What about you, Yukiko?'

Yukiko smiles.

'I miss the cherry blossom,' she says.

'I shall miss all of you so much,' I say. 'And you'll miss each other. Will you see each other again?'

It is Christiane who speaks.

'No,' she says, 'we can never see each other again.'

In the silence that follows, Yukiko says, 'We each have something for you.'

She nudges Ceren gently forward and Ceren says, gazing solemnly from the folds of her scarf,

'I bring you a gift, Mrs Gray.'

Then Yukiko hands over her parcel.

'And I bring you a present.'

'And from me,' smiles Christiane, 'a token of esteem.'

'And this,' says Desirée, 'is an offering.'

'I looked for word,' Irina says, 'like Russian word, but I don't know if is right. I bring you honorarium.'

'*An* honorarium, Irina,' I say, and as they laugh my eyes start to fill with tears.

'You are good lady, Mrs Gray,' Irina says, 'and we honour you. We wish you good life.'

And they're gone. I don't open the parcels. They are for another day. I shall go home now, back to my empty house and my silent cat. More than anything I want to ring David Scott and invite him round for supper, but I dare not do it. I don't trust myself. I don't know what I might say after a couple of glasses of wine or, if I got lucky, in the heady relaxation of pillow talk. I can't invite him round tonight. I'm not sure I can ever see him again.

I hear voices below, so I look out of my window and I see the girls striding off across the grass, arm in arm. I think, as I watch them, that they are capable of anything.